"It w-wasn't supposed to [...] herself. "Please...you can't tell Tony."

"You mean he doesn't know? Doesn't suspect?" Zach sounded incredulous.

"No." Feeling suddenly faint, she leaned against the sink.

"But, Laura—surely he'd be thrilled."

"No. Trust me, he wouldn't. I—I'm going to have to find the right time to tell him." She realized the nausea had made her vulnerable. Now Zach possessed yet another family secret. He'd be mulling over this latest damning piece of information.

"I swear he'll never hear a word from me." His voice was harsh with repressed anger. "Are you through being sick?" he asked more gently.

To Laura's amazement, he moistened a cloth and wiped her face. He took the bottled water from the counter and gave her a moment to rinse her mouth, then slid his arm around her waist and helped her to the bed. "You lie there while I get whatever you need," he said. "Name it."

She had no idea a man could be this caring and selfless. It was a revelation to her.

ABOUT THE AUTHOR

Rebecca Winters is a much-published and internationally popular writer; she's also won quite a few awards, including the National Readers' Choice Award and the *Romantic Times* Reviewers' Choice Award. Not only that, she was named the 1995 Utah Writer of the Year. Rebecca is well-known for her fascinating story ideas and her intense, emotional writing. As bestselling author Debbie Macomber has said, "Rebecca Winters writes from the heart. She has the ability to make me laugh...or cry. Mostly she makes me care." Readers of *Laura's Baby* will agree.

Books by Rebecca Winters

Don't miss any of our special offers. Write to us at the following address for information on our newest releases.

Harlequin Reader Service
U.S.: 3010 Walden Ave., P.O. Box 1325, Buffalo, NY 14269
Canadian: P.O. Box 609, Fort Erie, Ont. L2A 5X3

LAURA'S BABY
Rebecca Winters

Harlequin Books

TORONTO • NEW YORK • LONDON
AMSTERDAM • PARIS • SYDNEY • HAMBURG
STOCKHOLM • ATHENS • TOKYO • MILAN
MADRID • WARSAW • BUDAPEST • AUCKLAND

ISBN 0-373-70756-8

LAURA'S BABY

Copyright © 1997 by Rebecca Winters.

This edition published by arrangement with Harlequin Books S.A.

® and TM are trademarks of the publisher. Trademarks indicated with ® are registered in the United States Patent and Trademark Office, the Canadian Trade Marks Office and in other countries.

Printed in U.S.A.

To Terry, my friend and colleague.
Thanks for sharing your cycling expertise,
which was invaluable.

CHAPTER ONE

TOURISTS AND MEMBERS of the press crowded the reception area of the Hotel Metropole. Only one clerk, his hands gesticulating wildly with frustration, appeared to be manning the front desk.

Laura Donetti was almost dead on her feet as she approached him, thanks to the long crowded L.A.-to-Brussels flight and subsequent drive in a rental car to St. Léger. She fought an oppressive fatigue as she half listened to the cacophony of voices, speaking a dozen different languages, surrounding her. She'd probably caught her little niece's cold.

"Oui, mademoiselle?" the harried clerk said, then no doubt recognizing her as an American, added, "How may I help you?"

"I'm Tony Donetti's wife. He's here with the Ziff team." When the man frowned she explained, "You know, Ziff? It stands for Zindel Foto-Films? They're the Belgian team for the Tour de France." The owners of the Belgian team had been plagued with problems in the past, so they'd gone on a talent search and had found cyclists from several different nations who had gained outstanding reputations in the sport, Tony among them. "Could you tell me which room is his?"

Thank heaven *she* didn't need a room. There wasn't one to be found anywhere. The world's greatest annual biking event had attracted thousands of cycling enthusiasts to the starting point of the race in St. Léger, only a few miles from the Luxembourg border.

After checking in to the smaller Hotel Beaulieu around the corner, where a reservation had been made ahead of time for the team members' families, she'd tried to phone Tony at the Metropole, but kept getting a busy signal. Either he or the teammate he roomed with was holding a lengthy conversation with their coach, or one of them had taken the receiver off the hook.

The exasperated hotel clerk shook his head. "You are the second woman today insisting that she is his wife and must see him. *Je regrette.*"

Groupies. The inevitable result of Tony's rising popularity among the sports crowd. She was sickened by the knowledge that her husband loved that side of his rise to fame.

"Perhaps this will convince you." She whipped out her passport, plus some wallet-size photos of the two of them together. "I'm staying at the Beaulieu. If you wish to ring over there to verify who I am..."

"You think I have time to make a phone call with this crowd?" He threw his hands in the air. "*Très bien.* But it will be on your head, eh? Room twenty-two." She knew it would be futile to ask for a key.

"Thank you."

Laura turned away from the desk and began working her way through the throng of people. When her husband was on the racing circuit, trying to get in touch with him was like trying to speak to the president. And before a race such as this one, well...her only choice had been to walk the short distance through the crowds and stifling late-June heat to the Metropole.

Tony would probably be surprised to see her on the doorstep of his hotel room. The last time they'd been together had been five weeks ago when their two-day reunion had turned into disaster. Too restless to stay in their apartment for five minutes, let alone talk about the sorry state of their marriage, he'd made perfunctory love to her, then told her he needed to get out and talk to his cycling buddies. That had spelled the end of their private time together.

"Look, April!" Laura heard someone whisper in an American accent as she passed a group of people on the stairs. "Isn't that Margo from 'The Way Things Are'? Can you believe it? She's even more beautiful in person!"

Laura groaned and darted up the second flight. Being recognized for her role as the spitfire attorney in a popular soap opera was a daily occurrence back home in California. But somehow she hadn't expected to be spotted quite so easily here. For the international scene was *Tony's* arena.

Speculation that he could win the Tour de France, beating out Ernesto Farramundi, the four-time winner and favorite, had spurred Tony's ambition.

Even if the Ziff team didn't win, she knew that when the Tour de France was over, Tony would want a chance at the Olympics. Obsessed with racing, he'd continue to pursue new heights. Much to the disappointment of his family, not to mention hers, his plans to attend law school had been cast aside.

When she'd accepted his proposal of marriage six years ago, how could she have known his love of cycling would become so all-consuming? She certainly didn't begrudge him his brilliant success. But the compulsive need to win and indulge in every perk that went with that success had taken him down a road that had changed him into someone she didn't know anymore.

Yet Laura's respect for her wedding vows, plus her conscience—which wouldn't have allowed her to be as cruel to him as he'd been to her, especially on the eve of the big race—had brought her to Europe. And in case he lost out tomorrow and made a poor showing during the prologue—the torturous time trials—she didn't want him to use her nonappearance as the reason for his failure. She knew he'd love to do that, because that was how his mind worked. She refused to give him that opportunity. Instead, she planned to be close at hand every kilometer of the race.

Besides, every competitor needed family support. If she didn't show up, no member of the Donetti family would be there cheering him on. Even though the love had gone out of their marriage a long time ago, she didn't want their marital problems to threaten his chances to make a name for himself in the annals of sports history.

She could well imagine what the media would make of her absence. They were always gnawing at the heels of celebrities, especially a rising sports star like Tony. Because she and Tony both had highly visible profiles, it was even more vital they present a united front.

There were other less altruistic considerations, as well, she mused as she approached the room where he'd been staying....

With determination, she lifted her hand and knocked on the door. Until five weeks ago she'd doggedly clung to the faint hope that their marriage could be salvaged. But she didn't believe that anymore and had made the decision to file for divorce. Deep down she knew it was what he'd wanted for a long long time. Now he would get his wish because finally *it was what she wanted, too!*

ZACHERY WILDE had just stepped out of the shower when he heard a knock on the door. He paused in the process of reaching for his shaving kit. Tony was next door in teammate Klaus Waldbillig's room with some young thing he'd met last week.

Maybe Klaus had come back, forcing Tony to return to the room he and Zach shared, and he'd forgotten his key. Then again, it could be another female fan beating down the doors to get to Tony. It was a common enough occurrence.

The knock sounded again.

Grabbing a towel, which he hitched around his hips, Zach strode across the room to answer it.

"Who is it?"

"Laura Donetti."

Tony's wife?

Zach's frown turned to a grimace. He'd never met Mrs. Donetti.

Until he'd come to Belgium in March to train with the team chosen by their sponsor, Zindel Foto-Films, he'd had no idea the arrogant high-living womanizing Tony Donetti even *had* a wife.

Because they were the only Americans on the Belgian-sponsored team, they'd roomed together on and off throughout the spring. Zach had been forced to listen to many uncomplimentary, even scathing remarks about Tony's spouse, most of which Zach wasn't certain he believed, at least not coming from the mouth of such a world-class jerk. If anything, he felt sorry for any woman foolish enough to marry the guy in the first place.

On the other hand, maybe she was Tony's match. Maybe she didn't care what he did out of her presence, so long as she had a trophy husband to brandish before the world. If that was the case, he supposed they deserved each other.

But whatever the situation, Zach couldn't ignore the reality that Tony's wife was at their door, and Tony was in the next room—with another woman.

However much he disliked his roommate and despised his life-style, Zach had no desire for any member of the team to get caught in an ugly situation this close to tomorrow's prologue. Many cycling experts, Zach included, believed that Tony was one of the top contenders for the *maillot jaune*, the coveted yellow jersey proclaiming the winner.

Unfortunately Tony's appetite for women was becoming well-known. If at this point the media got hold of anything salacious, they'd create a scandal that could taint everything the team had been working for.

At thirty-three Zach was probably the oldest competitor in the Tour de France. This was his one shot at the race. He'd needed a challenge to test his mettle after surviving a broken engagement more than a year before. When the Tour de France was over, he would quit the cycling world altogether and take off for parts unknown.

But right now Laura Donetti's unexpected arrival could mean that their most important team member might be in a hell of a lot of trouble. Zach realized it was up to him to avert disaster.

"Just a minute," he called.

He pulled on a T-shirt, shorts and running shoes, then dashed back to the door and opened it. "Sorry about that, Mrs. Donetti," he murmured. "I had to get dressed first. Come in."

"Thank you. I-isn't he here?" she asked in a slightly husky voice. Eyes of dark brown velvet, heavily fringed with black lashes, looked at him in confusion.

Lord. Tony hadn't exaggerated. His soap-opera-star

wife was gorgeous. Zach's gaze moved from her short curly black hair to her face with its smooth olive-toned skin and wide full mouth, then to her voluptuous body, which did wonders for the simple white two-piece suit she was wearing. She was even more striking because of her height. Five foot seven, at least.

Suddenly he had reason to reassess his thinking. A woman as exquisitely beautiful as she was, who made her living as a soap-opera queen, could quite easily be guilty of every sin her husband had accused her of and then some.

More than likely she drew attractive male stars on and off the set. Maybe Tony's flamboyant charm had lost some of its appeal. Particularly when he and his wife led such divergent lives on different continents.

Or maybe Tony was truly in love with her and she'd lost interest. Possibly that was why he seemed driven to act the way he did. An effort to dull the pain of losing her love.

"No," Zach replied. "He just stepped out, but he'll be back soon. I'm Zach Wilde, the guy he's been rooming with."

"I've heard a lot about you, Zach, professionally and otherwise, and all of it good. You're a little taller than I'd imagined. Is that why they call you King of the Mountain?"

Zach smiled, surprised she even knew the term.

"I'm just kidding," she murmured. "I know why they say that about you. Because you're the best on the climbs." She extended her hand.

As they shook, he had to admit she was good. She knew how to make a man feel important, special. It was a trait that was dynamite on and off the set, no doubt, and probably had Tony on his knees the first time he'd met her.

"All I have to offer is warm Perrier water. Would you like some?"

She nodded, looking flushed. "I'd love it, if it's not too much trouble."

"No trouble at all."

While he took the cap off the bottle he'd swiped from the table he and Tony used for their meals and poured the sparkling water into a glass, his eyes followed her progress. With all their racing gear scattered about, the room was a disaster. She had to do a little rearranging to make a place for herself on one of the chairs.

When she crossed those long shapely legs, he could better understand certain offhand remarks Tony had made, such as the thing he had for well-built brunettes.

Apparently he'd met his stunning wife during a publicity shoot after winning the Shopwise Drug Classic Race in California. He'd pursued her relentlessly, and they'd married quickly without ever getting engaged.

Zach had been engaged twice. Once in his early twenties to a young woman who'd died unexpectedly of a brain tumor. Years later in Utah he suffered through a long hellish second engagement, only to lose out in the end.

It had been fourteen months since Zach had left

Utah. In that time he'd come to grips with the fact that Rosie's husband, who'd been presumed dead after he went missing in action during Operation Desert Storm, had suddenly come back to life seven years later and returned home to claim his wife.

Given his own history, Zach could see Tony's point in not wasting time once you found what you wanted. But the racing star seemed to live his life too impulsively. For certainly it seemed something had gone wrong in their marriage.

What was she? All of twenty-seven, twenty-eight? A dangerous age to live so many thousands of miles away from her husband and looking like the embodiment of most men's fantasies.

Even yours, Wilde?

Zach had always appreciated beauty in any form, and he always would. If he was being completely honest, he had to admit that Laura Donetti's looks were exceptional. More than that, her sex appeal reached out to him like a living thing.

How odd. Up until this minute he'd thought he'd lost the ability to respond this strongly to a woman, no matter how gorgeous.

"Here you go." He handed her the glass, then returned to the project he'd begun before his shower— lining the inner sole of his right biking shoe where it rubbed against his heel. He wondered if he should ask her to wait while he went "looking for Tony."

"I assume you've already checked in at the Beaulieu," he said, instead.

She nodded. "Yes. The place is a madhouse."

He flashed her a smile. "You're right. My brother, Richard, and his family are staying there, too. I'll have to introduce you to his wife, Bev. She and the kids are going to be doing some other activities while Richard drives one of the support wagons. How long are you going to be here? Maybe you can do a little shopping and sight-seeing with them. Bev would enjoy the company."

"That's very kind of you to offer, but I arranged for a leave of absence from the set so I can follow Tony around in one of the support vehicles, too. His aunt and uncle don't..." She paused. "His family can't be here."

Zach blinked in surprise. Tony had always been vague about the people who'd raised him, but he *had* said that Laura hated cycling and hadn't been to his last six major races. In one of them, the Paris-Roubaix, he'd set a world record and Laura hadn't even known about it.

"Y-you don't think he'll mind, do you?"

"Of course not," Zach came back forcefully, trying to recover from his surprise.

"That's good. When you didn't say anything, I thought..." She bent her head. "Well, it's not important what I thought."

He put down the shoe he'd been working on and eyed her levelly. "If I seem surprised, it's because he's told me how difficult it is for you to break away from your tapings."

A wry smile animated her features, giving her another dimension, almost an impish appeal. "Not when your parents help produce the show."

Another thing Tony had neglected to mention. One dark blond brow lifted. "Your parents are in showbiz, too?"

She nodded. "So are my sister and her husband. They're screenwriters. I couldn't escape it I guess, but since I'm the only one without any real talent, I act." She laughed lightly.

"According to Tony, you're a famous soap star."

"If I were famous, even *you* would know about me."

"Even *I*?" He smiled back, disarmed by her humility. If it was all a facade, she was a better actor than he'd realized.

"Tony tells me you eat, drink and sleep racing. No women, no alcohol, no distractions. Which probably means you haven't watched television in years."

His smile broadened. "You're right. I haven't."

"Except maybe a special on racing."

"Or the coach's videos on our team's performance to point out our weaknesses," he said wryly.

"You see?" she said. "It only makes sense that you wouldn't know I'm really a two-bit actor playing the part of an outrageous fire-breathing attorney. But they put me in a car crash and now I'm in a coma, so I could come and be with Tony."

Zach chuckled.

"That's what happens when your parents have

clout," she confessed. "Of course, it's a secret—about the accident and coma, I mean—so please don't tell anyone. The viewers won't know it happened for a couple of months because everything's shot so far ahead."

"And so when you return to the set..."

"Yes. I'll have miraculously come out of the coma."

His chuckle turned into laughter. Maybe it was contagious, because her face broke out in a full unguarded smile. Zach felt his pulse leap.

"They would have put me in a coma earlier so I could fly over for the Tour of Luxembourg race a while back. But Tony told me not to..." She halted in midsentence again. A habit of hers. "Anyway, it doesn't matter, because I'm here now and anxious to be of support to him."

Zach turned away. This was all news to him, unless everything she'd told him was a lie. He didn't know what he believed and couldn't figure out why it mattered one way or another.

It had nothing to do with him. Their marital problems were none of his business. What concerned him was that the team be psychologically ready for tomorrow.

In a way he worried that when Tony found out that his wife had come and planned to follow the entire race, it might throw him off.

Zach inhaled sharply. Tony reminded him of a high-strung stallion. The last thing the team needed right now was a display of Tony's volatility. It could affect everyone.

"Tell you what," Zach said. "I'm going to go ask around and find out what's keeping your husband. Make yourself at home. I'll be back in a minute."

"No, please don't bother," she said, and rose to her feet. "I appreciate your willingness to look for him, but he could be anywhere and—"

"I'd like to help," he insisted, realizing that the real reason he didn't want her to leave was that he was enjoying her company. Maybe Klaus had a point when he teased Zach about "all work and no play."

"I know you would. You're very kind. But I'm tired and need to lie down for a while, anyway, so I'll go back to the Beaulieu. When you see him, tell him to phone me. I'm in room eight."

Her determination frustrated Zach in ways he couldn't understand. If it was up to him, he wouldn't let her go. "You're sure?" he asked.

"Yes. Thank you."

Behind her poised demeanor, feigned or not, he sensed resignation mixed with a certain degree of agitation. She was, in fact, a mass of contradictions. Right now he didn't know what to make of Laura Donetti, let alone his own troubling reaction to her.

As for Tony, the sooner that idiot knew his wife had arrived, the better. Their team manager, Leon, who also doubled as their psychologist, would need to be informed of the new development, as well. He'd definitely want a chat with their number-one boy before the day was out.

Zach preceded her to the door, opened it and stepped into the hall, hoping to warn Tony should he suddenly emerge from the other room with his latest plaything in tow.

To his relief, all was quiet at their end of the dimly lit hall. "Come on. I'll walk you downstairs," he said, thinking he'd run interference on the way if necessary. "Maybe we'll catch sight of another team member who knows where he is."

"Thank you, but I hate putting you out."

He found himself avidly defending his position. "You're not! I need a new pack of razor blades, and now is as good a time as any to get one."

They walked the length of the hall and started down the stairs. "I brought a bunch of them and some shaving gel in case Tony runs out," she said. "They're the kind he swears give his legs the best shave. Before I met him, I had no idea how important it was to remove the hair so the skin could be cooled by perspiration."

"Little details like that make a big difference," Zach concurred.

"If you'll come to the hotel with me, you can have as many packs as you need."

Once again Zach was struck by her natural down-to-earth attitude, which was at total odds with the picture Tony had painted of a selfish man-eating television star in love with her own image.

Unless this was her way of coming on to a man so he didn't know what hit him until it was too late. But in his gut, Zach felt her offer was a hundred-percent genuine. So, until she showed the side that Tony had talked about, he'd reserve the right to think whatever he wanted.

"Well, if Tony endorses them, then who am I to refuse such a generous offer?"

It might be just as well if he escorted her to her hotel. After seeing her to the door, he could go to his brother's room and ring Klaus. If Tony was still there, he could alert him, and if Klaus answered, he could tell him to search for Tony until he found him.

At the second-floor landing she said, "I also brought a sackful of my homemade packets of granola with the little dark-chocolate morsels he loves. You're welcome to some of those, too." A trace of anxiety lurked in her eyes while she was making the offer. *Why?*

"I'd never turn down a gift like that. Something tells me I've miraculously glommed on to Tony's secret weapon. We've all wondered where he suddenly finds the energy to go on when the rest of us are ready to lie down and die."

She actually blushed. "I—I don't know about that, but I do express-mail him a dozen of them before every race."

Zach had had no idea. "Lucky guy," he murmured before he realized the words had escaped his lips.

More than ever Tony's wife was turning out to be the surprise of the season.

"It's just a little something to remember me by when he...I can't be there."

Zach caught the change in pronouns and continued down the next flight of stairs a little ahead of her, puzzled by the large number of conflicting factors in the Donetti marriage.

The minute the crowded lobby came into view, several cameras flashed in succession, briefly robbing him of his vision. If Tony had made an appearance down here, the press would have been all over him, which meant he was still upstairs...

Suddenly Zach heard people pointing out him and Laura. He cursed under his breath and felt her trembling hand on his arm with a sense of wonder. An actor could fake a lot of things, but not nervousness, which in this case appeared to border on panic.

A member of the international press started to approach them. "Mrs. Donetti, Mr. Wilde...how about an interview before tomorrow's race?"

Damn.

"There'll be a team press conference later tonight." Without conscious thought Zach grasped Laura's hand and whispered, "Come on."

She didn't seem to need any urging. In fact, she ran to keep up with his long strides. Once they were out on the street, she let go of his hand but kept up her pace to stay abreast of him.

"Thanks for getting us out of there."

"Sometimes the paparazzi can be a pain."

She shook her head, drawing his attention to the glistening black curls that framed the perfect oval of her face. "I'll never get used to them. Tony always orders me to smile and says I should tell them what they want to hear. I suppose it's the only way to survive, but I'm afraid it's not me, if you know what I mean."

Zach knew only too well, but she'd surprised him once again. Apparently she was as violently opposed to unsolicited publicity as he was. More and more he was beginning to feel shame for some of the thoughts he'd harbored about her when she'd announced her presence on the other side of his hotel-room door a little while ago.

Klaus and fellow team member Jean-Luc Vadim, both in their early twenties and unmarried, had laid bets that Tony's wife wouldn't show up at all, or if she did, it would have more to do with *her* need than her husband's, to be in the limelight.

They went so far as to speculate that if she should actually make an appearance in St. Léger for the big day, she would probably be motivated by a money-grubbing publicity agent who could smell a red-hot opportunity. "Soap queen unites with cycling king for Tour de France debut." The stuff that sold newspapers and paid six-digit salaries. Any woman married to Tony Donetti had to know exactly what went on when he wasn't burning up the road winning one big race after another. She obviously didn't give a damn. How wrong could everyone have been?

The Beaulieu was indeed a madhouse. And the minute they stepped into its crowded foyer, an elderly American woman recognized Laura and ran up to her, thrusting a travel map and pen in her face.

"Please, could I have your autograph? And sign it to Dawn from Margo? I watch your show every day when I'm home. You're my favorite character. I always wanted to be an attorney, but in my day women were expected to stay home. My daughter's taping it for me while we're here...."

When her babbling wound down, Laura smiled and said, "Thank you for the compliment, Dawn." She signed the map quickly along the border, then handed it back to her. "Just between you and me, I'd much rather stay home and be a mother like you've been."

The woman looked stunned, but no more so than Zach, who was again obliged to make some readjustments in his thinking about Tony's wife. He admired her grace and dignity with the autograph seeker. He was sure the intrusion was the last thing she wanted or needed.

"You handled that like a pro," he said as they started up the stairs.

"It's easy enough to sign something. Much harder to speak in front of a microphone when you know someone will twist your words and take everything out of context."

"Amen."

When they reached the next floor, she hurried to a door down the corridor and pulled out her key to open it. "Come in. I'll get those things I promised."

Zach had a better idea. "While you do that, I'm going to step across the hall to my brother's room. If they're in, I'd like to introduce you."

She flashed a grateful smile. "That would be nice, Zach. Then, I'll see you in a minute."

With a nod, he turned away and headed for room number ten. *I don't know the whole story yet, Tony,* he thought. *But there's one thing I'd stake my life on— you don't deserve your wife!*

There was no response to his knock. Zach let himself into the empty room with the spare key Richard had given him. He'd have to make introductions later.

After a quick scan of the directory for the number of the Metropole, he dialed the hotel and asked for Klaus's room. He waited a few minutes and was told no one had answered.

Tony was probably still in there and didn't want to be disturbed.

Frustrated, Zach instructed the concierge to ring the team manager's room. Rather than try to hunt Tony down, he would explain the situation to Leon and let *him* shoulder the potential crisis. This one was a beaut. But everyone on the team had a job, and problems were what Leon was getting paid to solve.

A minute later Zach was connected with him. When he told him the situation—that Laura was looking for Tony, who was probably in Klaus's room with some groupie—Leon let loose a stream of invective against Tony and his stupidity. As soon as he'd calmed down, he told Zach he'd get right on it, then hung up.

Zach wrote a note to his brother telling him that Tony's wife was just across the hall and could probably benefit from some company. Then he went out of the room and locked it.

Laura had left the door to her room ajar. Zach gave a couple of raps to announce himself, then entered. She lifted her head and seemed to study him, as if she was seeing him for the first time.

"Hi," she said in a soft voice that sounded somewhat timid. Then, apparently realizing he'd caught her looking at him rather intently, she averted her gaze almost guiltily.

"Hi, yourself. I'm sorry—it looks like my brother's family is out, but there'll be another opportunity to introduce you later tonight."

She paused in the process of unpacking her suitcase, the only one he could see anywhere in the tidy room. Bev had brought several, much to Richard's chagrin. Between the kids and all the paraphernalia, their hotel room looked like a tornado had blown through.

"I'm sure there will. Here you go." She handed him a plastic bag.

He glanced inside. She'd wrapped each granola-and-chocolate square in plastic wrap.

"Mind if I try one now?" he asked.

"If you'd like." Her voice kind of wobbled.

"I *would* like," he said, aware of an odd lack of

confidence in her tone. Every time she opened her mouth, he heard or felt something unexpected.

"Uh-uh-uh-uh," said a familiar male voice. "I was under the impression that those particular treats were meant only for me, darling."

CHAPTER TWO

ZACH WATCHED her face pale as a sun-bronzed Tony breezed through the open door smiling his dashing smile. She appeared anything but happy to see him, which seemed a bit strange, considering she'd been looking for him.

As for Zach, he felt a disgust that bordered on anger. Tony had presented such a false picture of his wife! It prompted Zach to retaliate. To hell with the kid gloves.

"Sorry, old man," he said. "But your secret is finally out."

Tony, Zach knew, had let his pro status go to his head, and he enjoyed dominating the people around him. On more than one occasion Zach had seen him use intimidation to get what he wanted. But it had never worked on Zach, and certainly not now that certain things had come to light.

Without any compunction at all, Zach removed a snack, undid the wrapper and popped the whole bar into his mouth. Laura looked apprehensive, which made him wonder what kind of treatment Tony subjected her to. All the more reason for him, Zach, to want to champion her cause.

With great relish, he reached into the bag for another bar and took a bite. He'd wait and see if his teammate turned nasty. Tony was known for his rapid mood swings.

Unable to resist baiting him, Zach asked, "How come you never told us what a great cook your wife is?"

Tony *was* angry now. "Because I didn't think it was anybody else's damn business!" he fired back.

"Well, it's my business now." Zach flashed her a warm smile. "These are delicious, Laura. I'm saving the rest for the race. Thank you. For the blades and gel, too."

"You're welcome."

She'd barely said the words before her husband's arm went around her shoulders, pulling her close. But Zach could see it was anything but a loving gesture, and the anxious expression on her face spoke volumes.

"Why didn't you tell me you were flying over?" he heard Tony mutter as he brushed her temple with his lips.

"As soon as I was given a leave of absence from the set, I tried phoning you from home, but I couldn't get through. Then I phoned from the airport in Brussels and later from the hotel here, but either there was a busy signal or no answer. When I finally went to your room, Zach was there and he wasn't sure where you were."

Tony gave Zach a murderous look. "So what are you doing over *here?*"

You're worried I've spilled the beans, aren't you, Tony? You should be worried.

Laura must have picked up on her husband's anger because she broke in with, "He needed some blades, and he wanted to introduce me to his family."

"That's right," Zach concurred, munching on the last bite of granola. The bar really was exceptionally tasty. "Some of the other guys' families don't speak English that well. I thought maybe Laura would enjoy Bev's company."

Tony ignored Zach and turned to his wife. "How long are you here for?"

"The whole race. I plan to follow you around the circuit."

If the tautness of his expression was anything to go by, Tony wasn't pleased by the news. This was further borne out when Tony said tightly, "We both know you can't be gone from the show that long."

"Haven't you heard the latest?" Zach preempted her response.

Tony swung back to him, his expression irritated. "What are you talking about?"

"They've killed off her character to accommodate you, Tony. You're a fortunate man to have in-laws who'd allow such a drastic change in the script of a nationally televised program so your wife could be here for you. I envy you that kind of support."

There was a tension-filled pause while Tony eyed Zach narrowly. "Then you'll understand that I'd like some time alone with her."

You're running scared, Donetti.

Zach smiled as pleasantly as he knew how. "No one would understand that more than I. The minute I saw Laura at the door, I realized I'd be minus my roommate tonight. I was just going to say that I'll go back to the hotel and bring all your gear over here so you don't have to spend a single minute away from her." He paused, then added, "I know that if my wife had just arrived, I'd put a Do Not Disturb sign on the door until further notice."

Laura started shaking her head. He caught a pleading look in her eyes that begged him not to taunt Tony any further. "Th-that's very kind of you, Zach, but—"

"No buts. That's what friends are for, right, Tony?" Zach was enjoying this once-in-a-lifetime moment. Tony couldn't make even a token response, because he was well and truly trapped.

Now that his legally wedded wife had shown up, the sleeping arrangements he'd made with his various girlfriends around the circuit would have to be called off for the duration of the Tour de France. With Laura driving a support car for the whole world to see, the Donetti marriage would look to be on solid ground, and the Ziff team would be spared any negative press.

"I'll be back in a little while." As Zach turned to leave, he was aware of the dangerous glitter in Tony's eyes. He felt sorry for Laura, yet for reasons of her own, she still clung to the marriage. But he had a strong suspicion she was just barely holding on.

What really troubled him, though, was why he cared so much.

THE SECOND Zach had disappeared out the door, Tony relinquished his hold of Laura and flung himself into the nearest chair. He stared up at her through hooded eyes. She gazed back dispassionately.

Her husband was definitely good-looking, she thought, with his dark hair and deep tan, attractive enough to play a lead role in a daytime soap. The running shorts and tank top he wore now revealed his superbly fit condition, and she couldn't blame any woman for wanting to be the object of his attention.

In the beginning she'd been blinded by her attraction to him; but it soon wore off when she discovered that beneath the surface, he didn't have the depth of character she'd naively attributed to him. They'd met at a cycling event in California. He'd been attending college at the time and had led Laura to believe he wanted to go to law school. He'd been a different person back then. Raised by his aunt and uncle, who had six children of their own and lived on a very modest income, he'd appeared to be a man who valued family and loved kids. He'd been especially attentive to Laura's two nieces.

He'd fit in so well, in fact, with her own relatives and friends, she'd assumed they would eventually enjoy a solid traditional marriage, that his hobby would take a back seat to the more important role of finishing school and settling down to a career and family.

But after they'd been married only a few months Laura realized that there was always one more race he wanted to win. Little by little the amateur competitions separated him from her and his family. At the end of their first year of marriage, Tony turned pro and admitted that he'd been training for the Tour de France for years. For the past four, he'd been winning important races, stacking up world-ranking cycling points. She no longer knew who he was.

Right now she was somewhat repulsed by him. He smelled strongly of mouthwash. She didn't even want to think what he'd been doing before Zach had accomplished the miracle that had unearthed her husband from wherever. From *whomever.*

"I can't figure out why you came, Laura. You hate what I do, so why did you bother?"

Probably nothing would suit his purposes better if she *hadn't* come to watch him compete in the most important race of his career to date. Then he could lie to himself and everyone around that his wife didn't care about him or their marriage. By placing the blame squarely on her shoulders, he could exonerate himself from all guilt and entrench himself in the life-style she so abhorred.

She sat calmly on the edge of a small love seat, needing to choose her words carefully. For the first time in years maybe, he seemed prepared to have the kind of long serious talk she'd been hoping for.

Ironically the timing couldn't be worse for him.

"Whether you believe it or not, I'm very proud of

your racing accomplishments. Here." She reached into a bag next to the love seat and handed him the gift she'd made for him.

"What's this?"

"A scrapbook of all your triumphs." The leatherette binder was thick with newspaper articles and photographs from magazines. He leafed through it, but she couldn't tell if it brought him pleasure or not.

"You're an athlete's athlete," she said. "Only a handful of men in the entire world have the talent to win the Tour de France. I'm married to one of them."

For once he didn't have a ready retort. His silence gave her the impetus to go on.

"Tony...we've never talked about this before, but I'm not unaware that deep down inside you, there's a void—because your own parents aren't here today to see you ride to victory."

His head flew back in surprise.

"I know it hurts that your uncle George and aunt Ann have never shown up at one of your races. I bet you're thinking that if they really loved you, they would've found a way to come up with the money to see this one."

"I don't want to talk about them."

Laura had an idea that his aunt and uncle, seeing Tony's neglect of her, had probably been instrumental in getting him to come home for that short visit five weeks ago.

But as awful as those two days had been, they proved to Laura that Tony wanted out of their mar-

riage. Unfortunately he would never be honest enough
with himself or with her to ask for a divorce. He'd
also been brought up a Catholic, and while his religion
meant little to him, his aunt and uncle were quite de-
vout. It was unlikely he'd want to risk their disapproval. So, what with all that, he hoped *she'd* be the
one who forced the issue, which would then free him
from all ties and blame. For the past few years he'd
become an expert at twisting situations. More often
than not she ended up feeling like the culprit.

Surely you understand we can't have a baby right
now. Come on. How many men get the chance of a
lifetime to really make it big? I have the talent, Laura,
and I'm going all the way to the top. We'll talk about
starting a family later.

Many times throughout their six-year marriage he'd
thrown that argument in her face. Yet never once had
he considered that her desire to be a mother might be
every bit as important; nor would he have given a
thought to the ticking of her biological clock.

If he'd hoped, five weeks ago, that in reasserting his
position about this not being the time to start a family
she would finally get the point and stop harassing him
about it, then he'd succeeded. In fact, he'd written the
death sentence of their marriage.

But right now nothing was as important as the race
tomorrow. She pulled a second scrapbook from the
bag. "Here. Take a look at this." She extended it to
him, but he didn't make a move to reach for it. She
dropped her arm.

"I went over to see your aunt and uncle before I flew here. Ann was there alone and we had a long talk. I told her I could easily afford to bring the whole family to Europe if they wanted to watch the race."

He rubbed the bridge of his nose. "I can just imagine how that went over."

She shook her head. "Do you know what she told me? Money has never had anything to do with their decision to stay away from your races."

"Tell me something I don't know." The bitterness of his tone broke her heart. "I'm not their kid and was never wanted. I've always realized that."

"Wrong, Tony. They've always loved you. No, that's not the reason for their lack of support." She felt like a parent dealing with a recalcitrant child.

He glared at her. "And you're going to tell me what it is, are you?"

"If you'll just look through this—she tapped the scrapbook—you'll understand a lot of things. I only wish it hadn't taken my going over there and pleading with Ann for an explanation to finally get an answer."

He let out an expletive. "What is it? Another scrapbook?"

"Yes. It's your father's."

Tony looked stunned.

"I want you to know," Laura went on, "that your aunt would have given it to you years ago, but your uncle wouldn't let her. However, she and I both agreed it was long past due for you to have it, so she let me bring it to you."

As Laura had hoped, he shed that armor of belligerent indifference and got to his feet in one lithe movement. He looked pale beneath his tan.

She stood up, as well, and handed it to him. "Consider it a gift from beyond the grave. I hope it inspires you to find that secret weapon of yours that Zach was talking about."

"What secret weapon?" he demanded.

"He said that when the rest of them are ready to quit, you always find the necessary energy to perform the impossible."

She wasn't sure why his eyes slid away from hers so quickly. She'd hoped to ease the antagonism he seemed to feel toward his roommate. She tried again.

"Zach says you're a champion of champions and he's dedicated to helping you win."

As far as Laura was concerned, *Zach* was a champion of champions for bowing to Tony's expertise and working for the good of the whole team rather than only himself. Tony would never do the same thing if their positions were reversed.

"Take a look at those pictures, Tony."

After eyeing her skeptically, he opened the cover. As he thumbed through it, she watched the expression on his face change to amazement.

On the flight to Europe, she'd memorized every page of the book. At an early age, Tony's father, Carl Donetti, had been the best swimmer at his neighborhood pool. Six years older than his brother, George, he excelled in almost every swimming event throughout his years in public school. From there he went on to regional and national meets. In time he made it to the U.S. Olympic swim-team trials. But that was where the scrapbook entries stopped.

When she heard her husband groan, she said, "Your father was a remarkable athlete. Now we know where you get your fantastic athletic ability. In some of the pictures, you and your father look so much alike I can't tell the difference."

Tony's eyes were suspiciously bright. "Why didn't Uncle George ever let me see this?"

She could hear raw anger in his voice, and took a deep breath before continuing, "Your aunt told me that your dad didn't make the Olympic team, and he couldn't get over the failure. Your uncle watched him beat himself up and felt powerless to help him—except by being your dad's greatest fan and never missing a meet, no matter where it was. He worshiped your dad. When your parents were killed in that freeway collision, the only thing that helped George to go on living was to take care of his brother's baby boy and raise him."

Tony's hands curled into fists. "He should have told me."

"Apparently when you started to show an interest in cycling so early in life and could beat everyone on the block, George saw history repeating itself. The pain of what he'd lived through with your dad was too great.

"That's why he moved the family from Thousand

Oaks to Pasadena. He hoped to thwart you by separating you from your cycling friends. He prayed you'd finally lose interest. Instead, you seemed more determined than ever. He knew the Tour de France was your dream, but he couldn't bear to watch you go through all the stages on the way up, only to lose out in the end.''

''But I'm going to win!'' Tony vowed with a fierceness Laura had never heard in his voice before. ''Pictures of me holding up the winner's cup are going to be in *my* scrapbook.''

As she'd hoped, the scrapbook she'd brought had focused her husband like nothing else could have. Temporarily, at least, he'd forgotten to be angry with her.

''I *know* you're going to win, Tony. That's why I'm here, why I brought these books with me. They'll bring you luck. No one has worked harder and longer than you have. No one deserves to win more. But just remember that when you pop the cork on that bottle of champagne on the Champs-Elysées, it will be a victory for your dad and your uncle, too.''

His glazed eyes met hers briefly and he nodded, but his thoughts were obviously on that triumphant moment.

''I have every confidence that when you return to Pasadena wearing the yellow jersey, you'll make a new man of George, and he'll be the one pushing you all the way to the Olympics.''

The fire of competition ignited Tony. ''That's where

I'm going, Laura. All the way. History isn't going to repeat itself this time, because unlike my dad, I'm going to make those trials!''

"I know you will."

I'm counting on it. After you've won, you'll be so high our divorce will go through without recriminations.

He dropped the scrapbooks on the table. "I've got to go talk to the coach."

Laura felt relief. She couldn't imagine anything worse than being closeted with Tony this close to the race. His restlessness made him difficult to be around at the best of times, but when he was filled with new purpose, there was no holding him.

"Zach said there was supposed to be a press conference later."

Tony paused midway to the door. "He's right. There's one scheduled at the Metropole tonight."

"Do you want me to come over for that?"

"No. I'm going to get it canceled. I've got some new strategies to work out with the team and I'll be late before I get back here. Don't wait up for me."

He bussed her on the cheek and started for the door. His single-mindedness also made him forgetful.

"Tony?"

He paused in the doorway.

"Take the key. I won't need it." She tossed it to him, watched it make a graceful arc and land in his hand.

He flashed her a trouble-free smile, the sort she

rarely saw anymore, then left the room. She said a little prayer of thanks that Ann had finally broken down and told her about Tony's father. The scrapbooks and the knowledge that his family loved him had now become her husband's *other* secret weapon. They would give him that needed edge.

Content that her gifts had produced the desired results, she locked the door behind him and headed for the bathroom. Within minutes she'd taken a shower and had put on a nightgown and robe, wanting nothing more than to lie down.

Dealing with Tony was an exhausting experience. Coupled with travel fatigue, it meant she needed at least twelve hours of uninterrupted sleep so she could be ready for the time trials tomorrow.

No sooner had she turned down the covers than she heard a rap on the door. Who...? It wouldn't be Tony because he had the key. Then she remembered that Zach had been going to come back with Tony's things.

"Just a minute!" she called, and padded to the door.

"Hi again," he murmured as she opened it, a smile curving his wide attractive mouth. His arms were loaded.

Despite her fatigue, clearing the air with Tony must have sharpened her ability to concentrate, because she couldn't stop staring at Zach. As she'd noted earlier, he was taller than her husband, with a larger build and quite a spectacular physique. He didn't resemble a lot of the bikers who, in the main, were small in stature.

In fact, while he wore nineties sportswear and kept

his hair cropped very short—no doubt to help give him minimum wind resistance when he cycled—Zach was a different type altogether. His big well-toned body could make a woman feel incredibly safe, protected. And with his dark blond hair and silvery eyes, she could be forgiven for thinking he had Norse blood running through his veins.

"C-come in," she stammered, suddenly embarrassed. He must have noticed her staring. "You shouldn't have bothered to bring Tony's things over, you know. Tony could have done that later."

He put the bags and paper sacks he was carrying on the floor next to the dresser, then turned to her. "It was no bother. He came back to the room before I left. Apparently there's been a change in our plans tonight and we're meeting with the coach. Tony's all fired up to win those time trials tomorrow."

She nodded. "He told me he was going to cancel the press interview."

"That was music to my ears," he said in his deep vibrant voice. "I'd say the arrival of his wife is just what the doctor ordered."

Laura looked away. "What do you mean?"

"He's a changed boy from an hour ago."

You're right, Zach. He's a boy. A very difficult one at that. But then, Zach, probably more than anyone besides herself, knew the dark side of Tony—his moodiness and compulsive habits. He'd been forced to room with him the past few months, and it couldn't have been easy. She found herself feeling a good deal of sympathy for Zach; he'd probably been subjected to the worst rather than the best of her husband.

Another part of her cringed, because she was certain Tony had made up a lot of half-truths and outright lies about her and their marriage. Long before they'd met today, Zach would have formed his own opinions about her and Tony, none of them good.

It would take an incredibly mature person to deal with Tony's confidences and temperament, and still have any respect for him. Maybe if she told Zach about the scrapbooks, he'd understand Tony a little better and not judge him too harshly.

Moving over to the table, she picked up the books and handed them to him. "These are what made the difference. I hope they bring your whole team luck."

Zach sat down on a chair at the table with Laura seated opposite him. As he leafed through the pages, she proceeded to tell him everything.

"I know Tony can be difficult," she finished. "Obviously he never felt accepted, never mind loved, by his aunt and uncle. That's why he's always had this drive to prove himself. But when he heard that his own father was close to being Olympic material, I think it gave him the sense of identity he's been looking for."

Zach closed both albums and looked up at her, his expression solemn. "You gave him a priceless gift today. He's not the same person who walked in here earlier. Not so…fragmented."

Fragmented. That was the perfect word to describe

Tony. Zach understood things much more than she'd realized.

"I hope he thanked you for them," Zach said.

She moved her head, neither a confirmation or a denial.

"Even if he didn't," Zach went on, his gaze missing nothing, "on behalf of the team, I thank you for doing something for him no else could have done. It's just possible that in turning Tony around, our team has a real shot at the championship. I've said it before and I'll say it again—He's a lucky guy."

She was touched by his kindness. "I think Tony has been very blessed to have had you for a roommate. In case he hasn't thanked *you* yet, then let me say it for him. Thank you."

Again their gazes met in quiet understanding.

"Laura?" he said softly.

She swallowed hard. "Yes?"

"Do you mind if I call you that?"

"I'd prefer it."

"Have you ever driven a support car for your husband?"

"No."

Zach appeared to be pondering something vital. "Would you be interested in driving the circuit with my brother, Richard? He's done it for me many times, but he's going to have to go it alone this time because Bev says she can't take the pressure.

"I know he'd welcome your company. Because you both have a vested interest in me and Tony, I think you two would be good for each other, and definitely good for the team as a whole.''

She blinked. ''You're kidding!'' His suggestion flooded her with warmth.

''No.'' He rose to his feet, and she had to look up at him. ''I'm being earnest. Following us around can be very grueling. It's nice to know there's another person to rely on. You two could spell each other and use each other for a sounding board. Richard's a great talker. It's hard on him when he doesn't have anyone around to listen.''

She ran a shaky hand through her curls. Lately she'd been tired a lot, and nauseated. The opportunity to be able to share the work with someone, not have to do the whole circuit alone, was a godsend.

''He...he might not want to ride with me.''

''Actually I've already talked to him about it. I was over in his room just before I came here. He couldn't be happier with the idea and is anxious to meet you. So, what do you say?''

Her gaze swiveled to his once more. *You're such a good man, Zach Wilde. A remarkable man.*

''To be honest—'' her voice trembled ''—it's like an answer to a prayer.'' She paused. ''It seems all I ever do is thank you.''

Something flickered in his eyes. ''I think all our prayers were answered when you showed up today.''

His remark produced a small smile. ''Are you certain your sister-in-law won't mind?''

He smiled back. ''She's the one who begged Richard to say yes. Actually it will relieve her of a lot of guilt.''

"Guilt?"

''She wants to help, but I guess she's been to too many of my races and can't take the suspense. To know someone else is there to assist Richard takes a huge load off her mind.'' Now it was his turn to pause. ''If there's anything I'm worried about, it's Tony's reaction.''

She shook her head. ''He'll be relieved I'm driving with someone who's experienced at this sort of thing. I'm afraid he still believes a man is better behind the wheel of a car.''

He smiled. ''Good. Then it's settled. Tony told me you're in for the night, so I've suggested to Richard that the two of you meet tomorrow morning at seven-thirty. We'll all have breakfast in the dining room downstairs.''

''That would be perfect,'' she said.

He studied her for a moment. ''You look a little pale. Are you feeling all right?''

''I'm tired, I confess, but it's jet lag. A good night's sleep will work wonders.''

''You probably need to eat, too.'' He gestured at the paper sacks he'd brought. ''You'll find some cheese, French bread and grape juice in those.''

''Zach…''

''Uh-huh?''

''You're not some kind of guardian angel sent down

here just for me, are you? Should I touch you to see if you're real?''

She did just that, reaching out and grasping his forearm. It was hard and warm. She quickly removed her fingers and stepped back.

He smiled again. ''As you've discovered, I'm quite real and nothing out of the ordinary. Only a teammate of your husband's who's very thankful you arrived in time to give Tony the best shot at the title.''

She wrapped her arms around her waist. ''You're not ordinary at all, you know. Most men would want the glory for themselves.''

His smile faded. She couldn't fathom it.

''I'm not here for the same reasons as Tony is, and I know my limitations.'' He headed for the door. ''I'll see you in the morning.'' In the space of a heartbeat he'd changed into someone unapproachable and remote.

Laura had the strongest urge to run after him as he let himself out to ask him what those reasons were. But she didn't dare. He'd closed up on her. Maybe the day would come when there'd be enough trust between them that she could ask.

And maybe you've come down with a full-scale flu, Laura. Zach Wilde is nothing to you. He can't be!

CHAPTER THREE

FOR ZACH TO AWAKE to an empty hotel room was not an unusual experience. Over the past few months Tony had slept elsewhere and it had never mattered.

The knowledge that he slept in his wife's bed last night shouldn't have made the slightest difference. In fact, if anything, Zach should have been relieved that for once Tony was exactly where he should be.

Cursing because he'd cut himself twice while shaving, Zach left the bathroom only to stub his big toe on the doorjamb. Then he decided to phone Richard at the Metropole to make sure he was up and ready. All he succeeded in doing was waking Bev, who was still in bed. She muttered something about her husband having gone downstairs already. After apologizing for disturbing her, Zach hung up, his state of mind a mix of self-loathing and befuddlement.

For a moment he was tempted to ring the room across the hall from his brother. But the picture of Tony in bed with his wife filled him with such distaste he squelched the impulse.

You're a mess, Wilde.

Today was the beginning of the race, yet he couldn't get another man's wife out of his mind. His skin still burned where she'd grasped his arm last night. He'd wanted to cover her hand and keep it there. *Be honest. You wanted to feel her hands on you, her mouth beneath yours.*

Donning his sweats, he left the room and headed out of the hotel for the Beaulieu. The minute he stepped outdoors, he could smell rain in the air. He looked up at the sky. The heavy cloud cover didn't bode well for the time trials, which were scheduled to start at noon and would probably go on until well into the evening.

Even at seven-thirty in the morning, the normally quiet streets were alive with activity. It didn't surprise him, not when it was estimated that at least 350,000 people from all over Europe and America had descended on St. Léger to watch the start of the race.

To avoid members of the press, he sprinted around the corner, making it difficult for anyone to pursue him with a TV camera in hand. But he couldn't escape the newsmen completely. One was waiting for him as he entered the crowded dining room of the Beaulieu.

"Here's Zachary Wilde, the Newport Beach American dark horse who was out of the racing circuit for a time, only to come back and win an impressive number of European championships, earning him the title King of the Mountain. So, Mr. Wilde, who do you think will be the first five finishers in the first stage tomorrow?"

Zach could see Richard waving to him from a corner table. No sign of Laura yet. When she did show, she'd be forced to run the media gauntlet, too.

"Donetti, of course, and Farramundi or Poletti of the Italian team, possibly Glatz or Richter of the German team. Vadim maybe."

"I notice you don't put yourself among the top contenders of your own team."

"The sprints are Donetti's long suit. Vadim does well on the flats."

"Do you estimate anyone setting records today?"

"No. The rain will slow everyone down. Now if you'll excuse me..." He shouldered his way through the crush of interested spectators listening to the interview and strode toward his brother.

Richard was only two years older, and when he was seated, many people mistook him for Zach. But in fact, Richard was three inches shorter, and his eyes were blue not gray.

Richard was an excellent swimmer and diver, and over the years he'd shared a love of sailing with Zach. These days, however, his responsibilities as a husband and father to three children, plus the growing outdoor-sign business, which was a Wilde-family enterprise, prevented him from indulging in much sporting activity.

When Richard did have free time, he'd given it to his brother. Zach knew he'd never be able to repay him for all the emotional and physical support he'd provided over the years, the unqualified unstinting love, the steady encouragement—and faith that one day Zach would find ultimate fulfillment with the right woman, despite his thus far poor track record.

At his approach, Richard got up and gave him a hug. "This is your big day, brother. How are you feeling?"

They sat down opposite each other. "Pretty good."

Richard broke off the end of a fresh baguette and handed the rest to Zach, who refused it. He eyed him speculatively. "You could have fooled me. What's eating you?"

"What do you mean?"

"How come you're not hungry?"

"I had a bagel in the room."

"You've nicked up your face."

Richard didn't miss much. Zach rubbed his jaw where he'd been careless with the razor. "Prerace jitters," he lied.

"Come on, Zach. It's *me* you're talking to here. What gives?"

Avoiding his brother's probing stare, he murmured, "I guess the team's holding its breath wondering if Tony's still as focused as he seemed last night."

"Well, he passed through the foyer about ten minutes ago. From the looks of it, he appeared more rested, relaxed and confident than I've ever seen him. He chatted amiably with the TV people, then left. I would say it's the best of signs."

The news should have pleased Zach, but instead, he suddenly felt acutely out of sorts and shoved himself away from the table.

"Hey!"

Zach ignored his brother's protest and got to his feet, glancing at his watch. "It's quarter to eight. I'm going to go see what's keeping Laura."

Richard squinted up at him. Zach didn't like it when he looked at him like that, as if he could see right through him.

"I've got time to kill, Zach. If she just flew in yesterday, then she's suffering jet lag. Give the poor woman a break. Why don't you take off and meet up with your team? If she doesn't come down in a little while, I'll go upstairs and introduce myself."

His brother's suggestion made perfect sense, but Zach wouldn't rest until he'd talked to Laura and found out for himself that she was all right. Tony, he knew, could be an insensitive swine when he felt like it. Yesterday he'd gotten an inkling of Tony's cruelty to her. It had accounted, in all probability, for his restless night.

"No. You stay here and enjoy your breakfast. I'll be right back."

"Have it your way. I'll be waiting."

"Thanks."

Zach gave his brother's shoulder a squeeze, then dodged the crowd and bounded up the foyer stairs two at a time to her floor. No sooner had he reached her door intending to knock, when it opened.

"Oh! Zach!" she said breathlessly, and clung to the doorknob for support. Dressed in a casual pink-and-white-striped top and skirt, she looked good.

Be honest, Wilde. She looks a lot better than good.

"Sorry to have startled you." He smiled. "Good morning, Laura."

"Good morning." She put a well-manicured hand to her throat, a sign of nervousness. "I'm afraid I'm the one who should apologize for keeping you and your brother waiting. Bed felt so wonderful I couldn't bear to get up, but I'm ready now." A faint but enticing flowery fragrance clung to her.

Zach took a deep breath. "I just dropped by to make sure you're all right, and to say that it's fine with us if you want to meet later—you know, if you're still feeling jet-lagged...."

I should have phoned her first. Why in hell didn't I?

"No, no. I wouldn't dream of putting you out more than I already have."

She pulled the door closed behind her and walked down the hall with him. A strange tension hung between them that prevented him from making desultory conversation. Not until they reached the bright lights of the dining room did he notice her pallor and the faint smudges beneath her eyes. Tell-tale signs that all was not well. He supposed crying could have produced them, but then again, so could illness. Either would account for her not being on time for breakfast. Until he knew the truth, it would gnaw at him.

Even if you knew the truth, what is it to you, Wilde?

The minute Richard saw them, he rose from the

table, smiled and extended a hand as they drew close. Zach saw the admiration in his brother's eyes. In fact, he saw the same damn admiration in the eyes of every man in the room.

"I've been looking forward to meeting you for more reasons than one, Laura. My wife is hooked on your soap."

"That's nice to hear, Richard." She laughed gently and shook his hand. "Glad someone in the Wilde family watches TV. Until yesterday, Zach had never heard of the show I'm in, let alone seen it! Anyway, it *is* how I pay the rent."

Zach found himself wondering how much of her paycheck had gone to fund Tony before he'd turned pro and could rely on financial backing from other sources.

Richard's smile broadened. Zach could tell his brother was already captivated. "Now that I've met you, I'm going to have to give work a miss so I can watch an episode or two myself! You're awfully easy on the eyes, if you know what I mean. Just don't tell my wife, Bev, I said that or I'm in serious trouble."

She laughed again. "Your secret is safe with me."

Well, Zach thought, no need for formal introductions here. Their easy camaraderie should have relieved him, but instead, he felt excluded. For no apparent reason everything was irritating the hell out of him this morning. Maybe he *was* having prerace jitters.

"Why don't we all sit down?" He pulled out a chair for her.

"Thank you," she murmured, darting Zach an appreciative glance.

He gave her an answering nod and sat down next to her. "What would you like to eat? I'll call the waiter over."

"Some tea would be nice."

"Nothing else?" Zach asked, realizing it was none of his business what she ate or drank.

"No. I'm afraid I'm too nervous to eat anything."

"Nerves make me *over*eat," Richard said. "I'm starting to get a pot—unlike my little brother."

"Cycling burns every calorie," Zach heard her respond as he gave the waiter her order.

Richard grinned. "Well, I hope you don't mind if I snack while we're driving around in the van. My wife, Bev, bought me enough sweets to last the entire tour."

"That makes me feel better, since I've brought along a rather large assortment of crackers and ginger ale myself."

"You're not pregnant, are you? When Bev's expecting, crackers and soft drinks are her staple diet for the first trimester." He chuckled. "Hey, I'm just kidding." Richard kept up his lively banter, but Laura's lack of response had made Zach feel like someone had just kicked him in the gut.

"How many children do you have, Richard?"

"Three."

"I'd love to meet them."

"You're going to meet the whole family when we drive Tony and Zach over to the stadium for the beginning of the time trials."

"I think I'd better warn both of you now that today will probably be the hardest driving you'll do," Zach inserted, still disturbed by his brother's innocent remark.

Richard was no one's fool and had lived through three pregnancies with Bev. In fact, twice Richard had known Bev was pregnant before *she* did. Zach supposed it was possible Laura was pregnant but didn't want anyone to know about it yet. She was a private person, he'd sensed, and the last thing she would want was for the press to get hold of the news.

Being pregnant could certainly account for her symptoms.

It could also account for the reason she still clings to their marriage.

Maybe the scrapbooks weren't the only gift she'd presented to Tony last night. Perhaps knowing he was going to be a father was the real cause of his good mood after dinner while he'd briefed the team on his new strategies. And it could explain why Richard thought Tony looked so at peace this morning.

A dark thought entered his mind. If she *was* pregnant, how long would the reformed Tony's glow last before he became bored with the whole process of child rearing and resumed his old habits?

Zach's younger brother, Mike, was a new father. It took a tremendous amount of time and work, a huge commitment. Somehow Zach couldn't see Tony in the role, especially not with the Olympics foremost in his mind.

Already Tony was talking about forming a professional cycling "dream team" that would include a triumphant Tony and Farramundi among the select group. Zach wagered that Tony would be a worse absentee father than he'd been an absentee husband. His wife deserved better.

Of course he could be wrong and she wasn't pregnant. Maybe he was getting way ahead of himself. *Maybe you're cracking up, Wilde.*

"I'll tell you what," he said, cutting in on their conversation and rising to his feet. "While you two finish getting acquainted, I'm going to see about some last-minute details and instruct the garage to bring the van around in front of the hotel at eleven-thirty. We'll load up then."

Richard flashed him a puzzled look. "Sounds like a good plan."

"I'll be by your room about eleven-twenty, Laura. If Tony's been held up, I'll bring your things down to the van."

She shook her head and said hesitantly, "I—I appreciate that Zach, but I don't think it'll be necessary."

Still, you don't know for sure, do you? He stared her down till she looked away.

"Talk to you both later," he said.

He left the dining room and then the hotel at a walk,

but broke into a run the moment he hit the street. People seeing him would assume he was giving himself a workout. In a sense he was, but not for the reasons they thought....

"BEV, HONEY?"

"Oh—you're back!" She didn't look up from the suitcase in which she was fiddling madly. If he didn't know better, he would think she was hiding something from him. "The children are in the other room getting dressed. We plan to do a little sight-seeing."

Richard caught his wife around the waist from behind and kissed the nape of her neck where her blond hair fell away. "I'm glad we're alone. We have to talk."

She lifted her head and turned around, instantly alert to that tone in his voice. "What's wrong? Is Zach ill or something?" Her anxious blue eyes searched his.

"Or something."

"Honey—" she cupped his face with her hands and kissed his lips "—stop being mysterious and tell me."

He heaved a sigh. "I wish I knew."

"Is he having second thoughts about the race?"

"To be honest, I don't think his mind is even on cycling."

"What?"

"My little brother is acting very bizarre."

"Since when?"

"Since the moment we came back to the room yesterday and found his note."

"The one asking us to befriend Laura Donetti?"

He nodded.

"Did you meet her? Is she as gorgeous in person as I told you she was on TV?"

"Yes to both questions."

"And?"

"I like her, and I think she'll make a terrific traveling companion."

When nothing else was forthcoming she blurted in exasperation, "Honey, tell me what you're thinking! This is one time I can't read your mind."

He took a deep breath. "I'm thinking that Laura Donetti has happened to my brother."

His wife blinked. "That's impossible!"

"You're right."

"She's married to that heartthrob, Tony Donetti! Zach would never have a thing for a married woman, particularly the wife of a teammate. He wouldn't even consider it."

"You're right."

"He's far too honorable!"

"You're right."

"And furthermore, Zach isn't over Rosie. I'm beginning to wonder if he ever will be."

"You're right about that, too."

"Richard Wilde, stop saying that!"

He grinned and shrugged, then kissed her unsuspecting mouth.

After a moment she pulled away. "Honey?" Astonishing, he thought, how she could ask a loaded question with that one endearment.

"What?"

She frowned. "Richard, you don't really think…" Her voice trailed off.

He decided to relent. Rubbing her arms with his hands, he said, "Tell you what—I'll let you be the judge."

"When?"

"When Zach comes by for us in a little while. The plan is, the Donettis will come in the van with us to the stadium."

"But if we're all together, how will I possibly be able to tell anything?"

"I have no idea."

"*Richard…*"

WHEN LAURA HEARD the knock on the door, she was having another attack of nausea, worse than the one she'd experienced while Tony was in the shower earlier that morning.

He'd promised to be back by eleven, but over the years she'd learned not to rely on her husband for anything.

Last night she was asleep when he came in, and so had no idea of how late it had been. Around dawn she'd felt him stir. When she asked him how he was feeling, he told her he was ready to take on Superman.

He seemed particularly pleased that one of the members of the favored Italian team would probably draw a fine and even be penalized with a poor starting position. It was because the racer was insisting on wearing red shorts for the prologue when it wasn't the team's officially registered color.

She listened as he told her how he planned to ride the course later in the day, then informed her that he and Klaus had decided to get up early and check it out for any hidden problems.

No doubt they were still out there and had gotten so involved, he'd forgotten his promise. This was one time she could have used his help to run to the local market and get some apples, the only thing that sounded remotely palatable to her.

She glanced at her watch. It was eleven-twenty exactly, which meant Zach Wilde was on the other side of that door. How odd that she'd only met him less than twenty-four hours ago, yet already she knew the man was as good as his word.

Again she experienced an embarrassment that bordered on shame because he knew things about her and her pitiful marriage to Tony she'd rather die than have anyone know.

If she let him in, he'd see that she'd lost her color and was wet with perspiration. He wouldn't leave it alone until he knew the reason why. Instinct told her he was that kind of man.

His brother's chance comment earlier that she could be pregnant had shaken her, particularly since her period was a week late. Of course, she knew that stress and worry could affect her cycle, but the unusual fatigue and nausea were something else again.

The flu was usually accompanied by fever, sore throat, earache—none of which she had.

If Richard were right and Tony had made her pregnant on his last visit home—despite the precautions they'd taken—then it was an accident. She would be one of those statistics that defied all odds.

Under no circumstances could she tell her husband what she suspected.

Until she could get to a pharmacy and give herself a home pregnancy test, this had to remain her secret.

What if she *was* pregnant?

She buried her face in her hands. She would have no choice but to keep it from him. But for how long? *Until I start showing?*

Once Tony found out, he'd tear into her, blame her for ruining his life. She couldn't bear the thought of such an ugly confrontation.

"Laura? Are you in there?" He knocked harder. "Tony's gone on ahead with Klaus."

Well, no surprise there.

She hurried to the door, feeling queasier by the second. "I—I'm here, Zach, but I just got out of the shower," she lied. "Give me a minute after I unlock the door. Everything Tony will need for today's race is right there in the small bag and can be taken down."

If she could buy herself a little time, maybe the nausea would pass and she could prevail on Zach to get some fruit for her without his becoming suspicious.

After she'd dashed into the bathroom, she called out for him to come in, then ran water in the basin and rinsed her face of the perspiration. But still her nausea worsened.

For the longest time she clung to the sink, pretty sure she was going to throw up. The thought of driving to the time trials and being hemmed in by thousands of people made her feel panicky.

Maybe some more ginger ale would help, but she'd have to go into the room, where Zach was, to get it. Besides, she wasn't sure she could walk that far.

Oh, Tony—this is one time I need a husband....

Certain, suddenly, she was about to be sick, she lifted the toilet seat.

"Laura?" Zach called. "Can I do anything for you?"

For the life of her she couldn't answer him.

"Laura?" Now there was alarm in his voice. "Are you all right?"

All at once she lost the bread and cheese she'd consumed earlier, the bread and cheese Zach had been so thoughtful to supply her with.

There was a tap on the bathroom door, then she felt Zach's presence right behind her.

"Good Lord! You *are* sick, just as I thought. What can I do? Tell me!"

Laura had never been so mortified. "I'll be out in a minute," she managed.

He put steadying hands on her shoulders. "Richard was right, wasn't he?" he said, staying right where he was. "You're pregnant."

"I don't see how," she said, mostly to herself. "But if I am, it w-wasn't supposed to happen. Please...you can't tell Tony."

Silence followed, then, "You mean he doesn't know? Doesn't suspect?" Zach sounded incredulous.

"No."

"But surely he'd be thrilled."

"No. Trust me, he wouldn't. I—I'm going to have to find the right time to tell him. Maybe after the Tour de France." She realized that the nausea had made her vulnerable. Now Zach possessed yet another family secret and would be mulling over this latest damning piece of information.

She heard a muttered imprecation before he let go of her with seeming reluctance. "I swear he'll never hear a word from me." His voice was thick with suppressed anger.

Laura went limp in reaction. "Thank you," she whispered.

"Are you through being sick?"

"I think so. At least for the moment."

She wished Zach would go away, but she felt too weak to assert herself. To her amazement, he rinsed out a cloth, then reached down and gently wiped her face and lips. Then he reached for the bottled water on the counter and gave her a moment to rinse her mouth before he put his arm around her waist and helped her out of the bathroom.

She had no idea a man could be this caring and selfless. It was a revelation to her.

When she was settled, he said, "You lie there while I get you what you need. Name it."

Hot tears pricked at her eyes as she looked up at him. "You've done too much already. I feel so guilty, Zach. This is the day you've been living for. I refuse to ruin it for you!"

His eyes had gone a dark pewter. "How could you possibly ruin anything for me? Because of you, Tony's in the best mental shape he's been in all year, and that in turn helps the rest of the team. You're the one we need to concentrate on right now. What can I get for you?"

It was no use arguing with him. ''Would it be too much trouble to buy a little fruit—some apples or pears? A roll, maybe?''

''I'm on my way.''

''But I'm putting out your entire family!'' she cried.

If he'd heard her, she had no way of knowing. He was gone almost before the words left her lips.

From the first moment she'd met him, she'd sensed Zachary Wilde was different from all the other men she knew. After what had just happened, she was convinced there couldn't be too many like him around.

The only information she'd gleaned from Tony, aside from the fact that Zach could beat out just about all their competition on the mountain stretches, was that his California teammate was a confirmed bachelor.

In Laura's mind, a confirmed bachelor was fatally flawed. How could anyone, except perhaps the most selfish of persons, shun marriage, a union that she believed, despite her own unhappy experience, was the ultimate expression of love and intimacy? Yet Zachary Wilde seemed the embodiment of the perfect man and husband.

You're an enigma, Zach. A marvelous unique enigma who'd had the great misfortune of getting involved with the Donettis. Too bad fate had made it impossible for him to wash his hands of her just yet.

CHAPTER FOUR

ALL THE WAY OUT to the van Zach reeled with the knowledge that Laura was probably carrying Tony's baby and was too terrified to tell her husband. If she was this sick already, how in hell was she going to keep from showing it in front of Tony?

Not only did Zach need to get the items she'd requested, he needed some expert advice and thanked providence that Bev was here to talk to. He'd promised Laura he wouldn't say anything to her husband and he wouldn't; but this was an emergency situation that required more than one head to sort out.

Richie, his twelve-year-old nephew and the oldest of Richard's children, was hanging out the back window of the blue van double-parked outside the hotel. When he saw that Zach was alone, he frowned.

"Where is she, Uncle Zach? We wanna get going!"

"Yeah, Uncle Zach," Rachel, their ten-year-old, chimed in. "What's taking so long?"

Robin's voice got mixed up in there, too. She was nine, and Richard called her their little red caboose because she was a strawberry blonde and made up the last of their family.

Richard watched Zach approach through narrowed

eyes. "Is there a problem with Laura?" he asked, too quietly for the others to hear.

Zach nodded. "Tell Bev to come inside with me for a minute."

His brother did a double take before he complied with Zach's wishes.

"I'll be back in a sec, kids," Bev said.

The children moaned as their mother got out of the van and joined Zach. He put his arm around her shoulders and together they walked to the doors of the hotel. He took her aside once they'd reached the empty foyer.

Since the time trials would be starting in another hour, almost everyone had already gone to their spots to view the race. She gazed searchingly at Zach.

"What's wrong?"

"Laura's upstairs throwing up." Bev's eyes rounded in surprise. "She's pretty sure she's pregnant, but she doesn't want anyone to know, least of all her husband. Not yet, anyway. Can you help her out?"

"Actually I think I can." Bev suddenly averted her eyes. "You see...I'm pregnant again."

"*What?*"

"Yeah." She nodded. "Richard thought Robin was our last but...well, I wanted one more and I'm excited about it. I know he will be, too. I haven't told him yet for fear he wouldn't let me come on this trip.

"So far I've felt better than I usually do. When we get back home, I'll think of a creative way to let him know he's going to be a daddy again. For the last time," she added. "Unless he figures it out before-hand, which he probably will." She grinned.

Zach felt a stab of pure envy. Nobody had a better marriage than Richard and Bev.

"Anyway, my obstetrician supplied me with enough Bendectin for a couple of months. It's a new drug for me and it works like a charm. I'll give Laura a box. If she takes a pill tonight, it'll prevent her from being sick in the morning. But for the rest of today, I'm afraid she'll just have to suffer through and try to eat something that'll stay down."

Zach raked a hand through his hair in amazement. "She said to bring her back some fruit and rolls."

"Yeah. That'll help. And some Coke. Celery works for me, too—she might try munching on a stock later. The trick is to eat before the sickness hits. Let's order some food from the dining room and go take care of her."

Grateful for his sister-in-law, Zach followed Bev's lead. In no time at all they were laden with fruit and rolls and had made their way to the third floor.

When they walked in the door he hadn't locked, Laura was sitting on the side of the bed sipping some gnger ale. She still looked drawn and pale, but her natural beauty was very much in evidence.

"Don't get up," he urged. "Laura Donetti, this is my sister-in-law, Bev Wilde. I had to tell Bev what was going on. You can trust her not to say a word to anyone but Richard, and I trust *him* with my life!"

"It's all right." Laura smiled wanly. "It's nice to

meet you, Bev. I've already met your husband. He's wonderful.''

Bev moved closer to her. "He says the same thing about you. Zach tells me you could be pregnant. So am I! It's a secret I'm keeping from Richard until we fly back to the States.''

"You're kidding," Laura said with a giggle.

Thank heaven for you, Bev. Zach thought. *I didn't think it was possible for Laura to smile now, let alone giggle, but you've managed to make both happen.*

"That's why I concocted that business about my nerves not up to taking the drive around the circuit.''

"So *that's* it," he murmured.

Bev nodded. "Your race is more important than anything else. Since I knew I'd be a liability if Richard was worried about me, I came up with my master plan to go to Paris and wait with the rest of the family there. Then if I have a few bad days, I can lie around in the hotel room and watch the Tour de France on TV, and he'll be none the wiser.''

Laura gasped. "But if your husband is saddled with me—''

"You're not his wife," Bev broke in. "It won't be the same thing at all. Knowing you're pregnant, he'll be distracted just enough to not agonize so much over Zach's performance. Besides, Richard is positively euphoric about driving you around. You know how I can tell?''

Laura eyed Bev in awe and curiosity. Zach was just as curious about the answer.

"He's been very quiet about you. Now I know why. You're absolutely gorgeous and he's already halfway in love with you. Of course he's not going to tell *me* that."

Tony's wife smiled again. Another miracle. Zach felt some of the shackles fall from his body. Bev was the best medicine around, bar none.

"Try a croissant with that drink." She handed Laura the plate.

"Tonight I'll give you a pill to take. If it works for you like it does for me, you'll feel fine in the morning."

Laura shook her head. "I couldn't do that."

"I've got plenty, believe me. And I have another tip, as well. Keep some crackers and juice or soda right by your bed at night and try eating and drinking a little before you lift your head from the pillow in the morning. It stops the sickness from starting and then you're all right for the rest of the day."

"Really?"

"I swear. Just don't tell Richard I gave you the pills."

"My lips are sealed. I'll be indebted to you if I can wake up in the morning and not feel nauseated. Even if I hadn't flown over for the race, I would have had to quit work. It's been awful this past week."

"Now when you go back on the set, you're going to have to be a *pregnant* attorney!"

With a sense of wonder, Zach watched the animation return to Laura's face.

"I suppose both my baby and I could have survived the coma they have me in."

"Coma? And whose baby is it? Cash's or Stone's?"

"Shh, don't tell anyone about the coma. As for the father, I don't know. I slept with both my clients *and* my ex-fiancé."

They chortled merrily. Obviously Laura was starting to feel a little better.

So was he.

"You may have a problem," Bev speculated. "You would probably want an abortion."

"True, but remember, money is what drives me. Silvestro Marchiani has always wanted a baby and none of his wives could have one."

"That's right! You could give him yours for a price, and he could bring it up to head the mob in Sicily."

"I'll let him have it for ten million dollars."

"Oh, you've got to think bigger than that. Make it twenty, and then you can buy out Aurelia's newspaper and get your revenge for her sleeping with your father when you were a little girl and he was in Europe buying horses from the sheikh while your mom was dying in the hospital of that disfiguring disease."

"Perfect!"

That did it for Zach. He burst out laughing.

Both women swung their heads in his direction. Laura's expression turned to horror. "Zach! The time trials!"

"Relax. We've got time to spare. Besides, even if

it *had* made me late, I wouldn't have wanted to miss what I just heard.''

"But you should be over there with the team right now, shouldn't you? Your coach'll have a fit." Bev got up from the bed, and Laura followed suit.

Zach studied her upturned face. "How are you feeling? Honestly."

She met his gaze without wavering. "Throwing up helped a lot. I think the croissant I just ate is going to stay down, especially with this drink and apple. I'll bring along an extra supply of everything in case I start to feel really awful again."

Bev moved toward the door. "Luckily we'll all be together today, and tonight we can come back here and crash. If worse comes to worst during the trials, we can use the excuse that we're bored and want to do some shopping. Then we'll run behind a tree and Laura can do her thing."

Zach's mouth quirked. "The trials are boring, I agree."

"Except when *you* head down that ramp, brother dear. Then we'll be cheering you to the skies."

But Zach's thoughts were on Laura. Whatever her husband's faults, Laura would be cheering Tony, which was as it should be.

His jaw hardened. *You don't know how lucky you are, Donetti. You don't begin to have a clue.*

"I'm going to sit in back with Zach and the kids," Bev announced as they made their way out of the hotel and headed for the van. "You sit in the front, Laura."

"But I don't want to separate you from your husband."

"I'll be right behind him. Besides, you can see the horizon better from the front, and you won't get car sick."

"That's true. When I was little and we were on trips, my dad had me sit in front if I started to feel funny. The odd thing was, I always did feel better, but I thought it was because I got to sit next to him."

"That works with our children, too," Bev said. "Richard's a great dad."

Laura smiled. "I'm sure it works equally well with a mother like you."

Zach couldn't get over how well the two women were getting along. By the time they'd climbed into the van and the introductions had been made, he had the impression that Laura and his brother's entire family would soon be fast friends, and remain so long after the Tour de France was over.

Richard announced they were off, but no one was paying much attention, not when the children learned that Laura was a television celebrity. In awe of her beauty and status, they couldn't stop asking questions.

As Richard plowed and honked his way through the traffic-filled streets of St. Léger, Zach made up his mind that when he returned to California, he would watch her soap. Now that he was getting to know her, he couldn't imagine her as the conniving man-eating Margo.

The more he reflected on the situation, the more he

realized it was Laura's TV personality rather than her own gentle unassuming character that Tony had portrayed to him.

Why?

It didn't make any sense—unless Tony was simply assuaging his guilt by telling himself that her actions were more reprehensible than his. Was Tony one of those people with such deep-seated psychological problems he couldn't distinguish between fact and fiction?

Whatever the explanation, it had to be a hellish situation for Laura to live with such a man, especially now that a baby was on the way.

Richard spoke from the front seat. "Zach, we're here! This is as close as I can get. Your team van is three cars ahead of us. We'll stay put. This is about the best view we'll get of you coming off the ramp."

"You do great work, Richard."

"Yeah, yeah."

"Good luck, Uncle Zach! We love you! We hope you win!"

The whole family gave him hugs and kisses. He sensed Laura's eyes on him, then her hand grasped his forearm over the seat.

"Thank you for everything, Zach. Be careful," she said in a low husky voice. "Don't let anything happen to you."

"Haven't you heard?" Behind his carefree smile he fought the impulse to kiss those lips that had expressed concern for him. "I'm indestructible."

An anxious expression entered her eyes. "I know better."

She *did* know.

Cycling could be extremely dangerous, even deadly. Over the years, two of Zach's racing colleagues had been killed in crashes. Laura lived through that fear every time Tony entered another race. That kind of anxiety couldn't be good for the baby.

"I'll tell Tony you're here," he said, if only to remind himself once again that she was well and truly married to his roommate.

After he'd gotten out of the van and had come around to the window at her side, she said, "In case he can't break away, here's his bag." She handed it to him through the window. "Good luck," she added.

Zach gave her a slight nod before wheeling away. *Don't think about her, Wilde. Just don't think.*

By the time he reached the team van, he felt his first drop of rain.

"What took you so long?"

As head of the Ziff team, Tony had every right to know why Zach was late.

Zach climbed into the oversize vehicle holding his racing buddies and handed Tony the bag Laura had given him. "*This.* Your wife is three cars behind in Richard's van."

Tony took the bag and placed it on the floor. Then he darted Zach an unfathomable glance. Zach had no idea what his roommate was thinking. "Hold down the fort for a minute, guys. I'll be right back."

The second the door closed, Zach looked at Leon. "Is everything all right?"

Their manager nodded. "Tony's up for this like I've never seen him before. Never underestimate female magic."

"With a wife who looks like her, Tony's a fool to waste his time on bimbos," Klaus said, loving to use the American slang he was constantly hearing.

"Yeah, quite a babe," Vadim concurred.

Zach could have done without hearing his teammates' unabridged comments about the breathtaking Mrs. Donetti. He particularly didn't want to think about the farewell send-off she'd be giving Tony.

"Gentlemen," their Belgian-born coach broke in, "shall we get our minds on business? Jacques? You'll be leaving the ramp first."

"THERE'S YOUR HUSBAND! He's coming this way! Cool!"

Laura had been facing the rear of the van chatting with Zach's family. At Richie's exclamation, she turned in her seat.

Wearing the Ziff-team colors of red and yellow, Tony stood out from the crowd. A lean romantic dark-haired figure with a smile that dazzled his fans.

If her baby was a boy, no doubt he would grow up to be every bit as handsome and dashing as Tony. But in her heart of hearts, she hoped her child's *character* would be exactly like another man's, a man she'd met only twenty-four hours before.

Already she thought of Zachary Wilde as her own heroic Viking. He was a *real* man and ought to be giving the world lessons.

How could two men be so different?

Before her husband reached the van, she had to make a split-second decision—step out to greet him or stay put? She decided to stay put. Aside from the fact that it had started raining and her stomach was still a bit upset, this was Tony's greatest moment, and he wouldn't like sharing the spotlight with anyone, especially her.

She rolled down the window and called out to him. When he got to the van, he reached inside and caught her around the back of the neck with his hand, bringing her head forward to give her a hard kiss on the mouth. "Wish me luck, Laura."

Dozens of flashes went off as she'd known they would, as Tony had planned they would. He loved the idea that a picture of him kissing her would make the front pages of a dozen foreign magazines and newspapers.

"You know I do," she whispered against his lips, trying to reassure the insecure little boy inside him, the boy no one but a few realized inhabited his man's body. It was to that little boy she said and could still mean, "I love you, Tony, and I'll be here for you. Please don't take too many chances."

"That's lousy advice, Laura," he whispered back, his eyes alive with the heat of imminent battle.

She was so used to him throwing barbed comments in her face, they didn't faze her anymore.

"In that case I'll pray for you."

"I'll win, anyway."

He gave her one more kiss, then saluted everyone in the van before heading back to join his team.

"Good luck, Tony!" hollered Richard's kids.

"Dad, can we get out and walk around?" Richie asked.

"You'd never find your way back to the van."

"Yes, we will!"

While they bantered good-naturedly, Laura shut the window, her gaze following Tony until he was out of sight.

At Bev's suggestion Richard started the engine to run the air-conditioning. With relief, Laura breathed in the cooler air.

"Oh, no!" Bev cried suddenly. "One of Zach's racing gloves must have fallen out of his pack."

"I'll take it to him," Richie volunteered.

"Oh, sweetie, I don't know about that."

"Jeez, Mom. You sound like I'm a baby!"

"You could be a hundred and still lose your way in this crowd, Richie. I couldn't handle that."

"I'll go with him, honey."

Richard took the glove and got out the driver's side. Richie followed—and so did his two sisters.

"See ya, Mom."

"See ya, guys."

"Good," Bev said once they'd left. She pulled

down the blinds so curiosity seekers couldn't peer in. "Knowing Richard, he'll stay outside with the children for a while. Now that we're alone, come on back here and stretch out."

Laura didn't need any urging. Soon they were both lying down across from each other. "I feel kind of guilty or naughty or something."

Bev chuckled. "I know what you mean. Can you believe we're at the site of the time trials for the Tour de France of all things, and we're lying here exhausted because we're *enceinte,* as the French say, and nobody knows but us. Here—eat another apple."

Laughter bubbled out of Laura as she accepted it and took a bite. Bev was so easy to be with she felt as if they'd been friends for years. "It's an amazing coincidence. How far along are you?"

"Five weeks, I think. What about you?"

"The same."

"I've been going over names. If it's a girl, we'll call her Lisa, after Richard's mother. But if it's a boy, I'd like to call him Zach. I swear if I'd met him first…"

Laura's heart turned over. She hid her face in the crook of her arm. "He's a wonderful man. So's your husband."

"All the Wilde men are. Wait'll you meet the baby brother, Mike. He'll be in Paris for the finish of the race."

"How old is he?"

"Twenty-seven. He and Carrie just had a little girl.

Mike's terrific, just like his brothers. Of course, no one compares in the looks department to the famous Tony Donetti.''

At that comment, Laura stifled a groan.

"Don't let on that you know, but Rachel has a poster of your husband on her closet door. Zach got it for her because she begged him so many times.''

That sounds like Zach. "How sweet, Bev.''

"I bet there are several thousand girls who have that same poster on their walls.'' A pause. "Does it bother you?''

Because of the difficulties in her marriage, and the nature of her job, Laura hadn't confided her problems to anyone. But Beverly Wilde was growing on Laura, and she was amazingly easy to talk to.

"It used to, but not anymore.'' *Thank goodness.*

Within a couple of months she and Tony would go their separate ways. She'd raise their baby alone and give it all the love she had to give.

"How does he handle your celebrity status?''

"He's so busy cycling I don't imagine he thinks about it very often.''

"I didn't mean to pry. Forgive me, Laura—I must sound very rude. Chalk it up to my shock over the privilege of getting to know the lovely woman behind the famous Margo facade. I have more questions to ask than my own children.''

"Don't apologize for anything. I'm indebted to you. As you and Zach have found out, I'm awfully human.

Too human, maybe. Poor Zach—he walked in on me while I was throwing up.''

"He came into the bathroom?" Bev sounded incredulous.

"Yes. He saw what was happening and proceeded to take expert care of me. If he's anything like your husband, then I envy you that kind of devotion and attention.''

"What did he do?"

Laura found herself telling Bev the details. "I've never been so grateful for anyone's help in my life.''

Bev's voice sobered as she confided, "He should have been a father several times over by now, Laura.''

She bit her lip. "Tony says he's a confirmed bachelor.''

"That's Zach's reputation, but no one knows the pain he's been through to bring him to this point.''

I knew there had to be an explanation.

Laura lifted her head, her heart pounding hard. "What happened?"

Laura lost track of the time as Bev told her about Zach's first fiancée who died of a brain tumor. A few years later he met another woman—Rosie Armstrong, a young widow—and got engaged, but the husband who'd been thought dead suddenly came back. Bev didn't think he'd ever gotten over her.

"That's…that's rough," Laura's voice shook.

"Honestly, Laura, Zach's the greatest guy. It isn't fair what he's lived through. I'm so scared.''

"What do you mean?" Luckily it was too dim for Bev to see the tears in her eyes.

"Well, Zach's trained for the Tour de France and is competing in it, I think, as a way to get over Rosie. When the Tour's done, though, he's through with cycling. What scares me is that I have no idea what he's going to do with the rest of his life. He says he's not going back home, and he's ruled out the possibility of another romantic relationship. He won't put himself at risk again, you know?"

"I—I don't think I would, either, Bev."

"When I think of all the awful husbands and fathers out there, and then I think of Zach, who's so wonderful, I can hardly stand it."

Laura couldn't agree more. "Tony says he has a very successful outdoor-sign business in partnership with the rest of your family."

"That's true, but I think Zach has gone into a deep depression. After the final ceremonies, we're not going to see him for a long time."

"Honestly?" Laura found she was holding her breath.

"Yes. Richard's sick about it. You see, he and Zach are very close."

Laura shut her eyes tightly. Now she understood what Zach meant when he said he wasn't into racing for the same reasons as Tony. And for just a second she'd seen that aloof cold side of him. She shuddered just remembering it.

"I don't blame you for being scared," she said.

Bev sniffed. "Hey—I didn't mean to burden you with all the Wilde-family problems. I must be insane."

"No. I wanted to hear."

Maybe I'm insane, too, but I want to know everything there is to know about your brother-in-law.

Bev sat up. "Let's change the subject. You didn't tell me yet what you're thinking of naming *your* baby."

My baby. Laura was pretty certain she was pregnant, and in fact would be strangely disappointed if it turned out she wasn't.

"Well, now that you mention it, if I have a boy, I think I'd like to call him Carl, after Tony's father. He and Tony's mom were killed in a freeway collision when Tony was just an infant."

"You're kidding! How tragic."

"It was. But he has this terrific aunt and uncle—they're the ones who have raised him. I found out only recently that his father was a swimming champion, so I guess Tony inherited his athletic ability." She paused. "Anyway, if I have a girl, I'd like to be completely frivolous and call her something like... Astrid."

"Now *that's* a coincidence."

"What do you mean?"

"I've been doing some genealogy on my family and Richard's, and found out there was an Astrid way back in the Wildes' Norse ancestry. It means something like having the beauty of the gods. It's a lovely name. What made you think of it?"

Laura, feeling heat sweep up her neck and over her face, was unable to answer.

"Do *you* have Viking blood somewhere in your ancestry, too?" Bev prodded.

Laura laughed nervously. "None. I'll probably call her Jane."

"I prefer Astrid."

"Well... Tony may have something to say about it. Then again, if we have a girl, he probably won't care and he'll leave the decision to me."

"When do you think you'll tell him?" Bev asked quietly.

Laura ran an agitated hand through her curls. "That's a good question. If I'm really pregnant, then this baby was a complete and total accident. Don't get me wrong—I'm thrilled. In fact, I'm more than thrilled. I'm overjoyed. But we've always taken precautions, because that was what Tony wanted. He'll be in shock when I tell him."

"There's always a risk, no matter what."

"Yes. As I've found out."

Bev made a commiserating sound.

"I guess it's no secret that my marriage to Tony has pretty much failed. Basically I've always wanted a family and he's fought me every step of the way."

"Oh, Laura. I'm so sorry."

"I might as well tell you the whole truth. After the Tour de France, I'm asking him for a divorce."

"Wow. Life gets complicated."

"You're right. Learning I'm pregnant won't make

any difference. In fact, it will probably ease Tony's conscience to know I won't be living alone, that I'll have the baby I always wanted."

"A baby needs both parents."

"I wish it were that sim—"

"Hi, Mom. We're back!" Robin's bright little voice broke in on them as she pulled open the van door.

"Good grief!" Richard exclaimed, then threw back his head and laughed at the sight of the two of them lounging.

He sounded exactly like Zach just then, and Laura was filled with inexplicable warmth.

"If I didn't know better, Mrs. Wilde," he said sotto voce, "I would think you're in the same condition as Mrs. Donetti."

"Really, Mr. Wilde." She remained poker-faced, but Laura caught the mischievous glance she darted her. "To talk about such things in front of the children…"

Laura could almost hear the wheels turning in Richard's head.

"*Bev?*"

"Mmm?"

"Good Lord! You're not…"

"I guess my secret's out now, Laura."

"You mean you *both*—"

"I've decided there's going to be a change in plans. I think we'll all drive around the circuit, instead of my going to Paris. That way Laura and I can help each other and tend the children at the same time. We'll leave the driving to you.

"It's going to be a lot of togetherness, but that's what being family is all about. Right, darling?"

He shook his head in exasperation, but Laura saw the gleam in his eye. He was delighted to learn he was going to be a father again. He was delighted his wife would be joining him for the tour. Again she thought about Tony, *How could two men be so different?*

"You do pick your times, honey. My brother's going to be heading down that ramp any minute now."

"One day, won't it be fun to tell our little Zach or Lisa that we watched their famous uncle ride in the Tour de France on the same day you found out I was pregnant?"

"There won't be a tale to tell, if you don't hurry."

"We're up, aren't we, Laura?"

"Absolutely." Laura couldn't wait to have a legitimate reason to feast her eyes on Zach. With the binoculars she'd be able to see him clearly, in spite of the drizzle.

Richard grabbed his binoculars from the visor, then helped his wife out of the van. In plain view of everyone he gave her a resounding kiss before they all took their places in front of the van with Richie to watch the start.

Laura wedged between Robin and Rachel and raised her binoculars to focus on the activity at the ramp. There was no sign of Tony. Earlier he'd told her he wouldn't be starting until late afternoon.

Slowly she brought the lens into focus. To her shock, to her *joy*, Zach was staring straight at her. He held up one of the granola bars she'd given him, then put it in his mouth and waved.

Zach.

At this point, her heart was galloping.

She waved back, but the hand holding the glasses was shaking so hard she almost dropped them.

Just before she heard an announcement in French, he flashed her a broad smile. Then he lowered his head and body into position over his bike.

Within seconds, he was off.

Laura followed his progress for about a kilometer, then lost him as he rounded a corner. It looked to her like he was moving with the speed of a torpedo. Not for the first time since she'd met him, she found herself holding her breath.

CHAPTER FIVE

LATER THAT NIGHT, Richard heard the door to their hotel room open. "Honey?"

"I'm back," Bev whispered, coming into their bedroom.

She shut the bedroom door, then scrambled across the room and got under the covers with him. "I just gave Laura a pill and she's gone to bed. What about the kids?"

"They're out like lights. Where's Tony?"

"He hasn't joined her yet."

"The team is probably still planning tomorrow's first stage."

"I don't want to talk about the race. Zach placed seventh and Tony placed third. That's good enough for me. Right now I've got so much I'm dying to tell you, I don't know where to begin."

Richard chuckled and held her close. "Well, for starters I'd like to enjoy a little togetherness and celebrate the coming event."

"Richard...we don't have time for that right now. I need to talk."

He sighed.

"This is really important, honey," she said. "It's about Zach!"

He smoothed the hair off her forehead, loving everything about his adorable wife. "Okay. Was I right about him or what?"

"Oh, boy, were you ever! But guess what?"

"What?"

"Zach Wilde happened to Laura Donetti, too!"

"Tell me something I don't already know."

"All right. Try this on for size. She's asking Tony for a divorce after the Tour de France."

Richard blinked, then raised himself up on one elbow. "That's something I didn't know."

"Amazing, huh?"

"Does Zach have any idea?"

"No. She confided that to me in absolute secrecy when we were in the van. I think their marriage was bad from day one."

"That's a shame."

"It is. Especially if there's a baby on the way. I like her, Richard. I mean, I really like her a lot."

He tickled her nose. "I do, too."

"Are you thinking what I'm thinking?"

"Probably."

"Do you think this might be the miracle we've been praying for?"

"Ordinarily I would say it was way too soon to tell. But I have to admit the chemistry between them is powerful. Not even Rosie had this kind of effect on him in the beginning."

She cuddled into him. "I know. He acts like he's been hit with a hundred-megaton bomb.'

"Do you know what he did at the start today?"

"What? You wouldn't let me look through the binoculars."

"That was because I couldn't believe what I was seeing."

"What do you mean?"

"Zach was smiling and waving, but it was for Laura's benefit, not anyone else's."

"So *he* was the person she was looking at through her binoculars!" Bev exclaimed. "Breathlessly, I might add."

"Zach couldn't have cared less about the race," Richard said. "Neither could she. It's a good thing her husband wasn't around, because I swear she and Zach didn't know anything or anyone else existed. He was so busy eating one of her granola bars I'm surprised he even heard the official tell him to go."

Bev squeezed him. "Oh, Richard. This has got to work! It can't blow up in our faces. Not this time."

"Well, one thing's for sure. If this keeps up, by the end of the Tour de France she and Zach will be so close we won't be able to pry them apart with a crowbar, and he won't be running off someplace where we can't find him."

"I know. But what worries me is that when Tony finds out he's going to be a father, maybe he won't want a divorce."

Richard let out a weary sigh. "I'm worried about

that, too, although my instincts tell me it won't make a difference. If a marriage has gone wrong, a child won't solve the problem.''

"I agree. Am I evil, Richard, wanting them to break up?"

"Don't be silly, honey. Obviously they're both very unhappy and have been for a long time. Otherwise she wouldn't be contemplating such a decision, let alone revealing her deepest thoughts to you. And as far as I can tell, she's been giving out vibes to Zach without even meaning to. The miracle is, he's been picking up on them. Whatever they're both feeling, it appears to be mutual.''

"I have a hunch they'd be really good together.''

"They already *are* good together. I must say my brother has excellent taste. This one is a major, major knockout.''

"Whoa. That's high praise indeed. Well, she's met her match in Zach. Next to you he's the most gorgeous man on the planet.''

"More gorgeous than Donetti? Our daughter would never believe it!''

"Our starry-eyed Rachel is a *girl.* Right now she's crazy about Tony Donetti because he's slick and glamorous. But he's shallow. It takes a *woman* to appreciate Zach, to see that he looks like a Norse god, you know?''

"What?'' Sometimes his wife astounded him.

"I told you that when I was doing the Wilde genealogy, I found out there's a large dose of Viking blood running through your veins because you all descended from Queen Astrid of Kelby.''

Richard's only response was a chuckle.

''Oh—'' she made a sound of frustration ''—you're a man and wouldn't understand.'' *But Laura does. She already has a Norse name picked out.*

''Let me get this straight.'' Richard's chest was shaking with laughter. ''When you first saw me, you thought I was a Norse god? Is that what you're telling me?''

''Well, maybe a lesser god, because you're a little shorter than Zach and you don't have silver eyes. Yours are more fjord blue and—''

''A lesser god? Silver eyes? Fjord blue?''

''Honey—'' she kissed him lingeringly ''—don't get your feelings hurt.''

''Trust me. They're not hurt.''

''Oh, Richard... I'm scared. If the Donettis don't break up, then it means that Zach could be in trouble for the *third* time.''

Suddenly Richard didn't feel so jovial. ''Don't say that. Don't even think it.''

''What are we going to do? How can we protect him?''

''It's too late. The deed is done.''

''I couldn't bear it if he got hurt again.''

''Neither could I, but these are early days and anything can happen. Let's sleep on it, shall we? We've got a long day of driving ahead of us tomorrow.''

"What do you bet Zach is over at Laura's room first thing in the morning to find out if she's okay."

"I'm not going to bet when we both know he'll be there the second her husband is out of the room."

"It sounds positively indecent and here I am condoning it. Honey? You don't think Zach would actually... I mean...she's still married, and—"

"Bev," he interrupted her gently, "in the frame of mind my brother's in, anything is possible, but let's not borrow trouble. Good night."

"Good night."

Richard drew her closer and closed his eyes. But before he fell asleep, the last image his mind conjured up was the look on his brother's face earlier in the evening when he'd told him that Laura had been too ill to join the family for dinner.

Richard's news had extinguished the light in Zach's eyes. They'd suddenly looked as bleak as a winter battlefield after the last body had been counted.

Zach was emotionally involved with Laura Donetti.

That wasn't good. Not when Laura wasn't available yet.

But soon... God willing.

LAURA GLANCED at her watch. Eleven p.m. She'd been asleep four hours.

Tony still wasn't back, but it didn't surprise her. He was running true to form. No strategy meeting would have lasted this long. Everyone on the team would be in bed right now. *Maybe Tony is, too.*

Nothing he did bothered her anymore. How sad, she thought. How tragic.

Their marriage should have lasted forever. Their baby should have had the guarantee of a wonderful caring father. But all the shoulds in the world hadn't made it happen.

Earlier today, when Tony had crossed the finish line with the third-best time of the prologue, fans for the Belgian-sponsored Ziff team had gone wild with excitement. But it had been all she could do to wave to him, because her nausea had flared up again.

At that point everyone in the family had been hungry and exhausted. Richard had driven them all back to the Beaulieu. Laura had gone straight to her room to lie down while the family had dinner, and so she hadn't seen Tony or Zach, who'd been collected in the team's van.

Now she was hungry and threw off the covers to get something to eat. A pear and another croissant sounded good.

As she finished the last of her fruit, the phone rang. *Must be Tony.* Why did he bother to call with an excuse? She had half a mind not to answer it, but the ringing persisted. At the last second she wiped her hands with a cloth and dashed across the room to get it.

"Hello?"

"Laura?"

Stunned because the deep male voice wasn't Tony's, she sank onto the side of the bed. "Zach?"

"Forgive me if I woke you."

"You didn't," she rushed to assure him. It was ridiculous, but every time she heard his voice or got near him, she experienced this fluttery reaction inside.

"I don't know if you heard. The rain was coming down pretty hard when Klaus went around the last curve of the course. He crashed into a concrete divider and was taken to the hospital with a concussion. That's where I'm calling from."

"Oh, no!" she cried. "I had no idea. The poor thing. How is he, Zach?"

"He's going to be okay. They're about to release him. The whole team's here. Since Tony doesn't know about your condition, I thought I'd better call so you wouldn't worry." There was a tension-filled pause. "Do you need anything, Laura?" His voice sounded husky.

She got to her feet, indescribably touched by his concern. "No. Thank you. I'm fine. Between your brother and his wife, I feel pampered and spoiled already. Bev swears by the medicine she gave me earlier. They're terrific people, Zach."

"Yes, they are."

She started pacing to counteract the adrenaline pulsing through her body. "Congratulations on a fantastic finish. I couldn't see it up close because I let the girls watch through my binoculars. But I know that seventh place is remarkable."

"Tony's the man of the hour, but it's nice to hear. For what it's worth, that was my best prologue time to date. I think it must have to do with the granola bar I ate on the ramp.''

She smiled in remembrance. ''There're more where those came from.''

''Good. I'll be over in the morning for a refill.''

Her eyes closed tightly. ''If the pill I took performs the required miracle, I should be able to make it to breakfast with your family.''

''Around eight, I understand.''

She moistened her lips nervously. ''I-if I can't come down, I'll send you a care package via Richie.''

''I just got off the phone with my brother. He says Richie is crazy about you already. Apparently you know more about baseball than any 'girl' he's ever met. Richie doesn't like girls, so you must have made quite an impression on him.''

Laura knew she shouldn't be so thrilled by a simple compliment. ''I never had a little brother, but if I could've picked one, he'd be it.''

''No one else ever had the patience to go through all his baseball cards with him at one sitting.''

''It was fun!'' she asserted. ''Do you realize he can reel off more facts than my own father? Dad's a Yankee fan from way back. Until this afternoon I didn't think anyone else knew more about baseball than he did. Just wait till I get him and Richie together!''

Zach's laughter rumbled over the line and seemed to travel through her, making her feel more alive than she'd felt in years. ''Do *you* like baseball?'' he asked.

''I love it. So does my sister. We wear our baseball

caps and go to every evening game with Dad, help him yell at the referee, throw popcorn, stuff like that. Dad's just waiting for one of us to have a boy so—'' She stopped, shocked to realize she really was going to have a baby.

She didn't need a test to know it. There were other signs that before this morning had seemed unconnected to the nausea. After consulting Bev, she now knew differently.

"So he can go to his Little League games?" Zach finished for her, but the lighthearted tone had disappeared from his voice.

"Something like that. Yes."

"Well, in about eight months it looks like he may just get his wish."

She swallowed hard. "So far, girls run in our family—my sister's had two. Neither of them shows a penchant for baseball yet."

"Tony's child might be different."

Tony may be the biological father, but I have difficulty associating him with my baby.

"Maybe you'll give birth to an Olympic alpine skier," he suggested.

"Maybe my baby will turn out to be Jane or John average, like me."

She heard a sharp intake of breath. "There's nothing average about you."

This conversation needed to end, for reasons she didn't dare explore. But perversely she didn't want it to. "All I care about is that it's healthy," she said.

"Amen. On that note, you ought to be in bed. Good night, Laura."

"Good night." She replaced the receiver slowly. *You're reading way too much into this, Laura. Zach Wilde is just a decent human being who would be this kind and thoughtful to any woman in distress.*

He didn't want her worrying that Tony was doing something he shouldn't. He knew she was pregnant, and had simply called to make sure she was all right. Some men in the world were like that.

Besides, she'd heard what Bev had said about Zach's past. So she'd better forget what she felt when she was around him. She must not make this out to be something it wasn't, or she could be headed for the greatest heartache of her life....

"Zach, *MON AMI!*" Vadim called to him. "*Viens!* They are talking about us."

Zach relinquished the receiver he'd been clutching and turned in Vadim's direction. While they waited for the doctor to release Klaus, the guys had gathered around the TV set in the lounge to watch any late-night specials on the race.

On the screen now, a French sportscaster was interviewing the Belgian-born members of the team in Liège. Next came a film clip of Klaus having dinner with his parents and friends at home in Darmstadt. Then, viewed with a lot of guffaws and good-natured teasing, several segments of the guys answering ques-

tions for news commentators several weeks before the
Tour de France.

After one clip, which showed Zach in a race in the
Italian Dolomite mountains the previous fall breaking
away from the peleton—the main group of bikers, the
newscaster explained—Jacques poked Zach in the
ribs.

"You hear that, Zach? King of the Mountain they
call you. The best biker on the hill. You deserve the
title."

"Maybe not after Val d'Isère," Tony broke in, his
expression intense as his eyes darted to Zach, challenging him.

What's gotten into you, Donetti?

"So, Tony," Jacques inquired in mild amusement
"you're the all-round best, but do you really think you
can take Zach in the fifth stage, when we hit the mountains?"

"We'll see, Jackie boy. We'll see," came the cocky
reply.

Zach ground his teeth. *Since when have you ever
been in competition with me, Donetti?* But Zach already knew the answer to that question.

Since your wife showed up at our room.

*It wasn't part of the plan, was it, Tony. Despite the
priceless treasures she brought you, you're still angry.*

Suddenly highlights of the time trials flashed on the
screen. The camera zoomed in on the crowds near the
ramp. The guys assembled around the TV pointed to

Tony, whom the newsperson had caught walking toward Richard's van before the start of the trials.

Zach's mouth went dry as the camera panned to Laura. She took everyone's breath away, including, it seemed, the newscaster's. Zach had picked up enough French to realize the man was talking about Tony's wife. He used words like *"belle," "fameuse"* and "Hollywood."

The guys started whistling and clapping. Vadim spoke for the team when he said, "Your wife is a real beauty, Tony."

As the tape showed Tony leaning inside the window to kiss Laura, Zach felt as if he'd been kicked in the gut. The other guys, oblivious, cheered Tony on, nudging him in the ribs, making suggestive comments that made him grin.

At the height of all this, however, Tony shot Zach a venomous glance and muttered something about his wife only having eyes for the winner before looking back at the screen.

So, you haven't forgiven me for siccing Leon on you yesterday, spoiling all your fun. Well, that's just too damn bad. You want a fight in the mountains of Val d'Isère? You're on, Donetti.

"I am ready to go home, in case anyone wants to know," Klaus announced, walking into the waiting room. That brought a cheer from the guys. Someone shut off the TV.

Though Zach couldn't have been happier to get

away from Tony, the thought of him going home to Laura's bed made Zach's blood congeal.

"Glad to see you're all right," Zach murmured to Klaus. "Let's get out of here. Leon's waiting in the van out front."

"It has been a long day."

"And longer tomorrow, I'm afraid."

"Yes, I know—209 kilometers."

"Think you'll be up to it?"

"Whether I am or not, I will do it," Klaus said firmly. "I didn't come all this way to watch the race on television." They went out the doors of the hospital ahead of the others. Zach noticed the drizzle hadn't let up.

"Just take an easy pace tomorrow. It'll still be flat."

"I can sleep and let my legs do the work." Out of the range of the others Klaus whispered, "I heard Tony baiting you. Don't listen to him. He's just angry his wife showed up and he's been forced to kiss all his little bimbos *auf Wiedersehen.*"

"He's a fool."

"Let me teach you what to say the next time he attacks." They'd reached the van.

"What's that?"

"Du bist ein Schwein."

Zach's mouth quirked. "I took German in high school, Klaus, so I'm familiar with that."

"Ja? Well, it gets the message across, doesn't it?"

As far as Zach was concerned, Tony was a swine in any language. Unfortunately the fact that everyone on the team held the same opinion didn't help the situation.

Thanks to Laura and the scrapbooks, there'd been a moment of illumination for Tony last night. But it hadn't lasted long. Tonight Tony's dark side had taken over again. They would all have to live with it for the duration of the Tour.

Laura had to live with it on a permanent basis. Even more alarming, when she finally chose to tell her husband they were expecting a baby, the pendulum might swing even *farther* that way.

Zach supposed it was possible Tony would turn into a responsible parent, but his gut feeling was that this wasn't likely; his teammate would probably continue selfishly down the road he'd been headed, wreaking more destruction.

But whatever happened, none of it should have any bearing at all on Zach's life. The wise course would be to take Klaus's advice and ignore Tony's gibes. Wiser still would be to avoid Laura as much as possible from here on out.

Easier said than done, he knew, but as he prepared for bed ten minutes later, he made a vow to himself, one he intended to keep. As of this moment, he was removing himself from the Donettis and the emotionally dangerous situation surrounding them.

Already he'd stepped over that invisible line when he'd called Laura tonight. He could try to rationalize why he'd phoned another man's wife, but no matter what name he gave it, it was a mistake, one of several he'd made within the past thirty-six hours.

No more. He wouldn't make any more.

Tomorrow morning, and every morning for the duration of the Tour, he'd do what he'd been doing for months now. Eat breakfast and ride in the team van with the others to the start of each new stage.

The only difference would be that, at the end of the day, he'd make certain Laura and Tony weren't around when he spent time with Richard and his family. Away from the circuit, the Donettis and the Wildes would lead separate lives.

Resolve hardened, he stretched out in bed and began flipping through a travel magazine Bev had inadvertently left in his room the other day. An article on the Galápagos Islands, off the coast of Ecuador, caught his eye. Interesting area. He decided that when the Tour de France was over, it would be as good a spot as any on earth to explore.

The idea of sailing to the various islands appealed to him. In fact, on the Tour's rest day in Villeneuve, nine days from now, he'd look into making travel arrangements so he could fly there straight from Paris at the end of the Tour.

For a long time he'd been toying with the idea of turning over his part of the outdoor-sign business to the others in the family and buying a larger sailboat, one that could accommodate four to six people at a time. The revenue from operating his own boat commercially for tourists could take him around the world.

If he liked what he saw in the Galápagos, he might just begin there. Why not?

He particularly needed to stay faraway from California and anything to do with television....

ON THE FIFTH DAY of the race, the crowds lining the mountain roads presented a real hazard to the cyclists. Laura couldn't believe how spectators crowded the roadsides, pressing in so far that the road was little more than a narrow path in places.

They'd left Belgium for France four days ago. The heat had become insufferable and was getting worse. What with that, coupled with the crowds and the difficulties of pedaling uphill, it was no wonder several of the entrants had already collided, resulting in minor spills.

One overly exuberant fan had thrown a bucket of water in Farramundi's face with such force it caused him to run into Tony's bike. Fortunately both men were such good racers they didn't fall, but the collision slowed them down. As predicted by the media and his own team members, Zach was still in the lead by a good thirty seconds.

Eight of the cyclists had broken from the peleton, leaving the others behind by a fifty-five-second margin. If Zach kept this up, he would win the polka-dot jersey for the fifth stage. Secretly Laura was rooting for him to triumph in this leg of the Tour, at least.

So far Farramundi was leading overall, with Pieter

De Raet of the Dutch team making a surprising second-place showing and Tony coming in third.

"The crowd is terrible, Richard!" Bev cried, trying to get everything on video.

"It's always like this, honey. Zach's used to it. They all are."

"Well, I don't see how anyone can win when they're hemmed in at every turn. There ought to be police or something."

"No, that isn't how this works."

"Yeah, Mom," Richie interjected. "Uncle Zach says all's fair in love, war and the Tour de France."

Richard chuckled, but apparently Bev didn't see anything funny about it. "I hate this. Don't you, Laura?"

"Yes, especially when Tony didn't stop at the last feed zone for anything to eat or drink. He's driving himself too hard!"

"Don't worry. Your husband has never been in better form. That's what everyone on the team's told me. According to Zach, Tony's pretty well invincible."

If Zach had told Richard that, then he'd not done it within Laura's hearing. In fact, she'd hardly seen him the past few days, except during the race itself. He hadn't come to breakfast with his family since the first morning, and he was never around at dinnertime. That phone call from the hospital had been their last conversation.

It looked as if she'd been right about Zach. He'd shown surprising concern when she'd arrived in Belgium—making her comfortable and locating Tony, arranging for her to ride around the circuit with Richard—simply because he was that kind of man.

But since the pregnancy test she'd bought had turned up positive, and Bev's medicine had helped her morning sickness, Zach apparently assumed she was in good hands. He'd put everything out of his mind except the race.

What a fool she'd been to think for one second that he might have had a more personal interest in her. Zach wasn't the sort to get involved with a married woman, a *pregnant* married woman at that. Besides, Bev's assertion that Zach's emotions were in some kind of deep freeze made nonsense of the notion he might have felt an emotional response to her.

If anyone was emotional, it was she. Chalk it up to her pregnancy. It seemed Tony's callous treatment of her had made her vulnerable to any man who showed her the slightest kindness. It was humiliating.

"Laura?" Bev asked. "Are you all right?"

"Of course."

"Sure? You've gone so quiet I thought maybe you felt a bit nauseated. Why don't we change places? I'll sit in back with the children."

"No, thanks, Bev, I'm fine. Honestly. I guess I worry too much. Tony's a big boy and can take care of himself."

For the past few nights he'd made a habit of returning late to their hotel room. Just when she'd finally manage to drift off, he'd wake her up to listen to him talk about his racing plans for the next day.

He never volunteered where he'd been or with whom, but one thing was perfectly clear. He intended to win the King of the Mountain official title, as well as the Tour de France itself. Even for Tony, he sounded obsessed.

Sometimes she worried that the articles in the scrapbook about his father may have made him overconfident and caused him to take chances he wouldn't ordinarily take.

Richard eyed her through the rearview mirror. "If you noticed, Laura, Farramundi didn't stop, either. They've been pros long enough to know if they need sustenance or not."

"That may be true, but in this heat even they could get dehydrated and not realize it until it was too late."

"Well, it won't be long before they reach the top, then it's downhill to the finish."

"Zach's already over the summit!" Bev shouted, still filming. "I bet he's going to win!" Everyone in the van clapped and cheered.

Laura thrilled to the news, but trembled inside because she could imagine Tony's fury. Lifting the binoculars to her eyes, she saw that her husband had gained the lead over Farramundi and the others.

He was going after Zach.

She marveled at his speed, wondering where that fresh spurt of famous Donetti energy sprang from. Though there'd been rumors of drugs, she dismissed them. After all, the media cast that same suspicion on most famous athletes.

Tony's legs were like pistons as they propelled him to the top. Then, suddenly, everything changed. It looked as if he'd lost control of his steering. She gasped when the bike veered from one side to the other, then fell.

"Tony's down!" Laura's voice shook.

"I think one of his tires blew," Bev said, exchanging the camera for their binoculars. "Hurry and catch up to him, Richard."

"I am, honey."

Through the glasses Laura could see the Ziff-team support wagon draw up alongside Tony carrying all the bikes and spare parts.

"He's still down," Laura whispered as a fresh burst of anxiety swept through her. "I don't think it was the bike."

"Don't assume anything yet, Laura."

Richard's gentle voice was meant to calm her. But Laura knew something no one else knew about her husband—how determined he'd been to beat Zach in this stage. It was obvious to her he'd overextended himself.

Dear God, don't let this be serious.

She jumped out of the van and ran toward the group huddled around Tony's inert body. Jules Massonac, the Ziff-team doctor, took his vital signs, then flashed Laura a compassionate look.

"I believe he's suffering from heat exhaustion, Mrs.

Donetti. We'll take him to the hospital. He'll be all right in no time. Come, you can ride with him.''

"We'll meet you there," Richard murmured from behind, pressing a gentle hand to her shoulder.

She wheeled around. "No, Richard. Zach needs you. Please go on and watch him win. We'll all meet at the hotel later.''

"You're sure?" Bev asked anxiously.

"Yes. You heard the doctor. Tony'll be fine in a little while. Go on, both of you. Please. For me? This is Zach's big moment!''

She saw them exchange glances. "All right. But we'll come to the hospital as soon as it's over.''

Laura nodded and squeezed their hands before climbing into the van where they'd put Tony. As they drove off, the doctor hooked up an IV to get fluids into him. Soon a siren blared; they'd been given a police escort to the hospital.

Laura's gaze fastened on Tony's face and chest, watching for signs that he'd regained consciousness.

When he remained motionless, she asked, "Is it normal to be out this long?''

The team physician's only response was a worried expression.

CHAPTER SIX

ONE KILOMETER TO GO.

Zach never once looked around to see if his opponents were gaining on him. Such a move would cost him one- or two-tenths of a second of precious time, which he couldn't afford if he wanted to beat Tony. Today, more than any other time in his racing career, he wanted to be number one—if only to wipe away that smug Donetti smile for a few minutes.

Val d'Isère was like every town on the circuit, with cheering spectators and cycling enthusiasts congregated on its main street. That made it difficult for him to see the finish line. In case Tony was at his heels, Zach drew on any remaining reserves for the last sprint.

A huge roar went up from the crowd as he crossed it first. Exultant, breathing hard, Zach looked back, eager to see how far ahead he was of Donetti, but well-wishers and cameramen besieged him from all sides, blocking his vision.

As far as he could tell, Pieter De Raet crossed the finish line second, followed by Farramundi. Zach frowned when he couldn't see Tony anywhere. Had he just missed him, or had Tony fallen way behind?

His gaze darted to the peleton coming up on the finish line. Vadim was among the lead group. Klaus trailed in the back. The rest of the Ziff team was far behind. Still no sight of Tony.

"Uncle Zach! You won!" the kids yelled, as they ran up to him with Bev following.

After much kissing and hugging, Richie took charge of Zach's bike and fit it on the van's rack. Then they all moved around to where Richard stood, smiling.

Where's Laura? Zach felt a pit of dread in his gut. Something was wrong.

"Congratulations, little bro. That was one great race!" Richard gave him a bear hug, but Zach scarcely responded.

"Why isn't Laura with you? Where's Tony? What's going on?"

A shadow crossed Richard's face. "He collapsed at the summit."

Collapsed? Tony?

"Laura went with him to the hospital in one of the support vans."

Zach sucked in a breath. "At a time like this, she shouldn't be alone. Let's get over there." He tried to move, but Richard blocked his path.

"Hey—you can't leave until the ceremony is over and you're awarded the polka-dot jersey."

"I'll ask Vadim to accept it for me."

Richard shook his head and placed his hands on Zach's shoulders. "No, Zach, you're not going to do that. This is your big day. King of the Mountain!" He paused. "Tony fainted, that's all. It isn't serious. He was apparently suffering from heat exhaustion—he didn't stop at the last feed zone."

Guilt consumed Zach. "That's because he was determined to beat me," he muttered.

"What are you talking about? Tony was out to beat *everyone!*"

"No." Zach shook his head. "You don't understand." He stared into his brother's eyes. "I—I baited Tony, and this is the result. His chance to win the Tour de France this year is over now."

Zach's guilt deepened when he remembered Laura's eyes pleading with him not to provoke her husband that day before the time trials, but he hadn't been able to resist. Now that he was victorious, Tony's resentment over having lost this stage—coupled with the fact that he would no longer be able to compete in the rest of the race—would turn to a burning hatred. Team morale would plummet to an all-time low.

Worse, Tony would be impossible to live with. Poor Laura.

Before everything fell apart, there had to be something he could do to ameliorate the situation.

"I've got to get to the hospital, Richard."

Finally Richard gave up the fight. "All right. Let's go."

"Let me talk to the guys for a second."

He signaled to Vadim and Klaus. They rode their bikes over to him, their faces wreathed in smiles for his triumph. But when he told them what had happened, their pleasure vanished. This was the first they'd heard about Tony. The news effectively dashed their dreams to be champions.

Zach, of course, wasn't in the race for the same reasons as his teammates. With Tony down, the chances of the Ziff team coming out number one were pretty well shot. Deep in his psyche, Zach knew it was his fault. He felt almost overwhelmed with guilt.

Yet, all he could really think about was Laura. In her condition she would need protection from Tony. So, ignoring an inner voice that reminded him he had no business being around Donetti's wife, he asked Vadim to accept the jersey for him, then assemble the other team members and join him and Tony at the hospital afterward. According to Vadim, it was only three blocks away.

"Let's get out of here," Zach muttered to Richard as he climbed in the van after Bev and the kids.

"MRS. DONETTI?"

At the sound of Dr. Massonac's voice, Laura's head jerked around. She'd just gotten off the phone with her parents and Tony's aunt and uncle—she wanted both families to hear the bad news from her, not the television set—and was standing outside the cubicle in the emergency ward where they'd brought Tony.

Everyone from the Ziff owners and sponsors to the coach were there with her. Hospital security had called in more police to stave off the onslaught of media people anxious to cover the top story of the race so far. Laura realized that with Tony out of the running, the team would have to perform brilliantly throughout the rest of the Tour to finish among the top five or six.

"Doctor? Can I see him now? Has he regained consciousness yet?"

He eyed her solemnly. "No, he hasn't. The attending physician, Dr. Sardis, wants to talk to you." He indicated the older man with him." Please...come in this other room with us."

Her heart was pounding like a trip-hammer, as she followed them in and heard the door close.

"Perhaps you should sit down," Dr. Massonac said.

Her eyes darted from one grim face to the other. "I don't want to. What's wrong? Why isn't Tony conscious yet?"

She heard a deep sigh. "I am afraid we lost him," Dr. Sardis said in his heavily accented English.

She stood there, not comprehending. *"What?"*

"Oui, madame. We did everything possible for Tony, but we couldn't revive him."

The awful words had been spoken, but still nothing computed.

"I don't understand. Are you trying to tell me that Tony's *dead?"*

When neither doctor spoke, she felt the room start to spin. Dr. Massonac put an arm at her waist and guided her to a chair. Shock made her cling to the sleeve of his shirt.

"I thought he fainted from heat exhaustion. How...how could he die from something like that?"

"We don't know the cause of death yet. What we *do* know is that it wasn't from exhaustion or dehydration."

She was incredulous. "His heart, then?"

"Madame Donetti," the older doctor importuned gently, "we are making tests and will know the results shortly."

"What kind of tests?"

Dr. Massonac's expression looked pained before he murmured, "Blood tests."

She paled even further if such a thing were possible. That meant they were searching for— *Oh, Tony*. Tears began to gush down her cheeks. "You think he d-died of a drug overdose or some such thing?"

"It's possible."

"But he's always checked before a race!"

"He may have injected himself with something that doesn't show up right away, but we hesitate to speculate. I'm very sorry."

The finality of Dr. Massonac's tone chilled her. This had to be a bad dream or some kind of ghastly mistake. Tony couldn't be dead!

"Please. I have to see him."

"Of course."

They preceded her out of the room. Dr. Sardis pushed the curtain of the cubicle aside so she could enter.

Beneath the white sheet Tony lay perfectly still on the examining table, all animation gone from his handsome bronzed face and limbs.

In horror she approached his inert body and reached for his hand. She gasped to realize his skin was already cooling.

He really was gone.

It didn't seem possible. She felt like someone functioning in slow motion, her own body lethargic.

"Tony…" A sob escaped her, as she placed her cheek against his. "What happened out there, Tony? This race was supposed to be the supreme moment of your life. You…you were going to win and…and finally be happy."

Suddenly she was convulsed with sobs. She rested her head on his chest to cry out her grief for the little boy inside the man who'd never known his parents. The little boy who'd never thought himself loved.

She grieved, too, over the marriage that seemed to have brought Tony so much unhappiness. And for his aunt and uncle, who would, no doubt, suffer more pain for not being here and blame themselves in some way for his death.

She mourned the loss for the baby growing inside her, the child who would never know its father. And, dear God, that she'd been contemplating a divorce without ever having discussed it with him. It was unforgivable.

"I should never have shown you those scrapbooks," she whispered brokenly. "It was wrong of me. They made you try too hard, want too much, and…and I should've known that. No matter what the tests say, *I'm* the one responsible for your death. I didn't even tell you I was pregnant with your baby. Forgive me for my dishonesty, Tony. Forgive me for everything..." She sobbed afresh.

After a moment a warm solid hand clasped her shoulder. "Madame...what can I do to help you?"

Dr. Massonac meant to be kind, but she couldn't be comforted.

"Please. Let me be alone with my husband. I don't want to see anyone."

"Whatever you say. If you need me, I'll be right outside. The priest who administered the last rites is here if you wish to talk to him."

"Th-thank you. Maybe later," came her pain-filled whisper.

"GOOD GRIEF," Richard muttered, seeing the enormous crowd in front of the hospital. "The police have cordoned off the entrances."

The pit in Zach's gut grew. "I'm not surprised. Anything to do with Tony is big news. Let me out here and then go back to the hotel. I'll call you later when I have some news."

Richard nodded. "That's probably the best plan. You're one of the few who might get through that line."

"Thanks for everything." Zach embraced both Richard and Bev quickly before climbing out of the van. He was still dressed in his racing jersey and shorts.

"Give Laura our love," Bev said.

If Zach was grateful for anything, it was the friendship that had sprung up between Laura and his family. She would need it to get through this black period. For losing today's stage, which meant Tony was no longer a contender in the Tour de France, would put him in the blackest mood of his life.

Zach worked his way through the crowd but was stopped near the hospital entrance by a local gendarme.

"Il ne faut pas entrer, monsieur."

So, he wasn't allowed to go in, but not to be put off, he said, "I'm a member of the Ziff team."

The gendarme didn't budge. *"Je regrette, monsieur."*

Zach cursed under his breath. "That's too bad because I'm going in, anyway."

Stepping around the uniformed officer, Zach ducked under the rope and sprinted toward the double doors, unheeding of the whistle blows and shouts coming from the police.

His speed worked in his favor. He managed to squeeze in the doors before anyone could stop him, then raced down the hall, following the arrows to emergency.

As soon as he saw the sponsors and owners of the Ziff team huddled in the reception area, Zach realized that Tony's problem had to be serious. There was no sign of Laura, but he did spot a familiar head of black hair with distinguishing gray wings. It belonged to the team doctor.

Zach hurried up to him. Without preamble he asked, "How's Tony?"

Dr. Massonac put an arm around his shoulders and led him a short distance from the others.

"We lost him, Zach. He was unconscious before he was put in the wagon and he never came out of it."

Zach's head reared back in shock.

A long time ago he'd heard words like those—when his first fiancée had succumbed to an inoperable brain tumor.

"I don't believe it," he whispered more to himself than anyone else, but the doctor heard him.

"None of us believes it yet. Neither will the racing world."

Zach felt as if a giant hand had just squeezed all the air from his lungs. "Where's his wife, Laura?"

"She's still in the cubicle. I can't get her away from him. She has this crazy idea she killed Tony. She's absolutely inconsolable. I'm worried about her."

Dear God. What have I done?

Zach headed for the only cubicle where the curtain had been fully drawn for privacy. The grief he could hear coming from it clawed at his heart, ripping it to shreds.

He took a deep breath and slipped inside. She was seated next to Tony's body and was rocking back and forth, her head buried in her hands.

The picture of Laura Donetti in abject despair would be permanently etched on his brain.

Zach had reached the end of the line. He had nowhere to go with his pain. Instinctively, he moved toward her. "Laura…"

She lifted her head.

He barely recognized her swollen tear-streaked face. In the next instant she was in his arms.

"Tony's dead, Zach, and I killed him. I should've stayed in California. My coming here has *killed* him!"

Zach crushed her to him, half smothering the self-condemning words pouring from her soul.

He knew exactly how she felt, for he was consumed by the same guilt.

"If anyone's responsible, *I* am," he murmured into the glistening black curls. "I knew Tony wanted to win this stage today." Through gritted teeth he muttered, "I should have let him. But for me, he'd still be alive."

"You're *both* wrong, you know."

At the sound of Dr. Massonac's voice, Laura tried to pull out of Zach's arms, but he refused to let her go completely and kept a supportive hand at her waist.

"What do you mean?" he demanded as Jules and another doctor Zach didn't recognize approached them.

Jules pulled the curtain closed to onlookers. "We just got the test results back. Tony died from blood doping."

Laura's tormented eyes lifted to Zach's in entreaty. "Blood doping?"

The other doctor cleared his throat. "Sometimes athletes inject an extra supply of their own blood that has been treated to enrich it. Dr. Massonac and I believe that your husband probably had someone do this for him, *after* he took the normal drug test, to give him that extra boost.

"But it can have lethal consequences. Today the blood thickened and formed clots—which caused complications and ultimately his death."

"No one's to blame for what happened to Tony but Tony himself." Jules spoke with authority. "He knew better, but chose to take the risk, anyway."

"Zach—" Laura, wild with desperation, grabbed his other arm "—we can't let the press know how Tony died! We *can't!*"

Zach understood only too well why Laura wanted the truth hidden from the world. And right now what she wanted was all that mattered to him. He turned to the team doctor.

"You heard her, Jules. Tell everyone he suffered a fatal heart attack."

The two doctors looked at each other, then back at Zach. They were obviously in a quandary.

"Do it for the sake of Tony's aunt and uncle, who raised him out of love," Zach said in a low quiet voice. "Do it for Laura, who has to face millions of television fans when she returns to the U.S. But especially...do it for the baby she's carrying."

Both doctors gasped in shock and dismay, exactly the reaction Zach wanted.

"Let's at least allow her son or daughter to grow up believing Tony died honorably. Surely a lie like that could be no sin."

Jules's eyes grew hooded before he nodded his assent.

The other doctor said softly, "In this case I agree that the sin of the father should not be passed on to the head of the child, monsieur. I will have a private word with the person who did the lab work before I leave the hospital."

It was just as well Zach was still supporting Laura, for her body went limp with relief.

"No one must ever know the truth," Zach insisted. "Not the sponsors, the owners and certainly not the team. They believed Tony was a winner. Let them keep that belief. Tomorrow we're going to go on with the race and we're going to finish up in Paris—*in Tony's honor*. Do you hear what I'm saying?"

"You don't have to do that, Zach!" Laura cried, but the look of gratitude in those tear-filled brown eyes made him more determined than ever.

"Jules," Zach rapped out, "tell Leon we need his help. As the team manager, he can make a formal announcement to the press so they'll clear out and leave Laura alone. I've got family here who can help take care of her and inform Tony's family of his death."

He paused briefly to glance at Laura. "It'll be up to Laura and her relatives to plan funeral arrangements—those will have to be announced at a later date.

In the meantime, Jules, you can tell the team there's going to be a meeting at the hotel tonight. Nine o'clock. Everyone is to be there so we can plan tomorrow's strategy."

Jules nodded and patted Zach's shoulder. His eyes reflected a mixture of admiration and relief. "It's the best plan."

Zach had been well aware of the fear running through the team doctor's mind. It was everyone's fear. After a tragedy of this magnitude, no one would be surprised if the Ziff team broke up, bringing a premature close to all those years of preparation, of sacrifice, of money—everything ending up an utter waste.

Zach wasn't about to let that happen.

"One more thing," he added. "Since Laura would prefer to tell her family she's pregnant before it's spread all over the world, please keep that news to yourselves, all right?"

"You have our promise," Jules murmured. He kissed Laura's cheek, offered a few more words of condolence, then left the cubicle to do Zach's bidding.

As for the other doctor, his compassionate eyes fastened on Laura and he reached for her hands. "I am very sorry you have lost your husband, Madame Donetti. If you should require medical assistance, do not hesitate to call me at home. Dr. Massonac has my number."

"Thank you for everything you've done. I'm indebted to the two of you for keeping this a secret," she murmured through her tears.

"It is a little thing to ask for something as important as the birthright of an innocent child, *n'est-ce pas?*"

"Thank God you understand."

Amen, Zach concurred.

As soon as the doctor had gone, Zach dropped his arm from her waist, then immediately realized he didn't like the feeling of separation.

"Laura, I'll leave you some time alone with Tony while I call Richard to come and get us. Is there anything I can bring you? A drink, maybe?"

She shook her head, not looking at him. "After the grueling race you lived through today, *I* should be the one bringing *you* something."

She turned suddenly to face him. "I hope you won."

Lord. She was the most honest woman he'd ever met.

"I did."

"That's good," she whispered. "Thanks to you, Zachary Wilde, I think I just might get through the rest of this night."

Little did she know that those words were going to help *him* survive the next twelve hours. His gaze wandered to the lifeless body beneath the sheet, the body that had once housed the troubled spirit of Tony Donetti. Though Zach had been his roommate, it saddened him to know that, until Laura had shared some personal insights with him, he'd had no idea what demons had driven her husband.

"Come out to the desk when you're ready."

She nodded. "I won't be long. I need to call his

aunt and uncle, as well as my own parents, but I'd prefer to do that from my hotel room.''

Naturally she craved her privacy. No one understood that better than Zach.

"I'll tell Richard to hurry."

CHAPTER SEVEN

BEV EYED her husband anxiously. It was getting dark and he was driving a little too fast. Thousands of local inhabitants and racing enthusiasts were out partying, most of them still unaware that only hours ago Tony Donetti's brilliant cycling career had ended in tragedy. When the ten-o'clock news aired, it would be a different story.

The reality of his death still hadn't sunk in. She couldn't even begin to imagine *Laura's* state of mind right now. All she knew was that Zach's phone call had plunged her husband into an abyss. Whatever her brother-in-law had confided, it had caused Richard to close up, which wasn't like him.

After putting the receiver back on the hook, he'd told Richie to mind his younger siblings while he went out with their mother for a bit. On the way out to the van, he'd broken the ghastly news to her.

"Any way you look at it, it's a hellish situation. Zach's convinced that if he hadn't made Tony angry and tried to beat him in today's race, Tony would still be alive."

"How could he have made him angry?"

"You know Tony's reputation with women. Apparently Zach rubbed it in about how lucky Tony was to have such a beautiful wife following him around the circuit. I guess it didn't sit well, and Tony decided to turn the race into some kind of duel.''

"Then that's *Tony's* fault!"

"Try telling that to Zach. His guilt's compounded a hundredfold because of his attraction to Laura."

"She has feelings for him, too." Bev sighed. "Her guilt is probably just as bad as Zach's."

"Maybe worse." He darted his wife a tortured glance. "After all, she's carrying Tony's child."

As usual her husband's insight got to the core of the problem. Bev buried her face in her hands. "They're both going to need our help."

"You can say that again. Right now Zach has decided he's directly responsible for Tony's death."

"That's ridiculous! We saw Tony go down. His body simply gave out!"

"No, honey. Tony died from an illegal drug that clotted his blood."

She gasped.

"Apparently this wasn't the first time," he added.

"Oh, poor Laura. How awful!"

"Zach got the powers that be to issue a statement that Tony suffered a fatal heart attack. The only people who know differently are the doctors, Laura, Zach and the two of us."

"Thank heaven Zach had the presence of mind to prevent the truth from coming out. It would have created a scandal and ruined Laura's life, not to mention her baby's.''

"Exactly."

"Did she get a chance to talk to Tony before…''

"No." Richard took a shuddering breath. "After he fell, Tony never regained consciousness. According to Zach, he died shortly after the support van reached the hospital.''

"I don't believe this has happened." Her voice trembled. "I wanted…I hoped that one day when Laura was free, she and Zach might really get to know each other. But never at the expense of Tony's life!''

Richard groaned and shook his head. "Let's not start feeling guilty, too.''

"Oh, honey—'' she gave a deep sigh "—think how devastated the team must be.''

"Zach says they're in pretty bad shape. Later tonight he's going to get them together and urge them to finish the race as a tribute to Tony. He knows how much they were counting on placing among the top finalists. Until this is over, he'll be the glue that holds them all together.''

Bev's eyes filled again with tears. "That sounds like your brother. He's a rock. But how much longer does he have to go on being the giver, Richard? When will it ever be *his* turn to find happiness?'' Her voice throbbed with pain.

"Don't, or you'll get me going.''

"He's doing this for Laura,'' came her tortured whisper.

"We both know that."

"I can't bear it, Richard. Even if she was going to divorce Tony, she'll still mourn his loss. She cared for him in some ways."

"You're right. And I can tell you one thing—" he cleared his throat "—Zach won't be interested in consoling the grief-stricken widow this time. He wasted two years praying Rosie would lay her dead husband's memory to rest, and look what happened!"

"But Rosie's husband wasn't dead. Laura's *is*. He won't be coming back. So don't you think there's a chance—"

"No. Not for Zach. I know him." The veins stood out in Richard's neck. "When this race is over, he'll be long gone—burdened by needless guilt he'll probably never throw off."

She shook her head. "We've got to do something— maybe call in professional help?"

"He'd never agree to that. Before Zach's phone call, I would have said Laura Donetti was the one person who might have been able to save him. But it's too late now. Tony's death has cast a pall over what might have been. When Zach's duty is done, there'll be no holding him."

"Don't say that."

"It's the truth, Bev. It's something I need to face."

Bev looked over at her husband. *If Zach leaves, you'll be in mourning. The one shadow on our marriage.*

"It would have been a lot kinder to Zach if *he* had been the one to die out there today," he muttered.

"*Richard!* You don't mean that. It's just your pain talking."

"You didn't hear him on the phone a little while ago. He couldn't feel guiltier if he'd held a gun to Tony's head and pulled the trigger. There's no reaching him. Honey…" He groped blindly for her hand.

She grasped his and held on tight, feeling the fragility of his emotions to the depth of her being. In that instant her protective instincts came rushing to the fore.

"We'll find a way." *I promise you that, my love.*

"MADAME DONETTI? Just sign these papers and we'll take care of everything until you decide when and where you wish to have your husband's remains transported."

The hospital administrator couldn't have been kinder. Neither could Zach, who stood nearby, ready to fulfill her slightest wish.

For the last little while he'd been running interference, smoothing her path. Without his masterly yet sensitive way of dealing with the press and the crowds, she didn't know how she could have handled any of it.

She sighed and murmured, "I'll let you know tomorrow."

"That will be fine."

She felt a familiar hand at her elbow. "Richard's here."

It would be easy to pretend that the shock of Tony's death, coupled with her pregnancy, caused her body to react to Zach's touch and deep voice.

But the real reason was Zach himself, this wonderful caring man who had appeared so unexpectedly in her life, teaching her about the things she'd been starving for, about the things of which she'd been deprived throughout her marriage, had she but known it.

She knew it now.

And if ever she needed proof that her wifely love for Tony had died years ago, she had the proof tonight. When she reflected on the past, it stunned her how blindly, how innocently, she'd entered into marriage. Tony had presented a dashing exciting figure. Her young heart had been in love with love, and he'd come along just as those new feelings were burgeoning.

She'd been too naive to ask the right questions. She hadn't known enough about life to realize she should have taken more time to find out who Tony really was.

She took a moment again to stare down at his inert body. She knew who he was *now*. Coming to France had been an education she'd never forget.

Suddenly a great calm descended, and her tears dried. One thing had become perfectly clear to her. It would be foolish to go on blaming herself for a situation that had always been out of her hands.

She knew as surely as she knew anything that her husband, who had been, in a way, on a tortured quest for the meaning of his life, had finally found peace. She believed that Tony was with his parents now, that he was getting his answers. Armed with this conviction, Laura was determined to make sure her baby knew its place in the world and would be happy there.

But alongside this verification lay a new form of torment, even more profound and disturbing. She veiled her eyes to prevent Zach from discovering her sinful, guilty secret. "I'm ready to go."

In silence they walked out of the hospital, Zach's hand at the small of her back, their hips occasionally brushing. Laura's breath caught sharply at the sweetness of the honeysuckle in the warm evening air.

Concentrate on Tony. Be thankful he's in a place where he's no longer hurting.

Tonight when she called George and Ann, she'd urge them to overcome the guilt she was sure they'd feel. Perhaps if she explained some of what she was feeling, they could find peace. If she wasn't successful, she'd ask them if they wanted to go with her to seek professional help. *Heaven knows I need to talk to someone about my wicked thoughts.*

Several times on the way to the van, she felt Zach's all-seeing gaze studying her profile, trying to gauge the depth of her pain. *If you knew what I was thinking, Zach, you'd be repulsed.*

"Laura?" Richard was the first one out of the van. His heartfelt embrace said it all. So did Bev's. *Where did these wonderful people come from? What is it they say about true friends? Those who are willing to mourn with those who mourn, to comfort those who need comforting?*

The tears Laura shed now were tears of gratitude—to the Wildes and their genuine outpouring of love.

"We're at your disposal, you know, Laura," Bev said after they'd all climbed into the van.

"That's right. Tell us how we can help," Richard called over his shoulder as they drove off.

Zach sat across from her in the back of the van, his powerful legs extended, his eyes on her face while he waited for her to speak. He had to be beyond exhaustion, especially after winning today's race, but it didn't show. The faint shadow of beard only enhanced those rugged features.

She, on the other hand, knew she must look as dreadful as she felt. "A-after I make some phone calls home, I plan to get a good night's sleep so I'll be ready to travel with your family in the van tomorrow."

With that unexpected announcement Zach sat forward, his expression disbelieving. "You're not planning to fly back to California?"

"No," she replied. "If you don't mind, I'd like to follow you around the circuit as we'd originally planned and hold a memorial service for Tony in Paris after the Tour is over. It's what he would have wanted. With this much lead time, his family and mine will be able to join us."

A long tension-filled silence ensued. Zach stared at her, his gaze still disbelieving. "But the baby..."

"Thanks to Bev, I'm fine. Zach, I want to do my

part to honor Tony's memory, too. I couldn't handle going home right now, not when all his racing buddies are here." *Not when* you're *here.* "But if it's a problem, I'll rent my own—"

"What in hell are you talking about?" he broke in with uncustomary harshness. "You honestly think I'd let you drive the circuit alone?"

She moistened her lips nervously. "No. I didn't think that. But Tony's death has changed everything, and it's possible Richie and the girls might be uncomfortable riding in the car with me."

"Don't be absurd. They're crazy about you. If anything, they'll get on *your* nerves trying too hard to make you feel better. Richie'll probably offer you his entire baseball-card collection."

Laura smiled softly at that, and he reciprocated.

"I'm going to let you two out here, then look for a parking place," Richard announced.

Laura had been so immersed in her conversation with Zach she hadn't realized they'd reached the hotel where they'd be staying for the night.

Without comment, Zach got out of his seat and opened the back door of the van, then helped Laura down. Immediately there were cameras in her face, reporters bombarding her with questions.

"Will there be funeral services in California?"

"Did you know your husband had a preexisting heart condition?"

"How soon are you going back on your television show?"

"There've been rumors your husband was on drugs. Would you comment on that?"

Then to Zach— "With Donetti out of the running, Mr. Wilde, can we assume that as King of the Mountain, you're now the number-one hopeful to take home the yellow jersey for the Ziff team?"

Laura had never liked the insensitivity of the news media, but tonight she felt a particular aversion to them. Zach's arm went around her shoulders protectively, an eloquent expression of his own disgust at their callousness.

"The team manager has already given the press a statement," he said firmly as he led her through the throng of reporters congregated around the entrance.

She slowed. "It's all right, Zach. Let me deal with this now, then maybe they won't hound us so much tomorrow."

He stiffened. "You're sure?" The fierce expression on his face would have frightened off any normal person. But Tony's death during the Tour de France had provided the kind of news that produced three-inch headlines and created millions of dollars in revenue. There was no stopping them.

"Yes. Just keep holding on to me," she begged softly.

His answer was to draw her closer to his side. She heard his sharp intake of breath before he said, "Despite her grief, Mrs. Donetti is willing to say a few words. Would it be possible for you to give her a little space?"

Something in Zach's tone had a sobering effect on the crowd, and they backed off a few paces.

Swallowing hard, she began, "No one is ever prepared for the death of a loved one. But if Tony could have chosen his time to go, it would have been during this race. He'd planned and dreamed of it since childhood."

Her voice was shaking but she couldn't stop it. "His father, Carl Donetti, was a great swimming champion. My husband inherited his competitive spirit and talent from him. This morning Tony awoke at my side so excited about the race I believe his heart just couldn't handle everything required of it."

She paused for breath. "But on a happier side, maybe the baby we're expecting has inherited those famous Donetti genes. It's possible that twenty years down the road, the world will once again see the Donetti name on the sports pages."

Laura had been forced to make a split-second decision. Just as she knew it would, her revelation had created a minor explosion of excitement. But it was for Zach's protection, if anyone's.

She knew how gossip ran rife. As soon as someone found out she was pregnant, they wouldn't think twice about attributing her baby to another man, and Zach would be their number-one target. Even now, because he was with her, supporting her, they could be forgiven for thinking he held an important place in her life.

"It might even be a girl," she added to divert their

thoughts further. Because they were hanging on every word, she got an approving chuckle out of them. But it was the extra squeeze from Zach that told her she was on the right track with this.

"Since I'm going to be a mother—in my opinion the greatest career on earth—I plan to stay home and raise my child. Tony lost his parents in infancy, and he was reared by an aunt and uncle who adored him, who devoted their lives to him.

"I plan to do the same for our child, and I know this is what Tony would have wanted. But if you would be so kind as to give me twelve hours to inform the television studio of my decision to resign, I would be grateful."

Actually Laura wasn't worried. She'd be talking to her parents before long. In reality, they were her employers, so there *was* no problem.

An odd stillness had fallen over the crowd of reporters. She had the oddest impression they were really listening to her, something that had never happened before. Now would be the time to say what was vital.

"The man standing next to me, holding me up so I won't fall down in a heap, is no stranger to you. Zachary Wilde has been Tony's roommate all these months of training. There's no one my husband trusted more. Now I know why." Her voice broke.

She felt the tremor that shook Zach's body just then.

"He has let me know that the Ziff team is alive and well. They're going to finish the Tour de France as if

Tony were riding at the helm. In fact, who could refute that he won't be right there with them, egging them on?''

She paused for breath. ''When it's over, my family and Tony's will hold funeral services for him.''

She was starting to feel light-headed. ''Tony loved the thrill of competition with all its ups and downs. He would be the first person to tell everyone to get on with the race and remember the good times.''

There was a suspicious prickling behind her lids. ''I, for one, intend to do just that. Now if you'll please excuse me, my most difficult job is still ahead of me. I have to phone the relatives who loved him like a son and tell them Tony's gone.''

Absolute quiet reigned as everyone backed off, allowing her and Zach to proceed into the hotel.

Unbeknownst to her, the Ziff team, sponsors and owners had congregated in the foyer and must have heard her speech, because they began clapping. One by one they stepped out of line to embrace her and offer their condolences. Every eye was suspiciously bright. Especially Richard's and Bev's, who'd rejoined them without her being aware of it.

She heard smothered coughs and more clearing of throats. Emotions were running high.

By the time they finally reached the elevator, she clung to Zach for fear she'd collapse from too much feeling. No one tried to jam inside with them.

When the door closed, sealing them off from the others, Laura let out an audible sigh.

"My feelings exactly," Zach murmured into her hair. "You were wonderful out there."

"I thought that if—"

"I *know* what you thought," he interjected, his voice thick with emotion. "You were right to talk about the baby and me in reference to Tony. Your frankness will pay dividends when the reporters get busy on their story."

His eyes were deep wells of gray as he went on, "You spoke from your heart tonight. I felt the effect on the crowd. You mesmerised them. You mesmerised *me*." He shook his head slowly. "I stand in awe of you, Laura."

She grasped both his hands, studying them before she gazed up at him once more. "Then we're both in awe, because you were the one who convinced the doctors to save Tony's reputation. From the moment I arrived in St. Léger, you've been my guardian angel."

Keep saying it, Laura. Keep saying he's your guardian angel. Don't think of him as a man. You mustn't!

It was all she could do to rise on tiptoe and kiss only his cheek, instead of his mouth. Then she let go of his hands to exit the elevator.

He detained her long enough to say, "Here's your room key. Number forty-three. Richard handed it to me outside the hospital. Their room is across the hall in case you need anything."

Laura took the key from him, fighting the urge to ask him where *his* room was. It took all her willpower not to suggest he drop by her room when he'd finished talking to the team.

What would be her excuse for requesting even one minute of his valuable time?

I need you, Zach. Since I've met you, I don't want you out of my sight. When you're around, my world feels complete. Come inside and hold me.

Make love to me.

All she said was, "I won't be disturbing anyone. They need a good night's sleep, too. So do you."

His question was unexpected. "Do you think that's possible?"

Her head came up. She steeled herself to keep from breaking down. "No. Each of us is having to do the impossible. Right now it's your turn to go downstairs and infect the team with your brand of Wilde heroism."

His brows knit. *"Heroism?"* He acted as if he'd never heard of the word. *How like him!*

"A real hero just does what needs doing. That's *you*. Good night."

Zach did nothing to detain her, but when she closed the door on him, he couldn't make himself walk away.

Lord. How could she shut him out like that? Until a few minutes ago he could have sworn she felt exactly the same way he did.

He wanted, needed her so much that desire was coursing through his body, igniting dormant feelings, making them ooze from their hidden places to infiltrate his last line of defense.

But she obviously wasn't suffering from the same affliction.

Unlike Rosie's husband, Nick Armstrong, Tony Donetti would not be coming back from the dead to reclaim his wife. He'd done something much worse.

He'd left his ghost behind to do the fighting for him, an adversary more cunning, more dangerous and cruel than the living entity. In that kind of unequal struggle, no one came out the winner.

As Zach stood there agonizing, his hands tightened into fists. *Not this time, Wilde.*

A shudder racked his powerful body before he wheeled away from the door.

The minute Klaus saw him enter the foyer of the hotel, he moved toward him. Over the past few months, they'd become good friends. "That was one amazing speech Tony's wife made out there. You can castigate me if you want, but he did not deserve her."

Zach struggled for breath. "I agree."

"So—" he clasped Zach's shoulder "—we will ride to the finish line for her and the little one to come, *Ja?*"

"Yeah," Zach muttered. His path set, he said, "Klaus? Do you mind if I take you up on the offer to room with you and Vadim for the rest of the circuit? I think it's important that the team stick together until the end of the Tour."

The German gave an infectious grin. "I not only do not mind, I am delighted. As for Vadim, he has been moaning that the old team camaraderie has been missing lately.''

You're right, Klaus. A woman has a way of wreaking havoc. But never again. You're out of my life, Laura Donetti.

"After we plan our moves for tomorrow," Zach said, "I'll grab my gear and join you. What's your room number?''

"Twenty-one. I'll tell the concierge to roll in another bed.''

Two floors down. Good.

"I have another idea." Zach was suddenly full of them. "I saw a café a few doors away. Let's gather the team and head there.''

"I know the exact one. The beer is average, but the local *freuleins* are nothing short of *wunderbar,* if you know what I mean.''

"Why do you think I suggested it?''

"Ja?'' The German eyed him speculatively. "The press refers to you as the dark horse from Newport Beach. I believe they are right. Have you been holding out on me?''

Zach's face broke out in a wolfish smile. *I'm fighting for my life, Klaus.* "They don't call me King of the Mountain for nothing. *Ja?''* he mimicked.

Klaus nodded. "That's right. We haven't celebrated your victory yet. An oversight we will rectify after we dedicate the first round of drinks to Tony." He turned to the others. "Hey? Guys?''

While Klaus shepherded everyone out the hotel entrance, Zach lagged slightly behind. He should have told Richard and Bev about the change in his accommodations so they wouldn't worry when he didn't show up at the room next door to them.

But Zach couldn't handle the kind of gut-level bare-bones interrogation his brother would subject him to. Morning would be soon enough for that.

As he stepped out into the fragrant summer night, its nocturnal beauty called to his aching heart and body like a siren's song, bringing a staggering wave of fresh pain.

Keep walking, Wilde. Just keep walking.

IT WAS AFTER MIDNIGHT when Bev heard the hotel-room door open and close. "Honey?" She hurried out of the bathroom, leaving her brush on the sink. "How's Zach?"

Richard grimaced. "I have no idea. I haven't seen him."

She closed the distance between them and threw her arms around his neck. "That means he's with Laura," she deduced with a growing excitement.

"No. He's not. The concierge said he left the hotel with the team hours ago, but he thought most of them were back by now."

Bev took a deep breath, aware of the hurt Zach's nonappearance had caused her husband. After such a traumatic day, she knew Richard would feel helpless until he could talk to his younger brother and find out what was really going on inside him.

Her love for her husband made her want to take away his pain. "I'm not surprised. The team has always looked to Zach for leadership. He's either with the coach or Leon, working out last-minute details. He'll probably knock on the door any minute to say good-night."

"Maybe."

"There's no 'maybe' about it. Come on. The kids are asleep." She slid her hands over his chest. "Get undressed and lie down," she whispered. "I'm going to give you one of my deluxe back rubs."

He covered her hands, stilling them. "Have I told you lately that I couldn't live without you?"

Her eyes misted over. "All the time. I love you, too. So very much."

"I know. It's what keeps me going. Is there something wrong with me that I want that happiness for my brother?" His voice was thick with tears.

She shook her head. "No, darling. I guess we're going to have to be patient a little longer while we wait for it to happen. In the meantime, we'll continue to give Zach all the support and love he needs."

"What if he disappears and we can't?"

"We'll find a way, no matter what."

But by morning that promise had already been sorely tested. Not only had Zach avoided coming to their room before going to bed, he made only a token appearance at breakfast, and that was to inform them that he'd hooked up with Vadim and Klaus for the duration of the Tour.

Laura hadn't yet come down to eat, but Bev noticed that Zach didn't even mention her. Given his total absorption with Tony's wife yesterday after the race, for him to suddenly display a complete lack of curiosity over her and her creature comforts today set off warning bells. When he gave each of them a brief hug and he went off with the rest of the team, Bev felt her heart contract painfully. If she was suffering this much, then she could just imagine her husband's tortured state of mind.

There was no question that Tony's death had caused something to snap in Zach, with tragic results. The thing she and her husband had worried about had come to pass: rather than be vulnerable again, Zach had decided to distance himself physically and emotionally from Laura. Clearly there was nothing Bev or Richard could do about it.

Because Laura would be riding in the van with their family, Zach didn't have to worry about her and could relinquish all caretaking responsibilities to them. But in the process, he was distancing himself from the family, too, and she could tell it was already hurting Richard.

Laura didn't make her way downstairs to the dining room for another ten or fifteen minutes. Bev had the disquieting suspicion that she'd waited upstairs on purpose, knowing Zach would have been up early.

After she arrived at the table, she, too, avoided making any references to *him*. Quietly she told Bev and Richard about her phone calls home, the combined shock and grief of both her parents and Tony's aunt and uncle. It had been decided that after a memorial service in Paris, the families would accompany Tony's body home to California, where funeral services would be held at their family's church. Then he would be buried next to his parents.

Other than letting Bev and Richard know she'd asked the hospital to ship Tony's body to a funeral home in Paris, she didn't touch on the personal again. If she was plagued by nausea, she didn't mention it and involved herself in the children's conversation. She was, Bev thought, behaving far too normally for a pregnant woman who had just lost her husband. But Richie was oblivious. He seemed to think the sun rose and set with her, and he fought constantly for her attention, winning out over the girls.

Though Laura had a natural way with young people, even Bev could see that she was overdoing the pretense that all was well. Whenever the children made a reference to Zach, she glossed over his name as if he meant nothing more to her than anyone else on the Ziff team.

Several times Richard's anguished glance darted to Bev, the message poignant and unmistakable. When he finally suggested they leave the table and get ready to follow the racers for the next stage, Bev rose from her chair with the awful premonition that getting through the next two weeks under these conditions would be a true test of the refiner's fire.

CHAPTER EIGHT

THOUSANDS OF PEOPLE jammed the Champs-Elysées near the L'Arc de Triomphe to watch the racers cross the final finish line of the Tour de France.

A roped-off area had been reserved for the Ziff-team support group and families. When Richard parked the van on a side street near their vantage point, Laura hurried on ahead. For one thing, there had been so much togetherness in the two weeks since Tony's death that she felt Bev and Richard deserved some time alone with their family.

But the most compelling reason for separating herself from them was her need to watch Zach as long as she could through the binoculars. Too soon she would be joined by her parents and Tony's aunt and uncle in the cordoned-off area. She wanted these few extra minutes to herself.

So far, all seven of the Ziff team had made a fantastic showing with no serious mishaps. She was so proud of them she could burst. Klaus and Vadim had won several stages on the flats. Day after day, kilometer after kilometer, through sunshine and cloudbursts, they had all ridden with unflagging stamina and courage. It was possible Klaus might finish up in the first six.

But anyone could see that it was Zach who set the grueling pace for the team. He was the rock who anchored the younger racers and kept them focused.

The past two weeks had also been an agonizing experience for Laura, because with each passing day, she knew the end was drawing near. After the memorial service, Zach would be gone from her life for good.

Not once had he sought her out during their free times, either before or after each day's race. Not once had he come to her room to inquire if she needed anything.

Though she'd taken many walks alone in the quaint towns of France where they'd spent their nights—hoping to bump into him—the desired result had never occurred. Clearly he wanted nothing more to do with her.

Because he'd drawn the line, she didn't dare cross it. Something told her that if she tried to approach him, he would reject her, and this would bring pain beyond enduring.

Tony's death had resulted in a different kind of grief, a sadness more than a sense of loss, but in two weeks she'd come to grips with it. The excruciating pain she was experiencing now had everything to do with Zach, because he'd cut himself off from her and his family. No one said anything, but she'd learned a great deal from the confidences Bev had shared with

her during those first few days in St. Léger. His brother
and sister-in-law were hurting, too.

Needing to see Zach, she inched her way through
the crush of bodies in the ninety-plus heat. When she
could see the racers, she lifted her binoculars and spotted Farramundi in the far distance.

That might have been Tony out in front if only...
She felt a pang that this couldn't be her deceased husband's moment, but she kept her glasses raised in
search of Zach.

Klaus was coming up fast, jockeying for a winning
position among the German and Dutch team members
behind Farramundi. Another group rode behind. She
could barely make out Jacques. Then she saw Zach.

I love you, Zach. You'll never know how much.

She watched him as long as she could, then headed
toward the Ziff-support area. The grief-stricken faces
of Tony's aunt and uncle brought back bittersweet
memories of the past. Then she spotted her parents.
Everyone caught sight of her at the same time.

"Laura!" they all cried, and ran to embrace her. By
this time Richard and his family had joined them, but
the introductions had to be cut short because the racers
were fast approaching the finish.

A roar went up from the crowd as Farramundi
crossed over first. But Laura's gaze was riveted on the
four Ziff team members whom the other racers had
allowed to ride forward. They pedaled side by side,
Klaus, Vadim, Jacques and Zach, each holding high a

personal item from Tony's racing kit. As they passed Laura on their way to the finish line, they saluted her.

While Richard and Bev's children shouted exuberantly to Zach, the crowd went crazy and camera flashes went off by the thousands.

Throughout the pandemonium, however, it was the silvery eyes briefly piercing Laura's that stayed with her long after the champagne flowed and Farramundi donned the yellow jersey.

When she heard Klaus's name announced as the fourth-place winner—a feat that brought another roar from all the Ziff fans—she felt her mother's arm go around her shoulders. "Come on, darling. You look ill. This has been too much for you. Your father and I are taking you back to our hotel and putting you to bed."

Too many emotions and feelings had caught up with Laura for her to form an argument. She nodded docilely.

Bev grasped Laura's hand and squeezed it hard. "We *have* to talk later."

Laura knew exactly what she meant. By tacit agreement they hadn't discussed Zach during the race. But now that it was over, there were things that needed to be said.

She threw her arms around Bev, attempting to convey her love and gratitude for all she'd done for her.

Soon it was Richard's turn. "We love you," he murmured, enveloping her in a hug.

"I love you, too," she whispered, then lifted her

head and looked straight into his eyes. "*Every one* of the Wildes."

There. Her secret was out. She was no longer able to hold back the truth.

Richard's eyes darkened and he cleared his throat. "Do us a favor, Laura. Go lie down and take care of yourself. We'll see you at the church for the memorial service in the morning. Afterward we'll talk, and that's a promise."

"I can't wait." Her voice shook.

Holding on to Richard was like holding on to a piece of Zach. So it was with great reluctance that she finally let him go, and then her wet eyes frantically searched the crowd. As was true of every day of the race, Zach couldn't be found once the stage had ended. In a city like Paris, he could have gone anywhere, traveled down any street. To find him would be like looking for a grain of sand.

"SO... YOU'RE GOING to pull out before the service tomorrow?"

Klaus and Vadim had just come into the hotel room where Zach was packing up his gear. He'd hoped to be gone before they'd finished their celebrating, but no such luck.

"That's right. I made a reservation to leave Paris tonight."

"What's the hurry?" Vadim asked, his shrewd eyes narrowed on Zach's hardened features.

"New horizons. I've seen enough of Europe to last me a lifetime."

Vadim rubbed his lower lip absently. "That's too bad. The rest of us were hoping you'd take off on a small climbing trip we've planned into the Pyrenees. You know, a little vacation before we all have to go home. The valleys are peaceful, the food excellent, and the women warm and willing."

The words of a single guy.

He gave Klaus and Vadim about three more years before they each fell hard for a woman and settled down to raise a family.

At least that was the way it was supposed to happen. Zach was living proof that life didn't always fall into place quite that neatly or easily.

As for Vadim's words, they had no power to tempt Zach's scarred soul.

Because of him, Tony had died on a mountain, blood doping or no. Since that day, the only reason food made it to his stomach was to preserve his pointless life. The only woman Zach could imagine wanting was Tony's pregnant widow, and she was forever off-limits.

After coveting Tony's wife, he had no moral right to Laura or her love. And one day, when she had to explain to her child why she or he didn't have a father, Laura's resentment of Zach and the key role he'd played in Tony's death would flare up and intensify. Zach already knew what it was like to try to win over the child of another man. Rosie's son, Cody, had never accepted him, and that division had created monumental problems. No way could Zach put himself through something like that again. It was time to bail out.

If his plan for the future was successful, tourists would be coming to him for a sailing holiday in far-off and unusual places. It sounded like a palatable life.

"I appreciate the invitation," he said to Vadim, "but I'm afraid I'll have to turn it down."

Vadim nodded, and then Klaus moved closer, his eyes fusing with Zach's. "Thanks to you, the team pulled through and I was able to place. Next year, who knows? Maybe someone on the Ziff squad will take home the yellow."

Zach nodded. "I've already told Leon to give you my bike as my congratulatory gift."

The German's face suffused with pleasure. "I am honored."

"I'll be watching and rooting for you from wherever I am."

"You don't know where you'll be?" Vadim showed his surprise.

"Not yet."

It wasn't a lie exactly. He did have a destination in mind and would stay there if he liked it. But for reasons of his own, he had no intention of telling anyone where he was going.

"Do me a favor tomorrow and light a candle in the church for Tony?"

"Of course," they replied in unison.

"Wait, *mon ami*. I have your polka-dot jersey," Vadim said.

"Give it to my nephew, Richie, tomorrow after the service."

"Bien."

"Any word for Laura?" Klaus asked.

Zach had wondered when her name would come up. He turned away and lifted his backpack, ready to go. "Tell her we're grateful for Tony's life. Otherwise none of us would ever have had the opportunity of knowing each other. It's been an illuminating experience, *ja?*" He smiled at Klaus.

The younger man smiled back before the three of them hugged. Then Zach slipped out the door and headed for the foyer.

Besides a letter he'd written for Richard and Bev, he wanted to return a book she'd lent him to read, along with the travel magazine she'd left in his room. After leaving everything with the front-desk clerk to be given to the Wildes in room 703, he stepped outside and hailed a taxi for the airport.

When he landed in New York, he would board another plane for Miami, then Quito, Ecuador, where he would meet with Russ Magneson, president of the Windjammer Connection Tours in the Galápagos. The renowned naturalist and sailor was a leading expert on the famous archipelago.

For the next two months Zach had signed on to help crew the Windjammer line of yachts traveling to the most noteworthy of the eighty or so islands. In that amount of time he would either have saturated his curiosity about the area and moved on, or he would buy a sailboat with a cuddy to run his own private tours for a while.

Hopefully the experience would help bring on forgetfulness, that long-sought-after state of mind that would allow him to survive the rest of his life.

"MONSIEUR WILDE?" the front-desk clerk called out. "I have something for you. *Un moment.*"

Wondering if it could be a fax from the company at home, Richard waited somewhat impatiently. Bev had already gone upstairs with the children, who were desperate to use the bathroom. As for Bev, she was so broken up about Zach and Laura's situation, Richard had an idea he would spend the rest of the night trying to console her.

When he saw a paper bag in the clerk's hand, he blinked in surprise and took it from him. Curious, he wandered over to a pillar and rested against it while he looked inside.

A magazine and a book?

He frowned and pulled out both items. In the process, a letter fell to the floor. He recognized Zach's handwriting and suddenly had the feeling *he* would be the one clinging fiercely to his wife in the next little while.

Greetings, Big Brother—
There are no words to express my feelings ade-

quately. You've always been there. You were always my role model. You never let me down. Not once in my life.

Richard groaned. This was the goodbye letter. Richard had been expecting it, but not until after the service tomorrow. Apparently Zach had decided to leave the country today. He read on.

Everyone should be blessed to have a brother like you. Then again, no one should have to give years and years of themselves and their time for someone else. But that's what you've done for me.

As he kept on reading, Richard's heart grew heavier.

I'm not unaware that my needs have put a blight on your otherwise perfect marriage.

But no more, Richard. The Tour de France is over. I relinquish you of all further responsibility where I'm concerned. Bev needs her husband back. Talk about the patience of Job, but even Bev has her limits!

Bev would be devastated when she read this.

Don't grieve for me. I'm fine. I promise to keep in touch so the family doesn't worry. Just think of me as you would an adventurous brother back in the 1700s who took off for new lands.

Lately I've developed a hankering to see the world. With the race out of the way, there's nothing to stop me.

Take special care of yourself and your precious family. With another baby on the way, why don't you slow down a little and enjoy life? No one deserves all the good things more than you.

I love you, Richard. You'll always be my idol.

—Zach

Minutes later Richard entered into his family's hotel room. He could hear his wife in the adjoining room with the kids.

"Bev?"

She must have known something was wrong by the sound of his voice, because she hurried into their room and shut the door, bracing herself against it. Her gaze darted to the paper bag.

"What have you got there?"

"A book and magazine you lent Zach."

She blinked. "He's gone, hasn't he."

Richard nodded before tossing the bag on the bed. "The letter's inside whenever you want to read it."

"Honey, he may have left Paris, but it's not going to work. It's like shutting the barn door after the horse has gone."

"I realize that."

She moved toward him with a mysterious smile. "It

doesn't matter that he's flown to the other side of the earth. He'll think about her until it turns him inside out. His protective instincts will be working overtime because she's going to have a baby. He'll slowly go mad wondering what's happened to her.''

Richard gave a great sigh. ''But for all the obvious reasons, he won't act on his feelings.''

''No. You're definitely right about that. But we know someone who might, don't we? I suppose it all depends on how much she cares.''

''She's in love with him,'' Richard declared without hesitation.

''I know that, but what makes *you* so positive, my love?''

''She told me today.''

''She actually said so out loud?''

He nodded.

''Richard!'' Her eyes lit with joy. ''If she could admit that to you, then she doesn't have any of the hang-ups Zach thinks she has!''

His wife's words ignited a ray of hope, but it was extinguished by a bleak thought. ''Honey, we have no idea where he's gone.''

''That's true. But we'll find out.''

Richard shook his head. ''Even if we do locate him and she attempts to see him, he'll fight her. I hate to tell you this, but Zach makes a formidable adversary.''

''I've no doubt, but haven't you noticed she's a fighter, too?''

He stared at his wife, then nodded.

"Honey, after Tony died it would have been so much easier for her to fly straight home to California and not deal with any of the pain or unpleasantness. Instead, she faced the press, supported the entire team and kept our children better entertained than either set of grandparents could have done."

Richard's mouth broke into a half smile. "You're right. She's definitely Zach's match. Funny how you would never guess it to look at her."

Bev darted her husband a wry glance. "I'm not a man, but I would imagine Laura Donetti's beauty would keep him too busy to think about much else."

He chuckled and reached for her. "Now how am I supposed to answer that?"

"You're *not* supposed to agree with me." But she grinned as she said it and was rewarded with a kiss.

He hugged her. "When I walked in here a few minutes ago, I felt like it was the end of the world. But as usual, my wonderful wife has made the sun come out again."

"That's what wives are for. I have to tell you that your brother badly needs to be loved by a wife like Laura Donetti. For what it's worth, the look she gave him today contained enough love to fill the universe. Zach can put up all the fences he likes, but Laura will get around them. Mark my words."

"I'm marking them, honey. I'm marking them," he murmured into her hair.

AT QUARTER TO TEN the next morning, Laura stood outside the small church in Neuilly with her parents and Tony's relatives. They were greeting those attending the service—mostly Tony's cycling friends, the people who owned the various racing teams or coached them and members of the press. In Laura's opinion it was a great honor that Farramundi, the five-time winner of the Tour de France, along with his wife, were kind enough to pay their respects.

But the whole time she shook hands and thanked everyone for the outpouring of affection and flowers, her eyes glanced around desperately for Zach. She'd raved about him to her family and Tony's, and couldn't wait to introduce him to the people she loved most.

Finally Richard and Bev arrived with their children. Laura broke free of the informal line to hurry forward and hug them. Now that the Tour was over, she thought, of course, Zach would be with them.

Without her having to say a word, Bev's expressive eyes conveyed the bad news. Laura's disappointment that he hadn't come was so great she felt ill. But she had no choice but to carry on as if his failure to show didn't faze her.

At the end of the brief service, she learned she wasn't going to see him at all. For Klaus and Vadim told her that, before Zach had left Paris yesterday, he'd asked them to light a candle in Tony's memory. By the time they'd given Richie Zach's polka-dot jersey and had left the church, the pain Laura felt was excruciating.

Damn your nobility, Zachary Wilde!

I was afraid it was going to be like this, her heart cried out in agony. *I was afraid you would vanish the second you'd done your part for Tony and the team.*

But I'm not going to let you get away with it. Wherever you've run, no matter how long it takes, I'm going to find you. I will!

I'm in love with you.

Do you hear me? I'm in love with you.

Please God, help me.

"Laura?"

At the sound of Bev's voice, she turned to find the pretty blonde at her elbow. They stared at each other while streams of unspoken thoughts flowed between them.

"I have an idea where he might have gone, but I realize this isn't the time or the place to discuss it," she said in hushed tones. "When we're all back in California and you've had time to put this behind you, call us. You know the number. We'll be waiting."

A wave of pure love for Bev swept over Laura. She reached out once more to embrace the woman who'd become her dearest friend. "You'll be hearing from me sooner than you think."

"That day can't come soon enough for us." Bev's voice shook with raw emotion. "Take care going home and God bless."

CHAPTER NINE

"ZACH? MIND IF I JOIN YOU?"

Zach was sitting in the hotel lounge. He recognized Gwenn Barker's voice before he even looked up from the itinerary he'd been studying in preparation for tomorrow's new eleven-day trip.

A member of the Windjammer staff, Gwenn was the naturalist who'd been aboard the *Flying Cloud* with him on their last two trips.

Besides being a master dive instructor, she knew her stuff and held tourists captive with her knowledge about the Santa Cruz highland rain forest, the lava tubes and a wealth of other information concerning the plant and animal life. He was indebted to her for what she'd taught him.

But he hoped it was her fascination with his expertise as an ocean-certified sailor and not his being a single male that had prompted her to seek him out during their free time.

"Be my guest," he murmured. His invitation was as redundant as her inquiry, since she'd already seated herself.

Instead of the normal shorts and shirt, she'd worn a sundress to dinner, revealing a considerable amount of bronzed skin. In place of a braid, her long blond hair cascaded over one shoulder from a side part. She was most certainly a head turner.

He'd learned enough on two trips with her to know that her eight-year-old daughter lived with her part of the year in the Florida Keys, the other part with her ex-husband in the mountains of Colorado. A joint-custody situation that had been working for some years now.

Zach couldn't imagine a worse scenario for a child, but then, he tended to compare every marriage to Richard's, so he kept his thoughts to himself. In any event, he had no interest in Gwenn beyond a professional one.

"Can I buy you a drink?" she asked.

That should have been *his* line, but all attempts at civility seemed to have died after the fifth stage in Val d'Isère when he'd heard the news of Tony's death.

"I just had dinner and enough to drink with it," he replied. "But I'll keep you company while you have one."

"Actually I don't drink. Since you and I will be working on different boats for the next two cruises, we'll only bump into each other on the various islands. Tonight I'd like to get to know the man behind the facade."

His brows quirked. "You don't like the man you see?"

"If I didn't, I wouldn't have invaded your space, which you guard oh, so jealously."

Her blunt speaking prompted him to do the same. "I had hoped we wouldn't have to have this conversation, Gwenn."

"Whew. You don't mince words, do you?"

"No. I can't afford to, and you're too terrific a person for me to hurt, intentionally or otherwise."

"I don't want to rehash our lives, Zach. I certainly don't want to talk about mine. I'm lonely tonight and sense you could use some company, too.

Can't we at least spend it together? No words. No expectations or morning afters."

Zach shuddered inwardly at the depth of her loneliness. "How long have you been divorced?"

"Three years, and believe it or not, you're the first man I've approached since my husband and I split up. Do you have any idea how much courage it took me to walk over to this table, fearing we might have this exact conversation?"

Her honesty reminded him of someone else's. Just the thought of Laura Donetti ripped him apart all over again. Six weeks ago he'd ridden past her on his bike, sought and found her beautiful brown eyes for the last time. They still haunted him.

He pushed himself away from the table and stood up, startling Gwenn.

"You're much too remarkable a woman to use for a night's comfort."

She got to her feet, also. "You're too remarkable a man to hide away from life much longer."

"Isn't that what *you're* doing?" he demanded quietly.

"No. My parents were naturalists from the Keys who raised me in these waters. The man I married thought he wanted this life, but he found out he didn't. I'm living the only life I know how to live. *You're not.*"

He frowned. "What makes you say that? I've been a water baby from day one."

"You're a lot more than that. I've read articles about you in sports magazines. Cycling and sailing are only a couple of your passions. You have strong family ties in California and a lucrative outdoor-sign business spanning three states.

"You've been on the verge of marriage twice, but neither relationship worked out. Tragedy followed you to France where your teammate, Tony Donetti, died of a heart attack during the race. I happen to know that Zachary Wilde, the man who was crowned King of the Mountain, has hung up his jersey and quit the racing world to crew in the Galápagos, but I still say you're sailing in waters way out of your element."

Zach blinked in amazement that she'd been curious enough to do her homework on him. He didn't see it as an invasion of privacy. Gwenn was a good woman and honestly interested in him. He couldn't blame her for that.

Her mouth curved in a compassionate smile. "I had hoped you and I might be able to forget our pain for a little while. Oddly enough, I do believe yours is even greater than mine. But if you should change your mind and crave a little companionship with a woman who's very interested in you, remember I'm always here and we'll be crossing each other's paths for the next three weeks. Think about it.''

Zach knew himself too well. ''I've already thought about it, Gwenn, and the answer is no.''

''Don't be so hasty,'' she warned him. ''For the past three years I've told every man who approached me that I wasn't interested. Then I met you.''

She turned and left the dining room, but her words remained. He felt as if someone had just walked over his grave. After Rosie, he'd been just as convinced that no woman could touch his life again.

Then, by some incredible twist of fate, Laura Donetti had happened to him.

She's still happening to you, Wilde. Every damn night when you're forced to be alone with your thoughts.

You can't forget the brush of her hip against yours as you walked out of the hospital together breathing the intoxicating scents of the night.

You can still feel the touch of her lips against your cheek at her hotel-room door.

Every night you go inside that room with her and shut out the world. But the dreams aren't enough anymore.

Damn Gwenn Barker for reminding you that you're human, that you have needs that are eating you alive....

"LAURA? I THOUGHT you would never get here!"

Laura had barely gotten out of the car she'd driven down from Hollywood to Newport Beach before Bev was hugging her like long-lost family.

It was how Laura felt, too, and she returned Bev's hug fiercely. They clung to each other for long moments, both assailed by bittersweet memories.

And in the clinging they could feel how much thicker they were from their pregnancies. They eventually broke apart with giggles that ended in hysterical laughter.

When it finally subsided Laura wiped her eyes and exclaimed, "You look wonderful!"

"So do you," Bev said, her cheeks glistening with moisture. "When I told Richard you'd called and were coming down, he gave a whoop of joy and said he was taking off work. I expect him at any moment. The kids won't be home for a couple of hours. When they find out you're here, they'll go berserk!"

"I've missed you all so much."

"You don't know the meaning of the word," came Bev's emotional response. She linked her arm with Laura's and they started walking toward the large hacienda-type house with its wrought-iron balconies and masses of flowering shrubs.

"Your home is gorgeous."

"Thank you, we love it. Oh, Laura," Bev said. "I've been praying you would call! So many times I picked up the phone to talk to you, but then I thought I'd better not because you needed your space."

Laura groaned. "Every day I've wanted to phone you, too. But I've been in a lot of pain since the funeral. Even with all the details to attend to, I find myself remembering things. I've been concentrating on the good times with Tony. I—I did love him once, and though I did most of my grieving long before he died, I found there were still things I had to let go."

"Yes, I can imagine."

"Being with Tony's aunt and uncle has helped. George and Ann didn't believe he died of a heart attack. There'd been too many rumors about drugs, so I ended up telling them the truth. It hurt them terribly. That's when I suggested we could all benefit from professional counseling, so the three of us went."

"Good for you. So has it made a difference?" Bev asked as they entered the house, which was done in a breathtaking Spanish motif.

"Yes. I'd already decided in the hospital room at Val d'Isère that I wasn't going to let Tony's death make me take on any more guilt. But that's easier said than done. We talked a lot about guilt in our therapy sessions. It became clear that all of us should have been getting counseling for years where Tony's concerned. We've been walking victims."

"And now?" Bev met her gaze. Laura had the impression she was holding her breath.

Now I need Zach. My life will never be complete without him. He understands me. He understands about Tony. I love him.

"Well, now that I'm four months along and have

been given a clean bill of health from my obstetrician, I'm ready to get on with my life.''

"A-are you going back to university?" Bev stammered.

Laura's heart was pounding. "Yes. But there's something I have to do first." She swallowed hard. "You *know* what it is."

"Thank Heaven!" Bev threw her arms around her again.

After a moment Laura stepped away. "Have you heard from him, Bev?"

"Only through Mom and Dad Wilde. Apparently Zach has written them several times, but a courier always brings the letter to their door with no return address or clue as to where he might be."

At that crushing news, Laura felt the blood drain from her face. Bev took one look and made her sit down on the couch, then sat beside her.

"Laura, I told you in Paris that I had an idea where he is. I still think he's there. Richard happens to agree with me."

"Where?"

"The Galápagos Islands. South America."

Laura gasped. "Really?"

"It's just a hunch, but before Zach checked out of our Paris hotel, he asked the front desk to return this to me, along with a book I'd lent him." Bev reached for a travel magazine lying on the coffee table and put it into Laura's trembling hands.

"If you'll look carefully at the article on the Galápagos, you'll see there's a tiny checkmark made in pencil next to the island of Santa Fe.''

Laura hunted for the page, saw the mark, then looked up. "But what does it mean?"

"*I* didn't put that checkmark there, Laura. Nor did anyone else, because I'd just bought it off the stand in St. Léger for something to read. When I finished it, I left it in Zach's room, in case he was interested.''

"Y-you think because of that...?"

"That, and the fact that sailing, not cycling, is Zach's passion. According to the article, the Galápagos Islands offer some of the greatest sailing in the world. You didn't know him long enough to learn that he and Richard are both certified to operate any ocean-going boats up to 125 feet in length. They're both certified scuba divers, and while they were in high school and college, they worked part-time for the company, and the rest of the time as beach lifeguards.''

She paused, then smiled as she went on, "In fact, I met Richard and Zach when my girlfriend and I got caught in the undertow at the beach and they saved us from drowning.''

"You're kidding!"

"Nope. Richard gave me CPR. When I could finally talk, I asked him if he was my guardian angel.''

At those words, chills shot through Laura's body, making the hair stand up on the back of her neck.

"*Laura Donetti!* Is it really you?"

At the sound of Richard's voice, both women turned

around. In the next instant he'd pulled Laura up and
into his arms.

At last he released her and said, "I'm not going to
ask you why you took so long to get here. All I can
say is, you've come and Bev and I are very happy."
He cast his wife a loving glance. "Now the only important question is, how soon are you going to go find
my brother and bring him back home?"

This was a time for honesty. She lowered herself
again to the couch. "I won't stop until I find him,
Richard, but I can't promise to bring him home.
Not…not if he doesn't want to come."

Richard's jaw hardened, exactly like Zach's. Another heart-wrenching memory. "You're the only one
who can work the miracle."

She bit her lip. "We're going to need one. Zach has
lost two great loves. He's not about to become vulnerable again with a third. On top of that, he believes
himself responsible for Tony's death. His guilt runs
very deep. I've learned a lot about guilt in counseling.
It's one of the most difficult emotions to eradicate
from the soul."

Richard's hand tightened on her shoulder. "But
you're going to try."

Laura sucked in a breath. "I have no choice. I'm
desperately in love with your brother."

"Thank God."

He paced the floor for a minute, then came to a stop
and said, "I presume Bev has told you where we think
he is."

"Yes. I already have a plan."

"You do?" Bev said.

"Yes. Knowing Zach, he's probably warned the locals not to tell anyone he's there. If I asked questions about him ahead of time, someone would probably tip him off and I might never be able to find him."

"You're probably right about that," Richard muttered.

"So, I think I'll sign up for one of those trips and go from there."

"My thoughts exactly," Bev said as she handed Laura a travel brochure from the coffee table. "There are a lot to choose from, but on page five there's an eleven-day trip that lists Santa Fe on the itinerary."

Laura spotted it. "I'll start with that one. But the next sailing is just ten days from now. I doubt I could get a reservation in time."

"We've already made it for you," Bev admitted somewhat sheepishly.

But Richard's smile revealed no qualms as he added, "Just in case."

"Don't I need immunizations to travel there?"

Bev shook her head. "We checked and found out they don't require any shots unless you're taking a side trip into the Amazon, which you won't be."

"What name did you use?"

Richard's eyes twinkled. "We debated on that one before coming up with Mr. and Mrs. John Wallace. That way you would be ensured a double cabin to yourself...just in case."

Just in case, Laura thought, Zach was crewing the trip. Her heart turned over.

"As soon as Bev phoned me a little while ago," Richard said, "I dropped by the travel agency and told them to put the charge on my credit card. Here are all your travel documents." He handed her a packet. "Your flight for Quito has already been booked under your own name, because, of course, you'll have to show your passport."

Laura stood in awe of their determination to find Zach. It was just as great, if not greater, than hers. "You two are incredible."

"We feel the same way about you," Richard said, smiling.

"Well—" Laura still felt a little dazed by events "—since you've prepared my path before me, it looks like the only thing left to do is some shopping."

"How about right now?" Bev suggested. "We'll go to lunch and then I want to take you to this darling boutique along the waterfront. They have a maternity section with the most adorable mother-and-infant matching sailor outfits you've ever seen."

Fear warred with excitement, making it difficult for Laura to breathe. "If I do catch up with him, he'll see this pregnant lady and dive overboard."

Richard's expression sobered. "You don't know what you're talking about. I saw the way he looked at you in Paris. It could have set off a three-alarm fire."

A warm flush stole over her cheeks. "He's just got to be there, Richard."

"This may be a long shot, but my wife's instincts are never wrong. In my gut, I *know* he's there."

On a surfeit of emotion, she reached out to hug them again. "Then I'll find him."

TEN DAYS LATER on a golden Monday morning, Laura and the eight other people in their party—four of whom were members of the same family from Michigan—stepped off the plane at Baltra Island. Immediately they boarded a bus that drove them to a dock on an azure-blue bay.

The two older couples, the Devrys and the Olsons, were close friends and had kept pretty much to themselves during the preceding part of the trip—a stay in Quito and a city tour. But to Laura's chagrin, the Fisher clan, comprising the parents, Don and Sylvia, and their two sons, Brad and Pete—both in their early twenties—had been unable to get over her resemblance to Margo of TV-soap-opera fame.

Laura had laughed at their comment and answered that Don reminded her of Bob Stack, the host of the TV show "Unsolved Mysteries".

That observation had distracted them enough to finally leave the subject of her looking like Margo alone. Unfortunately the two sons, both on break from the University of Michigan, seemed delighted that the young widow was traveling with them.

Their unsolicited attention was something Laura hadn't planned on. So except for meals, she'd chosen not to join them on the city tour and opted to stay in her hotel room in Quito until it was time to fly to the Galápagos.

Both Brad and Pete attached themselves to her now as they all made their way down to the pier. A dark-bearded, middle-aged man stepped forward and extended a friendly hand to each of them. He commented that the birds they saw diving toward the water like shooting arrows from dizzying heights were called blue-footed boobies. It brought a smile to her lips.

Unlike her, their greeter didn't wear sunglasses, and his skin was burnished the color of teak. She noted the admiration on his face as his deep-set blue eyes scanned her face and figure.

Her newly purchased white maternity pants with a sleeveless loose-fitting blue-and-white sailor top, which hid her condition, felt comfortable in the mid-seventies temperature. But because of the Humboldt Current, she'd heard that the nights got cool, even cold, so she'd packed a sweater and windbreaker.

Those with a discerning eye might suspect she was pregnant, but according to Bev, it would be at least a couple of more months before Laura blossomed for the world to see.

She debated telling the Fisher sons that she was pregnant. The news would definitely kill their interest. But she also felt it would be better if no one on board knew she was expecting a baby. Aside from the fact it wasn't anyone else's business, she didn't want any sort of preferential treatment.

"Welcome aboard the *Puff Cloud.* I'm the skipper and my name's Nathaniel Simonds. I answer to Nate."

He seemed to be addressing only her, and so she murmured, "Nate it is. I'm Jean Wallace."

"Do you mind if I call you Jean? We're pretty informal around here."

"Not at all."

Laura had been christened Laura Jean Delaney after the first names of both grandmothers, so the middle name wasn't entirely foreign to her.

"Good. Correct me if I'm wrong, but I thought there was a *Mr.* Wallace coming aboard, as well."

On the flight from Miami to Quito, Laura had made the decision that until she found Zach, she would tell as much of the truth as possible without divulging her last name. Zach could be crewing aboard the beautiful sixty-six-foot yacht that Nate was skippering and that would be taking her to the various islands, but so far she hadn't seen any sign of the crew.

If it was at all possible, she wanted the element of surprise to be on her side when she first saw him again. *If* she saw him again, her heart cried.

There were many different tour companies that ran trips in the Galápagos, but because of the travel magazine's article on the man who headed the Windjammer Tours and his impressive sailing credentials, Bev and Richard had acted on the hunch that Zach might be working for this particular tour group.

"Recently my husband passed away, and I decided I needed a vacation. Since I didn't want to share a cabin with anyone, I booked the trip under both our names and paid the double fare. I hope that's all right."

"If it's all right with you, of course it's all right with us. There's no better place to relax and enjoy nature. Hopefully this trip will bring you peace of mind and help you to get on with the rest of your life."

"That's exactly why I've come. Thank you." She smiled in relief because he hadn't recognized her from TV. Furthermore, he accepted her explanation without question and didn't pry.

"I first heard about the Galápagos Islands when I was a schoolgirl. I think it was in science class and the teacher was discussing Darwin's theories on evolution. The slides on those enormous turtles and sea lions had me completely fascinated."

He nodded. "I had a similar experience in my youth. I can promise you we're going to see those sights and a lot more before this trip is over. We're also extremely lucky to have Gwenn Barker along as our naturalist.

"She's lived a lot of her life out here—initially with her parents, but they're retired now. You couldn't have a better guide to introduce you to this wildlife sanctuary. No one's more qualified."

"I'm looking forward to meeting her."

"She'll be aboard shortly, along with our crew of three. In the meantime, your cabin is the first door on your right when you board the *Puff Cloud*." Just the

mention of the crew sent a shiver of nervous excitement through her.

"We're all on hand to keep you safe and comfortable," he continued, oblivious to the chaos of her
emotions. "Call on us at any time if we can be of
assistance."

"Thank you," she said.

"In half an hour, we'll ask everyone to assemble in
the dining area to meet Gwenn. Right now, go to your
cabin and settle in. The crew will follow with your
bags. You'll see we've left you some literature to read,
and you've been supplied a selection of soft drinks
and beer, so help yourself."

Needing no encouragement, she boarded the yacht
and found her way below. Pete, the elder of the Fisher
sons, hovered expectantly in the corridor watching her,
obviously having already checked out his cabin.

Laura pretended not to notice as she entered her
room and shut the door. She had no intention of making an appearance until everyone had been called together. The only thing on her mind was Zach. While
she unpacked, she tried to imagine what would happen
if he was assigned to the *Puff Cloud.*

She hid her face in her hands. It had been almost
two months since she'd seen him. Too many long
empty agonizing days and nights.

Have you thought about me at all, Zach?

*If, or when, you discover I'm a member of the tour,
will you ignore me in front of the others and wait until*

*no one else is around before you confront me? Will
you be angry?*

There was a worse thought. Maybe he wouldn't
seek her out at all.

That possibility struck fear in her heart.

Knowing Zach, he might simply acknowledge her
with a nod, as he would any past acquaintance, and
then go on about his business, never giving her an
opening.

If that happened, Laura was determined to go after
him and force him to listen while she poured out her
heart. What he decided to do with that knowledge was
anyone's guess, but it wasn't in her nature to play
games.

A shudder passed through her. What if he couldn't
return her love?

Traumatized by her thoughts, she still hadn't put her
things away when Nate announced over the intercom
that everyone was to proceed to the dining area at the
other end of the yacht.

With alternating feelings of excitement and trepi-
dation, Laura left the cabin still wearing sunglasses for
camouflage, her gaze darting everywhere for signs of
Zach.

The second she entered the common room, she
caught sight of the three other crewmen and her heart
plummeted.

Zach wasn't among them.

After the captain had made the introductions, she
realized she would have to put her second plan into

action—make friends with the crew and, without arousing suspicion, find out if Zach was an employee of Windjammer Tours. As Richard had said, this was a long shot, but now that she was here, she wasn't about to give up until she was convinced Zach hadn't come to the Galápagos at all.

Disappointed beyond belief, Laura only noticed Gwenn Barker after she felt the other woman's long probing gaze. Did she recognize Laura from her role on TV?

Somehow Laura doubted it. The naturalist spent most of her life here, away from the so-called amenities of civilization.

Not until Nate called upon the athletic-looking blonde to give a preliminary sketch of their itinerary did those penetrating yellow-green cat's eyes finally shift from Laura to the rest of the group.

She imagined that most men found their naturalist, who was probably in her midthirties, rather attractive. It was more than possible that Zach knew her.

Does he find her appealing?

Tortured by the thought, Laura could hardly concentrate on the woman's talk. She returned to her cabin as soon as the session broke up and it was announced they were setting sail.

Pete followed Laura down the corridor and asked her to join him for a drink in the cabin he shared with his brother. Deciding she'd better set the perimeters right now, she kindly but firmly refused him, hoping he'd get the point.

Once she'd shut the door, she opened her bags and put her things away in the drawers and closet. As she was placing her toiletries in the bathroom, she heard a knock on the door.

Afraid it was Pete, she decided not to answer it.

"Mrs. Wallace?" a female voice called.

It sounded like Gwenn Barker. For some unknown reason, the hairs prickled on the back of Laura's neck as she opened the door.

"Hi," Gwenn said. "Mind if we talk for a minute?"

After a slight hesitation Laura shook her head and told her to come in.

"I'll get straight to the point," Gwen said as soon as the door closed. "Part of my job as your guide is to know the passengers on board and adapt the tour to their individual needs."

Laura decided that Gwenn's womanly intuition had devined Laura's pregnancy, and so she needed to ascertain her state of health before the tour got under way.

Laura spoke up. "I know what you're going to say. It's true I'm pregnant, but my doctor told me I was in perfect health and he encouraged me to enjoy this trip. I went over the itinerary with him, and he said the exercise would do me good. I hope that reassures you."

Gwenn eyed her with a puzzled frown. "That's not why I'm here. We've had pregnant women on board before. I myself found out I was going to have a baby during a trip about nine years ago. As long as your doctor has given you the okay, that's fine with us."

"I'm relieved. I-is there another problem, then?"

"Only to me."

"I don't understand."

"I have to work with the authorities when we're responsible for tourists entering Ecuador or Peru for one of our tours. They send me a list of passengers' names, in case there's an emergency of some kind."

Laura knew what was coming and braced herself.

"Windjammer Tours has you down on our list as Mrs. Jean Wallace. But according to the name on your passport, you're Mrs. Laura Donetti. I recognized the name immediately. My mother is a huge fan of your soap opera."

"I see."

"It isn't a problem, Mrs. Donetti. If I was a celebrity, I'd travel under an assumed name and do everything in my power to keep attention away from me, too. I won't say a word of this to anyone, not even the captain. For this trip, you'll be Mrs. Jean Wallace.

"Off the record, may I offer my condolences over your recent loss. I read about your husband's accident in a magazine. I'm very sorry."

Laura expelled the breath she was holding. "Thank you. It *was* awful. I won't pretend about that, but the worst is over, and I'm looking forward to this cruise."

"I lost my husband through a divorce. The pain is not dissimilar, but I can tell you that your child will bring you incredible joy. I think you're very wise to give up your career to be a full-time mother. If I didn't have to earn a living, I'd stay home, too."

"Thinking of my baby has been my one abiding comfort," Laura confessed, warming to the other woman. "Thank you for allowing me my privacy."

"You're welcome. Anytime you want some female conversation, don't hesitate to seek me out."

"I won't. Thanks again."

After Gwenn left the room, Laura gave in to her pain and flung herself across the bed, convulsed with sobs. Since Gwen had read about everything that had happened during the Tour de France in a magazine, then she would have seen Zach in the pictures. The fact that Gwenn didn't say a word about him or display any sign of recognition meant he didn't work for Windjammer Tours.

Richard and Bev had been so certain!

But maybe he'd hired on with another company in the Galápagos.

Laura suddenly sat up and wiped her eyes, determined to get to know their naturalist a great deal better. By the time this trip was over, she would prevail on Gwenn to help her find Zach.

If he's here to be found.

CHAPTER TEN

"HI, SAILOR. A penny for your thoughts."

At the sound of Gwenn's voice, Zach turned his head in her direction, hoping she'd happened upon him by accident, not by design. Because of the bright morning sun he had to squint to see her.

Two sea turtles were mating on the shore, a sight tourists paid thousands of dollars for the privilege of viewing. Once upon a time, the scene would have intrigued him. But coming to work in the Galápagos had only underlined an acute sense of loneliness brought on by his self-imposed exile.

If anything, his state of mind was worse than when he'd left Paris. After the trip ended tomorrow he had ten days' free time coming to him and he'd decided to fly to Quito.

Aside from the Galápagos, he hadn't spent any time in Ecuador. Maybe when he reached the mountains, he could find that joie de vivre he'd unexpectedly felt during the first few days of the Tour de France.

Be honest, Wilde. The magic started when you opened your hotel-room door and discovered Laura Donetti standing there.

"Hello, Gwenn. I didn't realize the *Puff Cloud* stopped on Bartolome Island this trip."

She hunkered down next to him. "That's the difference between the two of us. I knew the *Racing Cloud*'s itinerary by heart and figured the yacht you're crewing for had pulled into the other disembarkation point by now. My female intuition told me that when you went on break, I'd find you on this forgotten stretch of beach, instead of keeping watch over the people swimming among the penguins."

His mood black, Zach got to his feet. He and Gwenn were colleagues of a sort, but he'd walked through the mangroves to this part of the island to be alone. It would be better to put some distance between them before he hurt her anymore because of his inability to respond.

She shielded her eyes from the sun to look up at him. "Before you take off, could I ask you a question?"

"You already know the answer, Gwenn."

"I think maybe I do, but I'm going to ask it, anyway. How well acquainted were you with Tony Donetti's wife?"

The mention of Laura—particularly when she was never out of his thoughts—set Zach's heart thudding. He paused midstride and jerked around, stunned by the question.

Her shrewd regard missed little. "Well, now, I guess I have my answer."

He watched her get up, wiping the grains of sand

from her shorts. Though Gwenn couldn't help reading what was printed in the tabloids, he felt irrational anger at the media who'd turned the tragedy of Tony's death and its aftermath into the biggest moneymaker of the Tour de France. He was particularly angry at her for believing the lies and succumbing to the sensationalism.

"You disappoint me, Gwenn," he said in a withering tone. "I thought scientists like you always strive to get at the truth."

"That's right." She stood her ground. "The scientific method of discovery may be basic, but it gets the job done. Fact number one—Tony Donetti died during the race.

"Fact number two—you were a teammate of his.

"Fact number three—you were his roommate throughout the training period prior to the race.

"Fact number four—the press took pictures of you with your arm around Mrs. Donetti the night her husband died.

"Fact number five—you disappeared right after the finish of the race in Paris.

"Fact number six—no one has seen you since, not even your family.

"Fact number seven—out of the blue you showed up in the Galápagos, asking to crew for Windjammer Tours.

"Fact number eight—you're single and attractive, and I know in my gut you're not into an alternative life-style.

"Fact number nine—you've spurned me, the only eligible woman working for the same company as yourself.

"Now there's fact number ten…"

White-lipped, he muttered, "And that's?"

She shook her head. "I'll let you figure it out for yourself."

"What in hell are you talking about?"

"Who," she corrected him. "Ever heard of Mrs. John Wallace?"

Zach couldn't imagine what Gwenn was getting at. "I don't know anyone by that name."

Gwenn stared hard at him. "Oddly enough, I believe you. See you around, sailor."

"Oh, no, you don't!" In a lightning move, Zach grasped her arm to prevent her from leaving. "You had a definite reason for mentioning that woman's name to me. I want to know what it is."

"Just testing one of my theories. I've come up with a partial answer."

"Then let me in on it."

"Sorry." She looked pointedly at the hand still holding her wrist.

Only now did he realize how out of control he was. He'd never used force on a woman in his life. As if her arm were a burning coal, he let go of it. "Forgive me, Gwenn," he said. "I didn't mean to come on so strong."

"I know that. Obviously I've hit a nerve that runs deep. I have my own apologizing to do for driving you so hard. Trust me, I'll be leaving you alone from here on out. You're obviously on some kind of pilgrimage to forgetfulness and don't want to be found, let alone hassled. So, the next time we see each other, I'll just wave and keep on walking.''

He sucked in a breath. "I've behaved badly.''

"None of us is at our best when we're in the kind of pain you're in,'' she said before walking off.

He didn't call her back. She'd opened up a wound that had been festering since the moment he'd laid eyes on Tony Donetti's wife and had wanted her for himself.

Zach took off on a run down the deserted pristine beach, but the exercise didn't wipe out the name Mrs. John Wallace. Why had Gwenn mentioned it?

Another couple of miles and the answer came to him.

Laura has remarried.

That's what Gwenn, with her keen intellect and perception, had been trying to tell him. Maybe she thought it would help him get over his heartache.

But the knowledge that Laura belonged to someone else, that another man had the right to kiss that exquisite mouth, to touch that gorgeous body, came like a tremendous blow to the midsection, incapacitating him. He collapsed on the sand with a groan.

He'd felt the brush of her lips on his cheek in gratitude; he'd crushed her grief-stricken body in his arms because she'd sought comfort. But never once had he been able to let loose his passion.

Now some other man had that privilege. Most likely

someone who knew her well in California and had
wanted her, despite the fact that she didn't love him
back. Zach buried his face in his arm.

*Whoever he is, I know you couldn't possibly be in
love him with him, Laura. Did you do it to give your
baby a father?*

Richard probably knew who the man was. All Zach
had to do was get to the nearest phone and he could
find out. But it would change nothing. If Zach hoped
to forget her, the fewer details he was told about her
remarriage, the better.

All he knew was that the faceless man who now
claimed Laura for his wife had taken advantage of her
pregnant condition, unable to wait a decent length of
time before getting her into his bed.

And Laura let him. Dear God.

Three blasts of the yacht's horn returned Zach to an
awareness of his surroundings. The *Racing Cloud* was
getting ready to sail to North Seymour Island for its
passengers' last afternoon and night aboard ship.

Jumping to his feet, he took off toward the boat.
Realizing he was already late for report—his first in-
fraction since arriving in the Galápagos—he poured
on the speed. Zach had always prided himself on being
the total professional. Unfortunately Gwenn's news
had knocked the foundation out from under him, leaving him in utter chaos.

He went aboard and found a moment to apologize
to Captain Martelli, who praised him for his performance thus far and told him not to worry about it.

Later in the day Zach volunteered for the night watch. His thoughts of Laura were so tortured he needed to keep busy, knowing he'd never be able to get to sleep.

When morning came and they'd pulled ashore at Baltra Island, he'd finish up last-minute chores, grab his gear and head for the plane that would fly him to Quito. He needed a change, anything to distract his thoughts. Otherwise... *Otherwise what, Wilde?*

THROUGHOUT THE TRIP, Laura had slowly been getting to know Gwenn Barker. Tonight, her last night aboard the *Puff Cloud,* she felt confident enough to approach the woman in her cabin. It would be a good time to tip her for being an outstanding guide, and it would allow her the privacy she needed to talk frankly.

She waited until dinner was almost over, then slipped away from the dining table before Pete could drum up some reason to detain her. She'd amassed dozens of pictures of the Ziff team for Tony's scrapbook and had brought a couple of photographs of Zach with her.

One newspaper article showed him in his cycling uniform and cap. The other picture had come from a magazine where he stood bareheaded and casually dressed with a group of people. Both were excellent pictures, easily identifiable.

But even if they weren't that clear, Zach was extraordinarily handsome. If Gwenn knew him, she would recognize him immediately. If she hadn't seen him, she might at least have heard of him. Laura didn't want to even consider the possibility that the other woman wouldn't be able to help her.

When she was ready, she glanced outside her cabin door to see if the coast was clear. Good. No one in the corridor. The sunsets in the Galápagos were spectacular, which meant their travel party was probably on deck enjoying the view one last time.

Normally Gwenn didn't mingle with the passengers after hours. Laura hoped that was true of their guide tonight as she hurried down the hall to her cabin.

To Laura's relief, on the second knock Gwenn told her to come in. Laura entered and shut the door, her heart starting to pick up speed. The fear that she might be headed toward a dead end made her mouth go dry.

She knew she was talking too fast when she thanked Gwenn for the fabulous trip and left some American money on the table for her. The woman cocked her head quizzically.

"Something's wrong. What is it? Has Pete been pulling more moves? He has a terrible crush on you, you know. It's a good thing he's going home tomorrow."

"Pete's been somewhat of a nuisance, but that isn't what's wrong. Gwenn—" she bit her lip "—I'm going to be honest with you about something because I don't know where else to turn.

"I came on this trip to find someone I have reason to believe might be working here in the Galápagos. Or rather, his brother, Richard thought he might be here, crewing on one of the yachts."

Gwenn eyed Laura in her usual direct way. "What's his name?"

"Zachary Wilde." Laura handed her the news clippings. "Since you heard about what happened to my husband during the Tour de France, it's possible you saw Zach's picture, as well, and would recognize him if he was in these waters."

"I saw him in the magazine article."

"I imagined you would have."

Gwenn gave her back the clippings. "He's so attractive he'd be impossible to miss."

This was a time for total honesty. "He's much more than that." Laura's voice shook. "He's the most wonderful man I've ever met. Gwenn, have you seen him? I *have* to find him. I'm...I'm deeply in love with him."

"Is he the father of your baby?"

Laura felt as if someone had just stabbed her. "No, but I knew the gossip surrounding Tony's death would construe things that way. If the truth be known, though, I wish Zach *was* the father," she whispered brokenheartedly.

"He knew I was pregnant before I did, and he took expert care of me in France while I was green with morning sickness. Tony died without knowing.

"You see, the pregnancy was an accident. Tony didn't want children, and I was afraid to tell him until the Tour was over." Laura covered her face with her hands. "I didn't want anything to upset him. I knew he wanted a divorce as much as I did, but he'd been so consumed with winning the Tour de France we never got the chance to talk about it. Then he died from some drug he'd been taking. Zach left Paris before the memorial service and no one's seen him since.''

Gwenn cocked her head again. "I thought your husband died from a heart attack."

"That's what Zach told the press to avoid any scandal that might hurt me or my baby. That's the kind of man he is. If Zach has a fatal flaw, he's *too* noble." She sighed. "He's like the proverbial knight in shining armor and won't let anyone see his pain. Please, Gwenn, don't tell anyone else what I just told you. That secret is the only thing holding my sanity intact."

The woman nodded. "You have my word."

"Thank you."

"Look, Laura, I wish I could help you."

She felt Gwenn's sincerity, but lost the battle with tears and wiped them away furiously. "This means Richard's intuition was wrong. He and his wife had convinced me I'd find Zach here. They were depending on me. I—I dread calling them with the awful news. Richard and Zach, you see, are closer than twins. His disappearance has put a blight on their marriage. I'm not the only one suffering."

She took a shuddering breath. "Well... I've just got to start a new search someplace else, because I'm not going to quit until I find him. He has this mistaken idea that he was responsible for Ton—" She stopped abruptly.

"I'm sorry, Gwenn." She sniffed and pulled herself together. "This isn't your problem. Please forgive me. You're not only the best guide around, you kept my secret from the others. When I get an opportunity, I'm going to write your company and tell them how lucky they are to have you in their employ."

She started to leave when Gwenn said, "Wait."

Laura wheeled around.

"What is it? Did you remember something?"

"Maybe I'm doing the wrong thing, but I can't lie to you. Zach *does* work for Windjammer."

"*Gwenn*—does he know I'm here?"

"No. Just give me a little time and I'll find him."

"You would do that for me?" she blurted joyously.

"Sure. Do you have to go home tomorrow?"

"No!"

"I'm assuming that money is no problem."

"No."

"I tell you what. The *Puff Cloud* is taking on another group of passengers tomorrow and it's fully booked. But if you want, you can room with me. Sometimes my daughter joins me, but not this trip, so it wouldn't be a problem. I'll arrange it with Nate tonight. He won't care as long as the company gets paid for your passage."

"Really?"

"Of course. I'll make inquiries at head office to find out where Zach is exactly. Then I'll leave a message that you're on board the *Puff Cloud* looking for him. How's that?"

"That's...that's wonderful!"

Without conscious thought, Laura threw her arms around Gwenn. "One day I'll find a way to really thank you."

AS IT TURNED OUT, Zach was the last to board the plane taking off for Quito. He found the only available seat next to a talkative guy who introduced himself as Pete and looked about twenty-two or -three.

Zach wasn't in the mood to deal with anyone, let alone Pete and his brother, Brad, who sat directly behind them. After shutting his eyes, he sat back, pretending to sleep. He needed it desperately, but feared that sought-after state would elude him for a long time to come.

Unfortunately he couldn't tune out the conversation going on next to him, which not surprisingly centered on some breathtaking creature they'd met aboard their yacht, rather than the sights they'd seen in the Galápagos. Zach could hardly remember being that age, when anything, everything was possible....

"She thinks she's gotten rid of me," Pete was saying in low tones to his brother, "but she's in for a big surprise."

"Are you going to fly out to California?"

"Yup. On my next break."

"Where are you going to get the money?"

"I'll work more shifts at that pizza place after classes."

"If she didn't want to be with you on the boat, then I don't think she's going to be that happy to see you."

"Mom and Dad were around. That's why she avoided me."

"I don't think so. She's older than us. Besides, Mom says she's pregnant and wants to be left alone."

"Tough. I'm going to go see her, anyway."

"How are you going to find her? You don't have her address."

"I'll find her. Even if there is no John Wallace listed in the directory, I can get Walt to help me. His dad works for the passport office."

John Wallace?

Zach sat up with a start, experiencing a suffocating feeling in his chest.

He turned to Pete. "I couldn't help but overhear you guys talking. What yacht did you say you were on?"

"The *Puff Cloud.*"

His jaw hardened. *Gwenn knew...*

When he'd forced himself to calm down, he said, "My yacht was full of retired couples."

Pete grinned. "We lucked out," he admitted, eager to talk. "Man, she's one hot babe."

"She's a widow, too," his brother, Brad, added.

Zach's eyes closed tightly. Laura hadn't remarried, after all. The relief he felt was exquisite.

"How come she's not on this flight?" he asked when he'd recovered.

Pete shrugged. "She said something about wanting to see more of the islands, so she stayed on board for another tour. If I'd had the money, I would've stayed on with her.''

A fresh surge of adrenaline almost drove Zach from his seat. ''What did she look like?''

''Have you got all day?''

''At least until Quito.''

''Have you ever seen that soap 'The Way Things Are'?''

''I've caught a few segments,'' he lied without compunction.

''She looks exactly like Margo, the attorney,'' Brad said.

''Nope.'' Pete shook his head. ''She's much better-looking. Black curly hair, dark brown eyes. You oughtta see her in a bathing suit. Whoa—is she built! Her legs go on forever. I get the hots every time I think about her.''

At that point, Zach excused himself on the pretext of needing to use the rest room. If he'd had to endure one more word, he would have bashed Pete's teeth down his throat.

Once he'd locked the door, he leaned back against it, trying to make sense of what he'd learned.

It didn't surprise him that Laura would travel under an assumed name.

She'd lived through so much hounding from the media, she probably dreaded stepping outside her house to get the newspaper. *If that, in fact, is her usual habit,* he thought. He had no clue how she lived her life.

What really preyed on his mind was the reason she'd come to the Galápagos.

No one, not even Richard, could have known where he'd gone when he'd left Paris, least of all Laura. But both him and Laura being here in Ecuador at the same time was too great a coincidence.

His brows knitted into a fierce frown. Nothing added up. Laura had to be at least three or four months pregnant by now. Even if she was in excellent health, it shocked him that she would travel on her own to this remote region of the globe. In case of an emergency, the closest expert medical care was hundreds of miles away by air. For her to sign on for another cruise defied logic.

Unless she was looking for him.

But if that was true and she'd enlisted Gwenn's help, then why hadn't Gwenn told him yesterday?

He raked his hands through his hair.

Because it's more than possible Laura isn't looking for you, Wilde. And if that's the case, then Gwenn had no choice but to believe Laura is here for a vacation. Nothing else.

Maybe after recognizing Laura from the tabloids, Gwenn had been prompted to come on a little fishing expedition of her own yesterday.

The more he thought about it, the more he realized that, when he'd refused to answer her question about Laura, Gwenn had mentioned the name Mrs. John Wallace just to see what kind of a reaction she'd get from him.

When Zach said he'd never heard of the woman, Gwenn had closed up. In retrospect, he couldn't blame her, not after he'd all but told her to leave him alone.

Which was exactly what she'd done. She'd delivered her cryptic message, then left him to his own devices.

A few minutes ago Pete had unwittingly decoded that message. Now it was up to him whether or not he acted on the information.

Lord. Laura was here in the Galápagos. She'd been here for the past ten days.

What if she doesn't want to see you, Wilde?

What if she's trying as hard as you are to bury painful memories?

Even if you do see her again, it can only end in disaster. That's the pattern. Haven't you learned anything?

By the time he left the washroom, he'd made up his mind that when they landed in Quito, he'd take that trip into the mountains where, at 21,000 feet, the air thinned dangerously. They said a man could pass out from lack of oxygen long before he reached that height. Well, he'd find out. In fact, he looked forward to it.

But after he'd disembarked and had made it as far as the passenger-information desk at the terminal, he suddenly found himself walking toward the airline desk to book the next flight back to Baltra.

While he waited to board the plane for the return trip, he phoned company headquarters located in the heart of Quito and asked to speak to Paquita. She was the manager in charge of staffing.

He needed to know the *Puff Cloud*'s itinerary. When he'd ascertained the yacht's next disembarkation point, he'd ask Paquita to locate another boat going to the same location from Santa Cruz and hitch a ride.

Though everything inside him screamed the warning not to put himself in any more emotional jeopardy, Zach found he couldn't fight the overwhelming desire to see her again. The desire had translated itself into a compulsion totally beyond his control.

CHAPTER ELEVEN

LAURA HAD BEEN LYING on her bed taking a nap when she heard Gwenn's voice over the intercom.

"Attention, everybody. We're alongside the peninsula of Santa Fe Island. At lunch I promised you a swim with some sea lions, and we've got sea lions heading our way as I speak. Report on deck with your snorkel gear."

Much as Laura enjoyed snorkeling, she decided to take Gwenn's advice and only participate if she could wade out into the impossibly blue water from the shore. Here they had to jump from the boat and couldn't touch bottom. If Laura should develop a cramp or a complication...

Since the baby's health came first, Laura opted to be sensible and remain on deck to watch the others, maybe do some filming. It went without saying that Gwenn would be relieved, since she and the crew were responsible for everyone's safety.

Laura's real reason for joining in as much as possible was to avoid being alone with her own thoughts and emotions, which ranged from elation that he was here to fear that he wouldn't want to see her.

"Mrs. Wallace?"

Laura didn't recognize the male voice, but that didn't surprise her. Except for the captain, they had a different crew this trip and it was only their second day out. Most likely Gwenn had sent someone to tell her to come up on deck.

"Just a minute, please."

Sliding off the bed, she pulled on a clean pair of white maternity shorts and matching cotton overblouse before padding to the door in her bare feet.

But the sight that greeted her eyes when she opened it sent her into shock.

Zach!

A gasp escaped her throat. She put a hand over her heart because it hurt so much.

Gwenn, it seemed, had wasted no time finding him. Her hungry eyes feasted on him without reservation, cataloging every detail. His tall powerful physique clothed in a T-shirt and shorts. His tanned skin that the strong equatorial sun had burnished to a rich mahogany. His hair, no longer the short-cropped racer's style, its sun-bleached tips making him more attractive than ever.

"Zach." She finally managed to say his name.

"Hello, Laura."

His narrowed gaze played over her tanned features, then dropped lower to register the changes to her figure the pregnancy had caused. There was something in his look that was so erotic he might as well have been touching her. She couldn't swallow, couldn't think.

"A-are you very angry?" she asked.

His well-defined brows met in a puzzled frown. "Angry?"

"Because I—I've been looking for you," she explained in a shaking voice.

His chest heaved as if he was having difficulty dealing with conflicting emotions of his own. She closed her eyes. At least he wasn't indifferent to her.

When he didn't respond, she opened them again. "Please...come in."

Dear God. The way her voice throbbed, she sounded as if she was begging him.

She could sense the struggle going on inside him before he finally stepped over the threshold, dwarfing the tiny cabin as she shut the door. Terrified he would change his mind and leave, she rested her back against it, her palms flat on the metal.

His taut body stood planted in the center of the room, which meant they weren't more than three feet apart. She could feel the heat radiating from him, smell the scent of the soap he used in the shower.

"How did Gwenn find you so fast?"

"She didn't, but that's another story," he said darkly. Close to him like this, she could see lines around his mouth that hadn't been there two months ago, giving him an almost hunted look. "More to the point, how did you know I was here?"

"Th-that's another story, too." Now was not the time to mention his brother. An invisible shield had been lowered around his heart.

His every emotion had gone into deep freeze—except his guilt, which was alive and doing well. And that guilt, compounded by the problem of his fear of ever being vulnerable to loss again, had driven him away. She knew that now.

Since she and Tony's family had been through therapy, Laura had a strong conviction that the only way she was going to penetrate that shield was *through* his guilt. Fighting fire with fire.

"Okay, then why have you been looking for me?" he asked next.

Zach wasn't a man to mince words. He'd always been open and direct, one of the many qualities she adored about him. But this was one time she'd have given anything if he hadn't wanted to get straight to the point. Not when she was aching for him to take her in his arms—they'd been apart for so long! There was so much to say.

"I need help," she whispered achingly.

While he absorbed that, a tension-filled silence hovered between them.

At last he asked, "Are you in trouble of some kind?"

"Yes."

His jaw hardened. "Why me?"

She'd been expecting that question. Whatever she said now would determine whether or not Zach disappeared from her life within the next sixty seconds.

"I have a confession to make to you. When I flew

to Belgium to support Tony in the Tour de France, I—
I had another agenda.''

She saw Zach's hard-muscled body stiffen in reaction. The past was every bit as painful for him as it
was for her.

''The demons driving Tony ruined our marriage
from the day we took our vows. Over time I came to
realize that deep in Tony's psyche, he wanted a divorce. But for various reasons, not the least of which
was his fear of his aunt and uncle's disapproval after
all they'd done for him, he couldn't bring himself to
ask me for one.

''On a subconscious level I realized it was up to me
if we were ever to be free of each other. But like most
young wives, I had hopes that I could change him,
that I could make our marriage work.

''When he turned pro the first year, I saw the writing on the wall, but I still clung to the idealistic dream
that everything would be all right if I just had patience.
His aunt and uncle encouraged me in this of course.
However, it was the wrong thing to do, and for the
next five years everything went downhill.

''Four and a half months ago, Tony came home for
a two-day visit because his uncle demanded it. We
hadn't been intimate in almost a year. We had sex
once, but you couldn't call it making love. It was like
we were programmed to do our duty or something. It
was awful. That's when I realized I couldn't go on
like that and I was determined to ask him for a divorce, no matter how his aunt and uncle felt about it.

"But with the Tour de France coming up so soon, I thought it would be better to broach the subject when it was over. That's when the idea came to me that if his father's scrapbook could help Tony to focus, he might win the yellow jersey. If that happened, he would be on such a high, it would numb him to any guilt and he'd agree to the divorce."

She sighed. "Then I found out I was pregnant. I didn't know what to do. I didn't want the baby to be the reason he stayed with me, but I realized he had to know the truth. So again, I decided to put off telling him the news until after the race."

Zach shifted his weight. "And because of me and my desire to give him a hard time for treating you like he did, his life was cut short," he said bitterly, wounding her heart all over again.

I loved you for that, Zach. I loved you, and still love you, so much, you can't possibly imagine.

"Obviously we both have regrets where Tony is concerned," she rushed to agree. Arguing with him would get her nowhere. "It's true that neither of us can do anything about the past. It's over and done. But there's still something to be salvaged from all the pain, something that could bring us both a lot of peace. That's why I'm here."

"I don't follow," came the hollow rejoinder.

"I have a defenseless baby growing inside me, a little life who only asks for a mother and father to give it love." She took a deep breath. *It's now or never,*

Laura. "How would you like to help me raise this child?"

The second the words left her lips, his head lifted in shock.

"In my mind," she went on, as determined as she'd ever been in her life, "you've always been the father. You were the one who discovered I was pregnant. *I* didn't even know!" She made a noise somewhere between a laugh and a sob.

"When you wiped my mouth with a cloth and helped me to the bed, brought me food and looked after me, it felt like *you* were my husband. And if you remember, *you* were the one who worried about my driving the circuit alone and made those arrangements with your brother. It was *you* who phoned me the night of Klaus's accident to make sure I was all right, to see if I needed anything. Not Tony.

"Now that I'm alone, I'm afraid to raise this baby by myself, Zach. Naturally I'm not talking about the physical aspects. I have the money and a wonderful support system with my family. What I'm talking about is my baby's emotional development.

"You lived with Tony long enough to see what being deprived of a father did to him. It denied him an identity. Tragically his uncle treated him like an uncle, rather than the father he desperately needed. I don't want that to happen to my baby. My baby deserves a father. But not just any father."

She saw Zach's lips thin, but was pretty sure he was still listening.

"Because you know things about my marriage to Tony and the circumstances surrounding his death no one else knows except me, that makes you the only man who'd have a vested interest in my baby's welfare. Don't you see? Tony is a bond between us."

By now, fear of his rejection had released another surge of adrenaline, forcing the blood to pound in her ears. Taking a calculated risk, she said, "If you and I worked hard at it, we could shower this child with love and attention, the kind Tony wouldn't let anyone give him after he lost his parents."

"Marriage isn't in my plans, Laura."

She'd been waiting for that wintry salvo and was several steps ahead of him.

"That doesn't surprise me, not after losing two fiancées." Again Laura saw his body stiffen, but she went on talking as if she hadn't noticed. "Unlike you, I was never engaged, much to my regret. If Tony had been forced to wait three or four months before the ceremony, I probably would've seen enough evidence of his insatiable drive and inner struggles to realize a good marriage with him would be difficult, if not impossible, to achieve.

"Perhaps Tony knew this, subconsciously at least, which was why he rushed me off my feet. I was too inexperienced to understand what was going on. At the time we met, many of my friends were married or engaged. I'm afraid I was in love with love and got swept along with the tide."

She drew a ragged breath. "Once I was married to

him and realized my mistake, I didn't know how to end the pain. I was so riddled with guilt it took me six years to gather the courage to confront him. When he came home for that two-day visit in May, I should have asked for a divorce right then.

"But once again I chickened out. When you guessed I was pregnant even before I did, you encouraged me to tell him right away. But I couldn't bring myself to do it. I was afraid to hurt him—he was very fragile inside and I was terrified of the consequences."

She drew in another ragged breath. "After living through so much pain with Tony, I'm a little nervous of it right now." That wasn't true, but she didn't want to frighten him off by making him think he *had* to marry her.

"But please don't get me wrong," she said, her hands spread in front of her. "I've seen some wonderful marriages. Especially your brother's."

"Richard and Bev share something unique," he admitted in a gravelly tone.

"Yes, they do," she agreed, "and I know why. They're both unselfish and put the other person's happiness first, *every time.* No matter how trying the circumstances, they forget self and reach out to comfort the other. It's a revelation to me. I don't think many couples attain that kind of joy."

"You're right about that."

"Communication was certainly not a strong point in my marriage to Tony. He wasn't home enough."

"Surely that's not your fault."

"No. I no longer take the blame for a lot of things that did or didn't happen, but I am sorry he died without knowing he was going to be a father."

"I'm sorry, too, Laura. But he was on the verge of winning the most important race of his career. Knowing Tony as I did, plus having witnessed the precarious state of your marriage, I think the news would have thrown him. In retrospect, I believe you did the right thing by keeping quiet."

Thank you for saying that, Zach. "Maybe. But that wasn't your gut reaction when you saw me throwing up in the hotel bathroom on the morning of the time trials. You urged me to tell Tony."

He straightened to his full height. "I didn't know all the facts then."

Even now you're defending me, Zach. If you only knew how much I love you.

"Nevertheless you always have the right instincts. In that regard, you and Richard are very much alike."

"You know what they say, Laura. Hindsight's twenty-twenty."

"That's exactly what you have *all* the time! It's the reason you're an exceptional human being. That's why I want you to be in my baby's life on a permanent basis. I need a good man I can trust."

Her cheeks had grown warm. "I grew up with a wonderful dad. The thought of depriving my own child of that experience hurts me. If you're honest, you'll agree with me, since I happen to know that you and your brothers share a special bond with your father.''

"I don't deny it."

"That's why I would like permission to hang around you as much as you would allow. There would be no expectations, just the quiet knowledge that you're there." *She held her breath.*

"My work is here, Laura. You work and live in Hollywood."

"No, I don't."

"What are you saying?"

"As I told the press that night in Val d'Isère, I've given up my acting job. A few weeks ago I gave up the apartment. Everything I own is in storage. There's no place I call home anymore. The only spot I want to be is near you because you make me feel…*safe.*"

He blinked.

"It's true!" she said from her heart. "When we first met and I couldn't find Tony, you did everything in your power to help me, even to arranging for me to drive around the circuit with your brother. Don't you see? When you realized I was pregnant, you took care of me, watched over me.

"The night you called me from the hospital because Klaus had been hurt, I realized then how much I needed you and had come to depend on you. Because you're not a woman who's expecting a baby, you couldn't possibly understand how much that caring meant to me."

Swallowing hard, she said, "I realize you're a

sailor, but you have to come ashore once in a while. I understand there are houses for rent in Puerto Ayora on Santa Cruz Island. If I lived there, you could drop in for meals at the end of a cruise, stay all night. Whatever suited you.

"Just knowing I could see you from time to time would bring a measure of comfort and relief I haven't experienced since before you left Paris." She looked away, fighting tears. "When Klaus and Jacques came to the church and told me you'd gone, I felt like...my rock had deserted me. It was the worst feeling I've ever had."

She saw the color drain from his face and went on, "Of course I couldn't blame you for leaving. You'd shouldered everyone's pain to help the Ziff team succeed, but no one shouldered yours." Her voice caught. "I couldn't come after you right then because I was still getting over the trauma of Tony's death, and I had responsibilities. There were loose ends to tie up, and Tony's aunt and uncle needed me. But now that I'm free and have put the worst of my grief behind me, I want to be with you in any capacity you'll allow."

A groan escaped his throat. "That would be insanity, Laura. We're hundreds of miles from the nearest hospital," he muttered almost as an afterthought, making her heart leap, because though his rejection was clear, somewhere in his complicated psyche, he was still entertaining the idea.

"I'm not expecting this baby for more than four months, and the doctor has told me my pregnancy is going along perfectly. If an emergency arose, I could fly to Quito.''

He rubbed the back of his neck. ''I only have three more cruises with the company, then I'm leaving the Galápagos and sailing my own boat to other waters around the world.''

Every time he opened his mouth, she was put on an emotional seesaw. One minute hope flared. The next he said something to extinguish it.

''Would you consider taking me with you? If nothing else, I'm an excellent cook and I've always wanted to learn how to sail. The baby would get her sea legs early.''

''Her?''

She'd been waiting for the propitious moment to drop that little piece of news.

''Yes. I had an ultrasound and the doctor is pretty sure it's a girl. She could learn everything about the oceans and sailing from you. I can't imagine a better education for a California girl, can you?''

''For a dozen reasons, Laura, it's out of the question.''

Taking a calculated risk, she said, ''If the idea had any appeal, none of those reasons would apply. Please forgive me. You've heard about a mother who would face a burning building to save her ch—''

''Have you ever seen the ocean during a storm?'' he broke in harshly.

''No.''

''Right now it looks like your friend, blue and

placid. But then a wind comes up. In an instant everything changes. The ocean becomes the enemy and you start fighting for your life. Under those circumstances, how could I protect you and the baby?''

As their gazes fused, a certain calm descended. "Because you're a Wilde. I have no doubt you would find a way." She knew the conviction in her voice reached him because he looked away, but not before she saw the flash of torment in his eyes.

Undaunted, she made one final plea. "Obviously the answer is no, but maybe you wouldn't mind if I came along on your next cruise with the company before I make definite plans. When you're not on duty, I could use a sounding board."

"The *Wind Cloud* is fully booked," he said a trifle too quickly.

Nervousness was not an emotion she would have attributed to him. It brought her another modicum of hope.

"Are the crew's quarters fully booked, too?" When he didn't answer right away, she rushed on, "The captain gave me permission to share Gwenn's room with her. Maybe I could bunk with you on your yacht if you had an extra bed. I've already paid for another ten-day cruise."

There was a marked rise and fall of his chest. "I wouldn't be good company. After the watch I crave sleep."

Blackness descended. "All right, I understand. However, I'm not sorry I came to the Galápagos. At least I know I *tried* to do the right thing for Tony's child.''

His face became an inscrutable mask. ''Where are you going when you leave here?''

''I have several options. Maybe I'll figure everything out while I'm on this cruise with Gwenn. She has a lot of wisdom, having lived through a divorce, which I understand is even more difficult than getting over the death of a spouse.''

''Gwenn's roots are here, Laura. You need your family.''

''I would have thought you did, too.''

''I'm not pregnant,'' he said.

''That's right. You're a man who can move about freely with no unwanted baggage. No ties, no obligations. How lucky men are.''

''Don't talk that way.'' He sounded angry. ''Cynicism doesn't become you.''

''Ah…forgive me, but I had a great teacher in Tony. His legacy to me and my baby.''

''*Laura…*'' She could see his throat working.

''Don't worry, Zach. I'm not your responsibility. I never was. There are lots of men out there who want a relationship without the ceremony. Since I refuse to let my daughter grow up without a father figure, I'm sure it won't take long to find someone. Maybe I'll get lucky and he'll like children. Maybe he'll even stick around long enough to help me raise my daughter. Maybe not.

''I would have preferred that man to be you, but

you've made your feelings quite clear. I'd be lying if I didn't tell you I'm disappointed. Nevertheless, I knew I could count on you to be honest with me.''

She forced herself to stay calm. ''Thank you for that, and thank you for coming aboard to talk to me when you didn't have to. Obviously you sailed here on another yacht. You probably need to get going.''

She turned around with the intention of opening the door for him. To her joy, he made no move to leave.

''Are you feeling all right, Laura?''

Thank God your heart hasn't hardened completely.

''Since the morning sickness went away, I've never felt better. But I have to admit the movement of the yacht makes me sleepy. I generally take a nap this time of day. The rocking motion is sort of like a giant cradle. No doubt the baby likes it, too.''

She smiled as she turned back to him.

By contrast, his jaw hardened. After a long silence he said, ''You look good.''

''Thank you. So do you. I can see you're in your element.''

His expression revealed surprise. ''How did you know?''

''Bev told me about your passion for sailing.''

After a sustained pause, he asked, ''When are you due?'' He changed the subject so fast she didn't have time to blink.

''February twentieth.''

''What happened to Margo?'' he asked.

''One of the evil mob bosses hired a doctor to do

plastic surgery on her while she was in her coma. A few weeks ago she woke up with a new face and a new life.''

Zach didn't smile. "The old one was better."

She eyed him saucily. "Have you been holding out on me? I thought you never watched TV."

"You're right. However I *do* have eyes in my head, and what I'm looking at right now could never be improved upon."

Laura trembled in every cell of her body. "You *do* know how to make an old pregnant lady feel attractive."

"Every old pregnant lady should look so attractive."

"Then it's a good thing you won't be seeing me again. Give me a few more weeks, and I'll look like a beached whale." She hoped her joke covered her fragmented emotions.

A bleakness entered his eyes. "You must have some idea of where you think you'll live."

She nodded. *I can keep this up as long as you can, my darling.* "I've always loved the beach. The only reason Tony and I settled in Hollywood was because he wanted to be with his racing buddies who'd formed a cycling club there."

She shook her head. "If I'd had my way, we wouldn't have lived anywhere *near* Hollywood, and I would have found a job doing something else. But Tony insisted I stay on the set and keeping working because it brought in more money than either of us could have earned any other way. He needed funds and expected me to help him," she added quietly.

Zach's jaw tautened. "I wondered about that."

"When he left the States to race in other countries, it suited him to tell everyone I was too busy at home being a TV star to join him. The truth is, he wanted more and more money to support his expensive lifestyle—the clothes, the parties, cars...women. He bought that Ferrari in Italy with the money I'd given him to attend law school. Little did I know he'd never intended to be a lawyer.

"Since his death, I received a bill for a wardrobe he'd had designed for himself in Italy. Obviously he was attempting to create a sort of sports superstar image for himself."

Zach was still listening, so she decided to tell him everything. "You know what Tony was like. He had delusions of grandeur that turned him into a stranger. He never really wanted me—only what I could do for him. When we first met, he told me I was beautiful. Every woman wants to hear that from the man she loves. But as time went on, I realized that my physical beauty was *all* he cared about. If I'd been less attractive, he would never have pursued me because I wouldn't have fit the image he had in mind for the woman he wanted hanging on his arm—say, for a publicity shoot. I didn't realize this until it was too late." She sighed. "Tony never intended to get to know the person I really am. He led a frighteningly shallow existence.

"But that's all in the past now, and I like to think he's found peace at last. As for me, I want nothing more to do with acting or filmmaking. I've got a degree in English, and maybe one day I'll go back for a master's. In the meantime, I'd like to stay in contact with Bev. We're both expecting around the same time, you know."

His features looked chiseled. "You've been with them recently?"

"Yes. I asked for their help in finding you. I hope you don't mind." *Please don't mind.* "Bev thought you might have come to the Galápagos because of that travel magazine she lent you. It seems she was right. It also seems as if all I've ever done is prevail on them for favors. I love both of them. A lot."

Zach stared at her for an uncomfortably long moment.

I've said too much.

"My condo is for sale."

What? She reeled in shock and stayed firmly planted against the door.

"You can buy it if you want. It's right on the water and has three bedrooms, one of which could easily be transformed into a nursery. What furnishings are there you can keep or sell."

Her heart plummeted.

"It's been vacant for months," he went on, oblivious to her pain. "Richard and Bev have been keeping an eye on it the past six years while I've been in and out of the country. But I told Richard at the beginning of the Tour de France that I was going to let it go because I wasn't returning to California.

"You're welcome to it, Laura. In fact, I'd like to sell it so that it wouldn't be a burden to my brother any longer. You'd only be two blocks away from them."

Steady, Laura. Don't fall apart in front of him. If he's being deliberately cruel to get rid of you, he's doing an excellent job....

"Does your brother have power of attorney?" She managed to keep her voice level, unemotional, despite her pain.

He nodded, but she noticed the shadow that entered his eyes. It expressed her question had surprised him. *Good.* "Well—" she forced her lips into a smile "—that's an incredible offer, but I probably won't take you up on it, since I may not be residing in California at all."

"Why's that?"

"Because I'm seriously considering moving to Hawaii." *At least, I am now!*

He looked as if she'd just slapped his face. "That doesn't make any sense."

"Actually it does. Before I met Tony, I'd started dating a man named Michael Shipp. He worked as a realtor for his dad, who has an agency in Hawaii and California. Naturally because of Tony, our relationship came to a premature end.

"To my surprise he showed up at Tony's funeral service in Hollywood to pay his respects. When he learned I was going to move and wanted a place on the water, he invited me to fly over so he could show me some beach properties I might be able to afford."

And it would be far away from you, my darling. Maybe that's exactly what I need.

"Is he married?" Zach demanded.

"No."

"Does he know you're expecting a baby?"

"Everyone knows and seems eager to be of assistance."

"You'd be much wiser to stay near family."

After a pause she said, "No matter what happens, I think I've prevailed on the Wildes altruism long enough, don't you? I told you in Belgium that I looked upon you as my guardian angel. When I arrived in St. Léger, I needed one desperately and there you were—ready to keep my world from falling apart. But you left Paris before I could thank you for everything. I'm glad I've had this chance now. I think you know I couldn't have gotten through that period without you."

"Klaus would have taken over," he murmured. "He thought the world of you."

"I liked him, too, but there's only one Zach Wilde."

"That's nice to hear." He glanced at his watch. "Unfortunately I can't stay any longer to talk. Is there anything I can do for you before I go? Do you want me to ask one of the crew to get you a drink or a sandwich?"

Laura had thought she could handle it, but now she had to fight not to react to the horrifying realization that he was about to disappear again.

"Nothing, thank you. They feed you like kings on here. I had this huge lunch and I'm going back to L.A. plump as a hen. No one'll recognize me. Maybe that's not such a bad thing, after all. I'm so sick of publicity it's wonderful to be anonymous again." She chuckled softly though her heart was breaking. "God bless you, Zach. No one deserves the best in life more than you."

Needing something to do with her hands, she turned and opened the door for him. Out of a sense of preservation, she stepped back to make sure their bodies didn't touch as he moved past her.

When he was in the corridor, he faced her one last time, his gray eyes dark slits. "The captain says you'll be stopping at South Plaza Island tomorrow. I know the cactus is in flower and the sight is spectacular, but it's a difficult walk even for someone who isn't pregnant. Stay on the yacht."

She nodded. "Since you're the one warning me, I'll do as you say." The desire to touch him was so strong she thought she might die from the wanting. But he obviously wasn't suffering the same way.

Face it. He's beyond feeling, and somehow you're going to have to get over him.

"Goodbye, Laura." That note of finality in his voice devastated her.

"Goodbye."

After shutting the door, she sank onto her bed in

frozen silence, her anguish too deep for tears. She would give him an hour, then she would prevail on Gwenn to help her find a way to get back to Puerto Ayora on another yacht.

Zach had gone away believing she would finish out her ten-day tour on the *Puff Cloud.* But she couldn't bear to stay another minute in the Galápagos knowing he was so close, yet so unreachable.

If he could give up his home in Newport Beach, then he truly intended to cut all ties with his old life.

Your guardian angel has done all he can do for you, Laura. Now he's flown elsewhere and you'll never see him again.

CHAPTER TWELVE

THE BARTENDER at the Del Mar Hotel in Puerto Ayora looked surprised when Zach sat down and ordered a double whiskey.

"You haven't drunk anything for a whole week, and *now* you want a double this early in the morning?" he asked with a friendly smile as he handed Zach his drink. "What gives?"

Ignoring the question, Zach swallowed the entire content of the glass in one go.

The bartender kept up the chatter, oblivious to Zach's mood. "You must be the kind of guy who doesn't usually drink, but when you do, you go all out. Am I right?"

"Yeah," Zach muttered, setting the glass down with more force than was necessary. "Do me again."

This one he sipped, his mind elsewhere. Every day he'd gotten up thinking he'd fly to Lima for a little diversion. But since his meeting with Laura, he had trouble deciding whether to get out of bed in the morning, let alone decide how to fill the long pointless hours. The free time given him had been exactly what he *hadn't* needed right now.

What I need is for you to be gone from the Galá-

pagos, Laura. Then everything will get back to normal.

"How soon will the *Puff Cloud* be in?" he asked the bartender, thinking the man was a bit too nosy about the people who worked for Windjammer Connection Tours.

The bartender shot him a surprised glance. "She was in an hour ago. Why? You crewing her later today?"

"No. I'm assigned to the *Wind Cloud*. She won't be sailing until tomorrow." He slid off the bar stool and slapped a couple of bills on the counter for the drinks. "Do me a favor? When Gwenn Barker shows up, ask her to come to my room."

The bartender grinned. "So *she's* the reason you're drinking doubles."

Zach didn't bother to enlighten him and headed back to his room. The only thing that mattered was that Laura had left Ecuador; he could find out from Gwenn. Until he knew she'd flown out, he didn't dare show his face in town. He might run into her, which was the last thing he wanted. One more meeting with her and he wouldn't be able to walk away again.

Toward noon he heard a knock on the door. As soon as he opened it, Gwenn said, "Hi, sailor. You wanted to see me about something?"

"I do. Come in."

"I don't think so. I can smell the alcohol on your breath. Obviously the only reason you want to talk to me is Laura Donetti."

"Gwenn, I was hoping we could talk for a few minutes."

"There isn't anything to say, because Laura isn't here."

"You saw her get on the plane?"

"No. I mean she sailed back here on the *Riptide* the same day you saw her. I haven't seen her since and all I know is that she said she was leaving on the next flight out of here. Sorry," she said before turning and walking off.

Laura hasn't been in the Galápagos for the past ten days?

He felt exactly the way he had when he'd been sailing on the Pacific years ago with his brother and a sudden squall had sent the boom crashing the wrong way. He'd been knocked overboard, unconscious. If Richard hadn't grabbed him and held on, he'd have been lost in the depths of the sea.

Okay, Wilde, you got exactly what you wanted. You sent Laura Donetti away, and now she's well and truly out of your life. Some other man who saw her first is eagerly awaiting the opportunity to get to know her better. She and her unborn baby will be well taken care of. It's nothing to do with you.

No words of love ever passed her lips or yours.

Be thankful it's a clean break. You're free from the possibility of ever having to lose her because she was never yours to begin with. It's time to celebrate.

"SO NOW THAT WE'VE TALKED you out of moving to Hawaii, why can't we get you to even consider *renting*

Zach's condo?''

Laura stirred restlessly in the passenger seat of Bev's car. They were parked in front of the bougain-villea-covered house overlooking the ocean where Richie was taking his piano lesson.

Bev's argument against Laura's moving to Hawaii was valid. If Laura had been emotionally involved with Michael six years ago, then Tony's advent in her life wouldn't have resulted in marriage. So it wouldn't be fair to go to Hawaii now and raise Michael's hopes when clearly none existed.

Not when I'm painfully in love with, Zach. But I couldn't live in his house. It would tear me apart.

''The offer is tempting, Bev, but much as I'd love to act on it, I can't. Put yourself in my place. Could you live in Richard's house if he was no longer in your life?''

Bev sighed in defeat. ''Probably not. But it's a cry-ing shame, because Zach's condo is exactly what you've been looking for. Nothing you've found is as close to us or as ideally suited to your needs.''

''That's true, but if one day Zach does change his mind and wants to come back to Newport, he should be able to return to his own home. My presence would keep him away.''

''I think you're wrong,'' Bev said. ''If he truly wanted to get rid of you, offering you his condo would be the last thing he'd do, wouldn't it? So maybe he had another agenda for suggesting what he did. He may be thousands of miles away, but it's apparent to me that he wants you exactly where he can find you at any given moment."

Her argument made Laura's heart race, but every time she remembered the tone in Zach's voice when he'd told her goodbye, she was jolted back to reality.

"I—I wish I dared, but I'm too afraid of doing the wrong thing. I think I'm going to rent that apartment we saw yesterday."

Bev grimaced. "It's not what you want. It's too small and nowhere near the beach. I've already told you that you can move into our spare bedroom until you find something permanent."

"No, Bev. I wouldn't dream of disrupting your family like that. Besides, the apartment is near the college, and I can put a crib in the bedroom with me."

"You're so stubborn! Well...what kind of lease agreement is it?"

"One year." At Bev's groan she said, "I know. I'm not happy about it, either. If I find something I really like before the twelve months are up, I'll worry about breaking it then."

"Oh, well, since I can't change your mind about Zach's condo, I should be thankful you're moving to Newport at all. The other night I told Richard that if you went to Hawaii, I'd be devastated."

"Oh, Bev, I feel the same way. That's why I'm moving here."

It was true. An unbearable sense of loneliness swept over her every time she even so much as considered the idea of living apart from Bev and Richard and their children.

Just then she saw Richie burst out of the house. He spotted the station wagon and ran over to it. "Laura! Mom!" he exclaimed through the open passenger-side window. "I didn't know you guys were coming here!"

"Your mother suggested we come so I could invite you to go to the ball game with my dad and sister tonight. You can sleep over at my parents', and I'll bring you back tomorrow. Would you like that?"

"*Would* I!" He looked ready to burst with excitement. "Mom, is it okay?"

"Of course. That's why we're here. Stick your bike in the back and let's go home. I've already put your toothbrush and a change of clothes in your backpack so you and Laura can get away as soon as possible."

"All right!"

Fifteen minutes later Laura had said goodbye to Bev and she and Richie were on their way.

"This is a rad car."

"It's a Passat. You like it?"

"Yeah. Uncle Zach used to have one."

"Really?"

"Yeah. He says German cars are the best, but Dad only buys American." He cocked his head. "Rachel has a poster of Tony driving a Ferrari. Did you ever ride in it?"

"No," she said quietly. "He bought it in Europe. I never did see it."

"Where's it now?"

"I had it sold."

"How come you didn't keep it?"

Oh, Richie. If you only knew. "Because I like German cars best, just like your uncle."

"I miss Uncle Zach."

"So do I."

"Do you think he'll ever come home?"

"I hope so, Richie."

"You love him, huh?"

"Yes."

"I think he's upset because you're going to have a baby."

She blinked. "Why do you say that?"

"Because Rosie's son hated him."

The words made Laura cringe for the pain Zach had been forced to suffer.

"A baby doesn't know how to hate. If my little girl is lucky enough to be around your uncle, she'd adore him."

Richie pondered that for a moment. "If you married Uncle Zach, then you could have more babies and they'd be my cousins, right?"

"Yep," she said softly. "We'd all be related."

"That would be the *best!*"

Her heart filled to overflowing. "No matter what happens, Richie Wilde, we'll always be friends, won't we?"

"Uh-huh."

"You know what? I thought I had enough gas to

get us there, but I'd better not take a chance on running out on the freeway, so we're going to stop at the first place we find."

On the outskirts of Newport she pulled up in front of the pumps at a convenience store. Hers was the only car there.

"Can I get a candy bar?" Richie asked.

"Sure. Tell the clerk to put it on my bill."

"I can use my allowance, but thanks, anyway."

What a wonderful kid. Laura watched him fondly as he disappeared inside. She got out of the car and went around to put her credit card in the slot. The next thing she knew, she was on the ground and it felt as if someone was shaking her. Glass shattered behind her.

Earthquake.

The tremor went on for endless seconds, and Laura heard a scream and the sound of crashes coming from the store. She cried out Richie's name, and when at last the ground stopped moving, she staggered to her feet and dashed to the store entryway. To her horror she saw that the window on the door and the plateglass window on the front wall had shattered. Inside, grocery items littered the floor. The middle-aged female clerk stood in the midst of the debris, panting and dazed.

"Richie!" Laura shouted again, unable to see him anywhere.

"I'm in the washroom!"

Thank God. "Are you all right?" she cried.

"Yeah, but I can't open the door!"

She made her way gingerly through the mess toward the men's room in the back. Most of the shelving had fallen, and one large metal cabinet had shifted and now lay directly in front of the washroom door. It was open as far as the cabinet allowed, and she could see Richie through the crack.

"Are you really okay, honey?"

"Yeah. That quake was awesome. Are *you* okay?"

"Oh, just a bump on my elbow, but I'm fine, especially now that I know you didn't get hurt. Wait just a minute while I try to move this thing."

"I'll get the other end," the clerk volunteered. Together the two of them managed to push the heavy cabinet a good ten inches from the door. Richie squeezed out and within moments was hugging Laura fiercely. Over his dark-blond head Laura asked the clerk if she was all right.

"I'll make it, but I just checked the phone and it's dead."

"That's not surprising," Laura murmured. "If you're really okay, I'm going to try and get Richie home. His parents will be frantic."

"So will my husband. His work isn't far from here. I'm sure he'll come before long."

Laura nodded. "Good. But to be safe, let's exchange names and phone numbers. Whoever can get through first for help, we'll do it."

When that was accomplished, she put her arm

around Richie's shoulders. "Come on, honey. Let's get going."

No telling how many of the streets were impassable. She would just have to weave her away around and pray they'd be able to reach Bev and Richard's house before the aftershocks began.

AT NINE THAT NIGHT Zach went off duty. Tomorrow the *Wind Cloud* would put in at Puerto Ayora and he'd have two days off before the next cruise. Forty-eight endless hours he couldn't bear to face because they gave him too much time to think, and thinking only sent him on a downward spiral.

The last nine days of work aboard the yacht had done nothing to lessen his despondency. Inside him was a great yawning emptiness, robbing him of the smallest pleasure. Even the thought of sailing the boat he planned to buy in another couple of weeks meant less than nothing to him.

Up until the moment he'd confronted Laura aboard the *Puff Cloud,* he'd had the idea that he could carry out his plan to go into the sailing business for himself, if not in the Galápagos, then some other place. But the unsettling news that Laura had slipped away unbeknownst to him seemed to have drained him of that desire or any other. He felt as if all life had been sucked out of him.

Alarmed by his morbid state of mind, he started for his cabin.

"Zach?"

Pausing midstep, he turned to see Sean McClintock, the captain of the *Wind Cloud,* headed in his direction.

"I'm glad I caught you before you went to bed."

"Is there a problem?"

"We just received word over the radio that a major earthquake hit Southern California about three hours ago. There was a massive tidal wave, too, and casualties are mounting. You have family there so I thought you'd want to know."

Zach was jerked for once out of the immobilizing bleakness of his soul. "Do you have any idea which area was hardest hit?"

"I heard something about the epicenter being near Costa Mesa in Orange County."

"Costa Mesa is only a few miles north of Newport." His words were calm, but his insides were in turmoil as pictures of the people he loved flashed through his mind. And Laura. Where was Laura? *Had* she gone to Hawaii or was she still in California? Bev and Richard adored her. If they had anything to say about it, she'd be ensconced in his condo right now. Dear God. If anything happened to her or the baby...

Sean gripped his shoulder. "Come on. You're welcome to listen to any reports over the yacht radio and try to make contact with someone who can give you details."

Unfortunately, after settling in the pilothouse, Zach only heard the same news repeated at intervals throughout the rest of the night: phone service had been interrupted in the hardest-hit areas; anyone wanting information about relatives could phone a special number set up by the Red Cross...

It was the news he *didn't* hear that caused one horrifying scenario after another to run through his mind. By dawn his anxiety had reached its peak. The captain took one look at him and said, "As soon as we dock, you have my permission to take the first plane out of Baltra."

"Thanks, Sean. I hate letting you or the company down, but—"

"Don't worry about it," Sean broke in. "Someone else will always be happy to crew in your place, but you can never replace family."

His words pierced Zach like a knife.

"You're one of the finest sailors I've ever had the pleasure of working with," the captain added. "Nate Simonds agrees with me. We'd hate to lose you. But it's obvious you've been going through some sort of personal hell while you've been out here. Coupled with the news of this disaster, I don't see that you have a choice except to go home. Otherwise you'll never have peace of mind."

Zach knew this, though he'd failed to acknowledge it before hearing about the earthquake. Now he couldn't get back to California fast enough.

"You're right, Sean. I won't." He raked shaking hands through his hair. "As soon as I reach Quito, I'll contact the head office and explain my situation."

"You can do that now and make a reservation for your flight to the States at the same time."

TWELVE HOURS LATER Zach was heading north from the San Diego airport in a rental car. He'd purposely avoided flying to the airport in L.A. because he wanted to avoid what he was sure would be chaos. This drive was much longer, but in the end he'd get to Newport faster.

Every radio station carried the same news. Costa Mesa had been hardest hit, with severe damage to oceanfront property and marinas stretching as far north as Sunset Beach and as far south as Corona Del Mar. Fatalities were in the hundreds. Damage to boats and waterfronts were estimated to be in the millions.

He cringed when he heard that major sections of the coastal highway from Huntington to Newport Beach were closed due to damage. Following that report was an announcement that the governor had just declared a state of emergency and was deploying National Guard units.

Zach took it all in with a sickening sense of dread. All the people he'd ever cared about—his parents, his brothers and their families—lived in Newport. And maybe Laura, too. He could only pray she *had* gone to Hawaii.

When he'd first arrived in San Diego and was waiting for his rental car, he'd tried reaching everyone, including Laura's parents in Hollywood, but hadn't been able to get through. All he could do was call a local number for emergency services and give them the names. He'd been told it might be twelve hours before they had any information they could pass on to him. In that amount of time he would already have reached his destination and would know the situation firsthand.

Using alternative routes, he drove into Newport a little after two in the morning and headed straight for his parents' house. They weren't there, and one of their cars was missing, but everything looked good. He didn't notice any damage. Their caller ID showed they hadn't been getting their messages for the past three days. They were probably out of town. That should have relieved him, but it didn't.

He drove to his younger brother's condo several blocks away. No one was home there, either, and one of their cars was missing. Their answering machine had a few messages, but Zach couldn't ascertain times or dates. Again everything seemed all right structurally.

Where is everyone? On a trip?

He didn't want to think the other possibility, that they might all be over at Richard's, whose house was on a private canal leading to the marina. The damage would have been the greatest there.

On impulse he left the rental car in Mike's driveway and took off for the marina on Mike's bike. As he had learned better than anyone, a bicycle could go any-where—and get past police barricades if necessary.

No one was going to prevent him from reaching Richard and Bev's. Not only did they mean the world to him, they were his only link to Laura.

"LAURA?"

She whirled around, milk glass in hand, thinking she was the only person awake in the Wilde household. "Hi, honey. Couldn't you sleep, either?"

Richie shook his head. "I keep waiting for another aftershock."

Laura shuddered. "So do I."

"I'm glad you're up. My sisters are in bed with Mom and Dad and they're all asleep."

She smiled at him and ruffled his hair. "Want some milk?"

"No, thanks."

"Do you want to come back to bed with me?"

"Can I?"

"Are you kidding? Bring your baseball cards and we'll see who wins. I've improved since our last game in France."

Richie left the Spanish-styled kitchen at a run. Laura rinsed her glass, then reached for the makeshift ice pack.

Her elbow was throbbing and swollen. She didn't dare take any painkillers until she'd checked with her obstetrician. But thank heaven it was her elbow, not the baby, that had taken the brunt of the impact. So other than a bruise below her right knee, she couldn't really complain. Nevertheless, if her elbow didn't start to improve in the next few days, she'd have to see a doctor about it.

After turning off the light, she tiptoed through the house and hurried up the wide staircase to the upper level. Richie was waiting for her in the guest bedroom, his box of baseball cards at the ready.

No sooner were they sitting cross-legged facing each other on top of the covers when they heard an ominous creak. Richie's face paled. "Another tremor's starting."

"Maybe," Laura said calmly. "Let's play, anyway. My turn to ask a question first. What year did Mickey Mant—"

"There it goes again," Richie said.

She gave a resigned sigh. "I don't think it's a tremor. More like someone walking around. Probably your dad."

"Do you think?"

"I do. Okay, here's the question again. What year did—"

"Uncle Zach!"

CHAPTER THIRTEEN

RICHIE'S JOYFUL CRY would have woken the dead. He flew off the bed to greet the uncle he idolized, knocking the cards to the floor. Laura's eyes darted to the doorway where stood an achingly familiar man in hip-hugging jeans and a T-shirt.

Zach. She mouthed his name silently as their gazes met and locked over Richie's head. Within seconds the house was filled with shrieks of excitement and joy as the entire family converged on the guest bedroom. Laura's eyes filled with tears as she watched Richard grab his brother and crush him in a hug. Bev was next, and then she explained that his parents were in San Francisco, and Mike and his wife and baby were visiting her parents in Sacramento, so there was no need to worry about anyone's safety.

Laura climbed off the bed, making sure the belt of her lime green terry bathrobe was fastened over her nightgown. She'd blossomed a lot in the past few weeks, and judging by the way Zach looked at her, the changes in her shape were readily apparent.

"Thank God everyone is all right," he said as Robin squeezed him for all she was worth. "We heard the news about the earthquake over the yacht's radio. I left the Galápagos on the first flight out of Baltra.''

Robin stayed in his arms and patted his burnished face. ''Our swimming pool has a *huge* crack in it, and water ran over the edge and ruined the flowers Mommy just planted.''

''Yeah, and your condo kinda got ruined, Uncle Zach,'' Rachel blurted, despite Richard's attempt to shush her.

Zach's eyes hadn't left Laura's. ''As long as no one was in it, it doesn't matter.''

She cleared her throat. ''Richie and I were on our way to a baseball game in my car when the quake hit.''

''Yeah… It was scary, Uncle Zach. I got barricaded in the gas-station washroom and Laura had to push this huge thing outta the way. She's a really cool driver, too, and has a Passat, just like you.''

''Hmm. I saw it in the driveway and wondered whose it was,'' his uncle said.

''She got us back home like a shot. I bet she could handle anything, even a Formula One racing car!''

''*Richie,*'' Laura said warningly, her face flushed, ''that was supposed to be our secret.''

The family burst into laughter. In the face of such unrepentant hilarity, Laura shook her head and joined in.

''By now you ought to know there are no secrets in this house,'' Zach said. ''After the Tour de France I thought I'd picked a spot where no one could find me, only to discover that all along my clever sister-in-law knew exactly where I'd gone."

A further burst of laughter from Bev, who still looked too young to be the mother of three and expecting her fourth. But Laura couldn't help feeling a little nervous because, after all, she'd been the one to follow him when he hadn't wanted to be followed. Still, if he was angry, it didn't show. At least he wasn't allowing it to show in front of his family.

"Come on, guys," Richard said finally. "Everyone back to bed. Your uncle has just flown thousands of miles and needs his rest. Girls, you go in with your mother. Richie, I'm sleeping with you."

"That's okay, Dad. Laura said I could stay with her. We're gonna have a contest."

"That can wait until tomorrow."

"But—"

"No buts, son." Richard's stern voice surprised even Laura.

"All right," Richie muttered crossly. He began gathering the spilled cards.

Laura leaned over to help him. "I'll play with you in the morning," she whispered.

"Promise?"

"Promise."

"You're the greatest!" He gave her a hug, then flung his arms around Zach one more time before disappearing.

As abruptly as the room had filled, it emptied, leaving a trembling Laura alone with the man who'd become her whole world. But she wasn't about to delude herself that he'd come back to California because of her, not when his goodbye on the *Puff Cloud* had been so final.

"I'm sorry you had to find me here," she said. "Because of the aftershocks, Richard insisted I stay the ni—"

"Is this yours?" he broke in without apology, scooping her makeshift ice bag from the floor.

"Oh—" her hands made an impotent gesture "—it's nothing."

His gaze flicked to hers, his expression sober. "If that was the case, you wouldn't have found a need for this." He held up the bag. "Show me where you've been hurt."

She took a step back. "It's nothing. Really."

"Let me see." He came closer. His nearness constricted her breathing. "You and Richie were caught by the quake. He's obviously fine, but you're not. What happened?"

Something in his stance, his demeanor, told her he wasn't about to let it go.

"When the ground shook, I fell and landed on my elbow."

His brows knit. "I've done that more than once on my bike. Let me see how bad it is."

Terrified to be this close for fear she wouldn't be able to resist reaching out and touching him, she backed up all the way to the bed. To her consternation, there was no place else to go.

"Take off your robe, Laura, or I'll remove it for you."

"Please, no..."

Her resistance only made him more determined. Without conscious thought Zach found himself untying her belt. Beneath the cotton nightgown he felt the hardness of her enlarged belly with a sense of wonder.

A faint citrus scent emanated from her. This close, her warmth caught at his senses, kindling the ache that had never gone away since the first moment he'd seen her standing in the doorway of his hotel room in Belgium. As he slipped the robe off her shoulders, he leaned closer, letting the black glistening curls of her hair, soft as butterfly wings, brush against his unshaven jaw.

Compelled by an urge he no longer had the power to control, he skimmed his hands down her arms, unable to credit that Laura Donetti, the phantom lover of his dreams, stood before him in the flesh, vital and trembling.

He was so entranced he forgot the reason her robe had come off in the first place. That is, until his fingers inadvertently found the tender area around her right elbow. Though the pressure was ever so slight, it elicited a wince.

"Forgive me for hurting you," came the husky apology as he carefully examined her injury. All the time he was touching her, he could sense the blood coursing through her veins. It seemed to match the wild rush of his own.

"You're not," she said, lifting her face to his. That lovely face whose features he'd imagined exploring with his lips over and over again in the solitude of his empty bed.

"You have too much mobility for it to be broken," he murmured, "but it'll be sore for a while."

"That's what I thought." She sounded breathless. The effort to speak appeared as difficult for her as for him.

Only now did he recognize the difference between fantasy and reality. Dreams had a way of obscuring details—like the faint freckles on her nose, the laughter lines around her heavily lashed eyes.

This was no dream. When he gazed into those liquid brown irises, he saw that same look of nervousness and vulnerability he'd seen in Belgium. He saw something else. Fear of *him*, maybe? *Why?*

"Don't you know I would never intentionally hurt you?"

"I know." Her breath seemed to be coming in pants. The beguiling curve of her mouth was only a whisper away.

Her mouth. It was all he could think about.

"I want to kiss you, Laura. I *have* to kiss you."

"Zach..."

If crying his name was an attempt to stop him, it had come too late. He could no more deny the desire driving him than he could deny the air he breathed.

When his mouth closed hungrily over hers, Laura almost fainted from too much feeling. She'd been praying for this day, longing for this moment. Zach could have no inkling of the depth of her love or her desire.

She'd promised herself that if he ever reached out, she would respond slowly, carefully, so as not to frighten him off.

What a joke! How delusional could she have been? The way she was kissing him back, you'd have thought she was a lovesick teenager caught up in the out-of-control passion of first love.

Laura was just like that. Out of control. She knew she was, but she couldn't stop what was happening, couldn't stop her response to him. Zach's kiss went on and on. She wanted it to go on forever.

Her subconscious fear that he would regret this momentary lapse made her lose all inhibitions. She pressed her body closer and wound her fingers into his hair. She pulled her lips from his and moved them with restless intensity over the rugged features of his face.

"Dear God, Laura..." he groaned, then urged her with him onto the bed. Her voluptuous body felt hot to the touch. His insatiable need for her drove him to kiss the perfumed satin of her skin everywhere the cotton nightgown didn't cover.

She brought him so much pleasure it was almost pain. Her gorgeous long legs intertwined with his, locking them together. Her mouth was another miracle, like an endless fount where he could drink long and deeply.

He loved the healthy ebony sheen of her short curls.

Every inch of her hair and body smelled like flowers. The first time he'd ever laid eyes on her, he'd thought her the ultimate of femininity. The thought had only intensified.

"Do you have any idea how beautiful you are?" he said into the scented hollow of her neck.

"I was thinking the same thing about you," she confessed as her hands roamed over his T-shirt-clad chest and broad shoulders. "Bev told me you have Viking blood in your ancestry. If these were days of old and you'd come to kidnap me and take me away in your longboat, I would have gone willingly."

He crushed her mouth beneath his again, electrified by her nearness, by her breathtaking response. Laura was different from any woman he'd ever known. She had this amazing ability to give her body *and* her soul, holding nothing back. It was a revelation to him.

"Willing or not," he whispered against her lips, "I would have thrown you over my shoulder and claimed you for myself."

The fierceness of his tone thrilled Laura. She inched closer. "I wouldn't have wanted anyone to come after us and rescue me."

"You think I would have let them?" His voice was gruff.

"Maybe...after you'd grown bored of the distraction." Heat stormed her cheeks. "As you've learned for yourself, I'm afraid I'm not your typical demure maiden, shy and unsure."

He rose up on one elbow. "You really think I could be held by such a woman?"

"I don't know," she answered honestly.

Somehow their lovemaking had become something else. She began to feel uneasy about the serious turn their conversation was taking.

Talking only complicated everything. She didn't want to talk, but when she tried to bring her mouth to his again, he stopped her by pinning her shoulder to the mattress with his free hand.

"Come on. Explain what you mean." The steel in his voice alarmed her.

She sucked in a breath. "You and I said our good-byes back in the Galápagos. If there'd been no earthquake, you wouldn't be here now, compelled to deal with *my* presence."

"Compelled?"

Her brows knit delicately. "Did Richard leave you any choice when he ordered everyone else to bed?"

"Since childhood my brother and I have communicated without words. Richard did exactly the right thing—he knew I wanted to be alone with you."

She could feel his searching gaze, but averted her eyes for fear he'd read too much in them. "In case you were wishing you hadn't offered it, I never considered buying your condo, Zach."

His ruthless silence prompted her to keep on talking, which she did—faster and faster.

"Richard and Bev begged me to at least rent it, but

I told them that if you ever came back to Newport, you would want to return to your own home.''

She felt his hand tighten almost painfully on her shoulder. He could have no idea of his strength, yet she welcomed it because the unconscious gesture proved he wasn't indifferent to her.

"I'm glad you put my needs first," he said. "Otherwise, considering what the quake did to my condo, you could be nursing more than an injured elbow."

In the next instant he bent his head to kiss her shoulder where his hand had been. "So when are you leaving for Hawaii?" he murmured against her sensitized skin.

She couldn't think, not when his mouth was inching closer to hers. "I decided it wasn't a good idea, after all." The words came out so faintly and tremulously she wasn't certain he'd even heard them.

He had. "You're right," he said in a silky whisper, burying his face in her hair. "So what's your plan?"

With a thudding heart she said, "There's an apartment complex here in Newp—"

"Which one?" he cut in, brushing her cheek with his lips.

"The Riviera."

"It's too far from the beach, but it will do as well as anyplace else until the condo's repaired."

"No, Zach. I've already told you I'm not moving into your home."

After gently biting her earlobe he said, "I thought you wanted me around to help you raise your daughter. Has that idea lost all its appeal since you left Ecuador?''

Confused, Laura tried to sit up, but his hard body kept her pinned. ''You know it hasn't, but you made it clear to me you weren't returning to Calif—''

''Earthquakes have a way of putting a man's priorities in order. I owe Tony—not only for baiting him without mercy, but for the greater sin of coveting his wife. Since you're willing, I'm prepared to make restitution, provided we get married immediately. Anything less wouldn't do.''

Laura couldn't prevent the gasp that escaped her throat.

Before she'd gone to the Galápagos, her plan to win Zach's love had been based first on appealing to him to be a father to her baby. At the time she'd thought it a good idea. It seemed her plan had finally succeeded, but the results were tearing her apart—because she'd forgotten one thing. *Zach's not in love with you. Remember your conversation with Bev?*

The lovely Rosie Armstrong was the woman who would always hold Zach's heart.

''Think about it,'' he said, ''and let me know in the morning.''

And then he gave her a hard kiss and levered himself from the bed.

Her gaze followed his retreating back until the door closed behind him.

What am I going to do?

She buried her face in her hands, shattered.

The next hour passed like an eternity. She felt feverish. In this anxiety-laden state, it wouldn't be long before she was really sick.

Zach had told her to give him her answer in the morning.

But you already know the answer, Laura. You have no shame where he's concerned. Admit it. Go to him now and tell him the truth.

Bare your soul.

If he still wants to marry you knowing you love him, then so be it. At least we'll both know exactly where we stand. We'll have honesty. That's more than a lot of couples have.

Her mind made up, she got off the bed and reached for her robe. Then she tiptoed out of the room.

He was probably asleep on the pullout couch downstairs. It would be cruel to wake him up after his long flight, but this couldn't wait. If she didn't tell him now, she might not be able to find the courage in the morning.

The large family room off the kitchen was her favorite place in the Wilde household. Besides books and games, there was an old player piano everyone enjoyed. Laura particularly loved the comfy furniture.

The aquarium in one corner gave off enough light for her to distinguish shapes in the darkness. Her gaze sought the couch, expecting to see Zach's stretched from end to end.

"You're looking in the wrong place."

She wheeled around in surprise. Zach, still dressed,

stood in the doorway. "Why aren't you in bed?" she asked.

"Why aren't *you?*"

Zach had a way of knocking her off balance. "I haven't just flown in from Ecuador. You must be exhausted!"

"If I am, my body doesn't know it yet. I've been outside inspecting the damage to the swimming pool. Richard's lucky his house is still in one piece. Luckier still that everyone is safe."

"I couldn't agree more," she said quietly.

"Is your elbow keeping you awake?"

"No."

There was something about the middle of the night that created intimacy and made it difficult to lie about anything.

Nervous and frightened of the outcome, she rubbed moist palms against the side of her robe. "I need to talk to you, but I was afraid I would have to wake you first."

"I'm listening."

Isn't this what you wanted, Laura?

"All right. I've only told you one untruth since we've known each other. No, that's not exactly true. I've told *two* untruths," she blurted, then moaned because it had come out all wrong. "That's not exactly true, either." She fidgeted with the ends of her belt. "Since Tony died I've been keeping something from you—" her voice shook "—and I've been hating myself for it ever since. I should have just been honest when you came to the cabin on the *Puff Cloud,* but..."

"For the love of heaven, Laura," he said impatiently, "just *say* it. You think I don't know that deep down you could never marry me because you've never stopped loving your husband no matter what he did to you?"

"No, Zach!" she cried in horror, because he was so wrong. So very wrong. "That isn't what I'm trying to tel—"

"Don't deny it," he warned, sending a thrill of alarm through her body. "I witnessed your devotion to him, saw it in a dozen different ways, remember? But the proof was in your eyes the night I accompanied you to your hotel room after Tony died."

Her heart turned over just remembering that moment she'd almost committed the unpardonable and invited him inside.

"*What* proof?"

"Do you really need me to spell it out for you?"

"I do. What is it you think was going on inside me?"

Something in her tone must have alerted Zach, because she sensed his hesitation, a rare thing for him.

"You were in so much pain you didn't want or need anybody."

"You're right," she said. "You saw pain. Excruciating pain. Perhaps now you have some idea of what it cost me not to ask you to spend the night with me."

Even in the dim light of the room, she perceived

his shock. There was an electric silence. The time to tell all had come.

"I'm far from perfect, Zach. Maybe you'll understand why I underwent therapy after the Tour de France was over."

"Therapy?"

"Yes. I knew that if I didn't talk to a professional about my guilt over wanting you, I'd be endangering my health and ultimately the baby's. I'm not proud of what I'm about to tell you, but it has to be said because it's the truth.

"I fell in love with you, Zach." Her voice caught. "It happened after you answered the hotel-room door and introduced yourself as Tony's roommate. When you asked me to come in and wait for him, a little voice warned me this was wrong, told me I should run away and not look back. But I chose to ignore it. That's how fast and how…naturally it happened."

She heard a low groan. It could have meant anything, but she'd started this and had to finish it. "I'm at a loss to explain how or why. All I can tell you is that…my life changed that day.

"In the beginning I lied to myself. I told myself I was only attracted to you because you were so kind to me. I rationalized that my pitiful marriage had made me vulnerable to any decent man's attentions. But when you phoned me from the hospital to tell me about Klaus, I had to admit that my feelings for you went far beyond anything remotely resembling gratitude.

"As terrible as this sounds, I didn't want to hang up. I wanted our conversation to go on and on. I wanted to beg you to come back to the hotel and be with me."

She paused to draw a deep shuddering breath. "The more circumstances separated us, the more my feelings for you grew. By the time I'd finished shedding my tears for Tony, I had to face the truth. I loved *you*. My heart, my soul knew it. And so did my body."

Laura heard Zach groan again. In admitting the truth she risked everything, even his revulsion. But it had to be said.

"When you walked me to my hotel room that night, I struggled not to break down and invite you in. I feared what you would think of me if I did." She paused once more. "Do you understand what I'm saying?" she cried, barely holding on to her emotions. "Only a few hours before, Tony had collapsed and died! And there I was, wanting you in all the ways a woman could ever want a man."

Tears rolled down her hot cheeks. "I was convinced there had to be something wrong with me, something evil. How could I want you when the body of the man I'd promised before God to love and honor hadn't even been buried?"

She choked down a sob. "This gets worse. Only one thing prevented me from begging you to stay the night. To my shame, it wasn't God. It was *Rosie Armstrong*."

At the sound of his ex-fiancée's name, she saw Zach

recoil. Proof, as far as she was concerned, that he'd given everything to Rosie. There could be no more.

"Bev told me all about her, that she was the great love of your life, so it's pointless for you to deny it."

"I wasn't about to."

You knew this could backfire on you, but you didn't know how agonizing it was going to be.

Head bowed, she murmured, "Even Richie let me know how much her son's jealousy of you brought you grief."

Finish it. Just finish it. "It's obvious to me and everyone else you've never gotten over her. I *know* what that kind of love is like, because it's the same kind of love I feel for you. The forever kind. It defies time and…and logic. It drove me to lie to you in the Galápagos about not wanting to be married. I thought I'd be clever and pretend marriage didn't matter to me as long as you'd let me stay in your life, in whatever capacity you chose. But from the beginning, I fantasized about what it would be like to really belong to you, to have your baby."

She lifted her chin. "But therapy taught me many things. Like the fact I'd been in mourning my whole marriage and had done most of my grieving long before Tony died. Thus the reason I was ready to get into a new relationship.

"Therapy also helped me understand that it's unhealthy to live with guilt and secrets. In the end, you find you've only destroyed yourself.

"That's why I decided I'd better tell you all this

tonight. I'm not about to hang around you, let alone try to lock you into a loveless marriage. I realize that if both parties don't feel the same, it doesn't work and wouldn't be good for a child."

She had to get out of here, and she started for the kitchen. "Please," she called over her shoulder, "let me be. Forgive me for flying to the Galápagos uninvited. It was wrong of me. You went there to nurse your wounds. All I managed to do was stir up the past and embarrass you. I promise it won't happen again, Zach."

She hurried through the house and up the stairs, anxious to be gone from here before morning. It was time to close the chapter on the Wildes before she made any more mistakes.

A FEW MINUTES LATER Zach opened Richie's bedroom door, seeking Richard. He didn't care if his brother was asleep. He had to talk to him or he'd go out of his mind.

"Come all the way in," Richard said, "I've been waiting for you."

Relief swept through Zach. "Where's Richie?"

"I think the quake scared him more than he wants to admit. He had so much trouble settling down, I went to the kitchen to make him some hot chocolate. That's when I heard voices coming from the family room and figured you might need to talk later. I told him to get in bed with Bev and the girls."

"What would I do without you? How come I'm one

of the lucky ones in life who was given a brother and best friend rolled into one?''

Richard turned on the light by Richie's bed. Dressed only in a T-shirt and boxers, he threw off the covers and sat on the edge of the bed, eyeing Zach for a long sober moment.

''Welcome home. It's good to see you again, too. I've missed you more than you know.''

''Want to bet?'' Zach fired back. ''I don't think I realized just how deep my feelings went until the captain of the *Wind Cloud* told me there'd been an earthquake in Southern California. When he said the epicenter was in Costa Mesa...'' Zach couldn't finish.

''It was something, all right. I was in the office when everything went flying off the desks and cabinets. For once I was glad you were thousands of miles away. Luckily no one at the office or home was hurt.''

''Except for Laura.''

Richard leaped to his feet. ''She never said anything.''

''You know her. She's so self-sacrificing she didn't want to alarm Richie.''

''She's not going to miscarry, is she?''

''No, no. It's not that bad. But when the quake hit, it knocked her to the ground. She banged her elbow pretty hard and I saw an ugly bruise below her knee.''

Richard quirked and eyebrow. ''The knee, huh? That must have been *before* you left her bedroom to go downstairs.'' He chuckled.

''Zach, when are you going to break down and admit she's the reason you flew home on the next plane?'' He paused, ''You know you're in love with her.''

''I've known that since day one.''

''Is there the slightest doubt in your mind that she's hopelessly in love with you, too?''

''Not anymore. Tonight she told me exactly how she felt.'' Her confession had transformed him. ''*Lord*, Richard. She loves me the way Bev loves you. I didn't think that kind of love was possible for me.''

Richard's eyes moistened. ''Destiny must have known what was down the road when you were asked to train for the Tour de France. Let me tell you something. Bev and I *watched* the two of you fall in love. It happened fast. Now answer me one question. What are you doing here in Richie's room, instead of hers?''

''She thinks—no, she's *convinced* I'm still in love with Rosie.''

''That's Bev's fault,'' Richard confided. ''The day of the time trials she told Laura about your past without realizing the damage it would do. She's hated herself for it ever since.''

Zach shook his head. ''I love Bev and could never blame her for anything. It's *my* behavior that's the problem. When Laura came to see me in the Galápagos, she offered herself to me in any capacity I was willing to consider. I was so afraid she didn't love me the way I loved her, I turned her down flat.''

''Tell me something I don't know,'' Richard said, shaking his head. ''She came home shattered.''

"Then you have some idea of the state I was in when I found out she'd left the Galápagos without my knowledge. The hell of it is, tonight I made another fatal mistake by telling her I'd marry her to atone for my guilt over the part I played in Tony's death."

"You *what?*"

"Yeah," Zach admitted. "I told her to give me her answer in the morning. As you found out when you went downstairs, she chose not to wait until the sun came up to tell me no thank you." He began to pace. "You should have heard her tonight. If I'd tried to tell her how I really felt about her, if I'd made one move toward her in the state she was in, she would have run out of the house and I might not have been able to find her again."

"You mean like *you* did in Paris? Without leaving a forwarding address?"

Zach's hands balled into fists. "Okay, I deserved that."

"Hey—" Richard gave him another hug "—don't be so hard on yourself. You did what you felt you had to do. Tony's death shocked all of us. But that's in the past. You *are* home to stay, aren't you?"

They stared at each other.

"I don't ever want to be anyplace else."

"Then you need to tell Laura."

"I need to tell her a lot of things."

"I agree. So go in to her right now and start talking." Richard took him fiercely by the shoulders. "I mean a knock-down-drag-out heart-to-heart. Don't stop until she's listened to you—and *believes* you! Whether it takes two hours or twenty, I'll make sure the kids stay away.''

Zach's thoughts raced ahead. "Does the guest-room door have a lock?''

"No.'' Richard grinned. "When the house was built, I made a last-minute decision not to bother.''

"That was a wise decision.'' He grinned back. "Otherwise there might have been more to repair than your swimming pool.''

But Zach's grin faded as he left the bedroom and approached Laura's. Fearing she wouldn't answer him if he knocked, Zach made the split-second decision to go in unannounced and uninvited.

Quietly he turned the knob and entered.

The sight that greeted his eyes would live with him forever.

A gasp escaped Laura as she frantically attempted to cover herself with the end of Richie's bedspread. The movement knocked her clothes to the floor. She must have just come out of the shower and was about to get dressed, Zach thought.

No doubt she has a secret plan to leave Newport without saying goodbye.

"Going somewhere?'' he asked. Acting on instincts older than time, he closed the distance between them and picked her up in his arms. "I don't think, so.'' he whispered against her lips.

"No, Zach!'' She turned her head and fought with surprising strength, but she was still no match for him.

With only a bedspread separating him from her gorgeous body, he recognized his advantage for what it was and chose to use it.

In wonderment he watched a rose tint suffuse her cheeks and proceed down the breathtaking length of her.

As he'd once told Richie— "All's fair in love, war and the Tour de France." With the race out of the way, they were now down to the love and war part. He remembered that the family-room door *did* have a lock and he planned to show no mercy.

"Please put me down," she begged.

"I will when I'm good and ready, but first we're going to have a long undisturbed talk." So saying, he started for the door.

"What are you doing? And we've already talked."

"What happened to my raven-haired captive who said she'd come with me anywhere willingly? And no, we have *not* talked."

"But you don't want me!" she wailed plaintively before burying her face in his shoulder.

"You don't have the faintest idea *what* I want because I let you say everything that was on your mind first. Once we're where no one can bother us, it's going to be my turn to talk and yours to listen. Without interruption."

He opened the door and headed for the staircase.

"Let me at least take my clothes!"

"I'll let you come back for them later."

Enjoying the role of marauder, Zach stole through

the house with his treasure, pleased that she'd gone all silent on him.

Once the family-room door was closed and he heard the satisfying click of the lock, he could concentrate fully on Laura. The thought of making love to her on the sofa bed Bev had made up for him almost sent his heart into fibrillation.

But if he gave in to the desire racking his body, there'd be no talking. Richard's easy chair would accommodate both of them. Locked in his arms, she would have to stay put, and he'd still have the power to think and speak.

Or so he'd thought.

Too late he discovered that the small amount of light from the aquarium had given the smooth skin of her arms and shoulders a pearly luster. The reality of her physical presence, her natural beauty, every curve of her face and body, played havoc with his senses. The enticing dishevelment of her curls, still damp from the shower, the lovely mouth with its full lower lip made him forget what he was about.

Suppressing his yearning while he still could, he got up with her from the chair and carefully lowered her onto the sofa bed.

Her astonishment at being dispatched well out of his reach would have made him laugh if the situation wasn't so crucial to his existence. Though he'd lived through two relationships that had caused him great heartache, he'd been able to get on with his life. Not this time, though.

As long ago as Belgium, he'd realized that if he was privileged to live the rest of his life with her—as her husband—he would be one of those mortals lucky enough to scale the full height of human experience. In the Galápagos he'd discovered that without her, he would suffer a kind of death and be irrevocably lost.

She made no move to escape. Like an obedient child she lay there with Richie's bedspread cocooning her, her dark eyes anxiously peering out from the fringe.

The mixture of innocence and womanly beauty melted his insides.

"Before any more time passes," he said, "I want you to know everything there is to know about me. That way there'll be no secrets between us after we're married."

CHAPTER FOURTEEN

AFTER WE'RE MARRIED? Do you really mean it, Zach?

With extreme effort, she managed to sit up and still keep the bedspread in place.

His eyes followed every movement. "Because you were a married woman when we met, I didn't have the right to share everything with you like I'm going to do now."

"You'll never know how much I wanted you to," she said.

"You think I didn't?" He sucked in a breath. "I'm afraid you're in for a long siege, Laura. Many of the things I'm about to tell you, no one else knows. Not even Richard."

Because she'd never known two brothers more devoted, this statement made an impact. She stared at him, wide-eyed.

"As you've already divined," he began, "I have several glaring flaws. But one stands out from the rest. I've always put Richard on a pedestal. Everything I ever did, aimed for, achieved, had to be measured by his standards. He didn't ask for his little brother's hero-worship. Unfortunately for him it just happened, an accident of birth in the family constellation. I followed him around like a puppy and he had to bear the burden.''

''That happens in lots of families,'' Laura said, rushing to his defense.

''In our case I took it too far. I'm afraid I became a nuisance, as well as a responsibility. Being Richard, he took me on because that's the kind of man he is.'' Zach paused. ''After saving Bev from drowning, he fell in love with her.''

''Yes. She told me about that.''

His eyes flashed. ''Did she tell you how jealous I was because she'd taken him away from me?''

Laura's heart went out to him. ''No.''

''Maybe I did a better job of hiding my dark side than I thought. Anyway, there were moments in my teenage years when I disliked her intensely.'' His brows knit. ''If you can imagine anyone disliking Bev, then you'll have an idea of just how dark I can be. Anyway, at their wedding, I felt like I'd lost my best friend. I couldn't tag along anymore. The only people they associated with were other engaged or married couples. Life just wasn't the same, particularly when a few months after the ceremony I heard they were expecting a baby.''

''Zach, many younger brothers and sisters feel bereft when an older sibling leaves the nest. It's a huge adjustment for everyone. I went through it myself.''

He shook his head. ''My case was unique. I could have benefited from therapy. But that word wasn't in our family's vocabulary and I went from bad to worse.

I figured that if I found myself a girlfriend and got married, Richard would allow me into that inner circle and we'd be buddies again. So began my quest to find the perfect woman.''

"And she turned out to be a carbon copy of Bev,'' Laura guessed. But she'd spoken without thinking.

Zach stared at her before nodding. "She could have been Bev's twin. Superficially they resembled each other. Cathy had Bev's sunny disposition. Richard approved of her, so that was all that mattered. To my delight, they let me bring her over to their apartment for dinner. The four of us went sailing together. After Richie was born, we saw even more of one another. When it looked like my plan was working, I bought her a ring and we set a date for our wedding.

"The only shadow on that particular horizon were the migraines Cathy suffered. Sometimes she'd be too sick to go anywhere. Though I never said the words out loud, I'm ashamed to admit that I used to resent her for ruining an evening we'd planned with Richard and Bev.''

He blew out a sigh. "Obviously I was too emotionally immature to be involved in a serious relationship of any kind, certainly not one that had been engineered by my own selfish agenda. Because Richard had always handled everything so well, I thought I could carry things off just like he did.

"Reality struck when Cathy had to be hospitalized after a bad migraine attack. She was frightened and reached out to me for support. I couldn't comfort her the way she needed. Don't get me wrong—I cared for her a great deal, but I didn't know what real love was. I didn't dare admit that to anyone. That was the hell of it. About now my guilt kicked in.

"It was a sobering experience for a number of reasons. I'd never been around a really ill person before, in this case my fiancée. For the first time in my life I had to forget my needs and desires to be there for her. I had to pretend things I didn't feel in front of her family and mine because I didn't want anyone to know my turmoil, particularly Richard."

"Zach—"

"You see what I'm talking about? I had real problems and promised myself that when she got better, I would try to make it up to her." Another sigh. "It never dawned on me that Cathy would die. My imagination didn't stretch that far. When the doctor told me she'd passed away in her sleep because of a brain tumor, I simply didn't believe him. Like all young people, I thought we were immortal.

"Her death was not only a tragedy, it forced me to continue living a kind of lie. Everyone assumed I was grieving for my lost love. Of course I felt horrible about it, but part of my pain had to do with my own wretchedness."

Laura understood only too well.

"My guilt deepened and I went into a depression. Of course no one knew what I was going through. The family rallied around me, but for once their love couldn't fix what was wrong. Poor Richard, forever my champion, made a suggestion he thought would help me get over losing Cathy."

"What was that?"

"He felt a new hobby unassociated with the past would force me to channel my energy into something positive. The next thing I knew, we were out buying racing bikes. His idea. I would never have thought of it on my own." He shook his head.

"Oddly enough, her death brought us close together again. It was wonderful being with Richard in the old buddy way, but my guilt—compounded by more guilt because I knew he ought to be home with Bev—prevented me from enjoying the situation.

"I concentrated, instead, on pushing myself to the edge. Cycling happened to be the only sport at which I was better than my brother. It felt good to beat him at something. I needed to redeem myself, be a person worthy of his respect. When I saw he was proud of me, I worked out harder and began entering local competitions.

"That was about the time Bev announced she was pregnant again. She suffered terrible morning sickness, and Richard couldn't come with me as often. But it no longer mattered as much. Between my work in the family business and the cycling, a certain amount of healing started to take place. So even though Richard never knew the truth, his idea had turned out to be a good one.

"Those years following Cathy's death were a time of growth for me. I won a lot of national and international races. I traveled a great deal and met a scout representing a European-based sponsor of a cycling team."

Zach told Laura how they'd been looking to include some Americans on a new pro team they were putting together to train in Park City, Utah, for the Tour de France. Though he'd had no burning desire to win a competition like that, the idea of seeing new places had sounded interesting.

"Of course old habits die hard," he said, "and I had to discuss it with Richard before I did anything as drastic as uprooting myself to live in Utah. He thought I ought to consider it because my hobby kept me from dwelling on the past, and I was good, really good, at cycling. Dad encouraged me, as well, and offered to sponsor me so I could devote full time to the grueling training involved. I began to see that if I did this, it would make the family happy. Since I felt I owed them, I thought, why not try it?"

Laura pondered this last revelation. Guilt was responsible for more pain than just about anything she could think of.

"I realized an offer like that didn't come your way very often. Being at loose ends, I accepted it and moved to Park City. The Rockies provided me with a whole new set of problems, but I thrived on adversity. It took time to acclimatize. At such a high altitude, I learned endurance and found the steep grades challenging.

"I also discovered loneliness and began seeing

women. Over a period of time I met all types, from sports buffs to party girls.''

That's something I didn't know, Laura thought. *I don't think Bev and Richard know it, either.*

"To some extent I enjoyed the experience, but I never felt anything lasting. As soon as I sensed they wanted a commitment, I moved on with the excuse that I'd be leaving the States before long to live in Europe.

"One day on a mountain road, I was racing around a corner and almost bumped into this woman who was out riding bikes with her son and his friends. She apologized for being in the way. When the near-accident was clearly my fault, I found her generosity refreshing.''

He smiled at the memory. "Rosie had a sunny disposition. The absence of any artifice or superficiality made her really appealing. Unlike the other women I'd met, she had stability in both her career as a teacher and role as a mother. She didn't come on strong.''

In fact, Zach said to Laura, it had been her reticence that had drawn him to her. He'd known instinctively that she would make no demands on him. He'd needed that because he wasn't ready for a deep emotional commitment.

"She was a widow and quite content with her life. She didn't need me to complete it, didn't want something from me. I could tell she was a good parent, too. Her son, Cody, was friendly at first. But as soon as he realized I enjoyed being with his mother, he didn't like me at all. Since I was out of town a lot, it didn't bother me. Our dates were sporadic.

"But little by little, love grew. In time I discovered that I liked coming home from a racing event to one woman. The bachelor life began to pall, as did the cycling circuit. I gave up the idea of training for the Tour de France and, instead, started up a branch of our family business in Salt Lake.

"At that point Rosie's son declared war. Between him and her in-laws interference, I had the fight of my life on my hands. Despite the love Rosie and I shared, the second year of our relationship resembled a battlefield with Cody outmaneuvering me at every turn.

"Unfortunately Cody's behavior had created sort of a smokescreen that masked a much more serious problem for Rosie."

"What was that?" Laura asked in a haunted voice.

"Rosie was still in love with the husband who'd died in the war." He started to pace. Laura watched him, her heart breaking for him. "I knew all along she wasn't completely over him, but I told myself it didn't matter. What we had was here and now. It was similar to what I'd told myself about loving Cathy when I knew the kind of love I had for her wasn't enough."

Laura shivered involuntarily, afraid of what was to come.

"I knew in my gut it was pointless to keep seeing Rosie. But so much time had been invested, I made one last-ditch effort and invited her and Cody on a cruise. If nothing came of it, I was going to leave Salt Lake.

"To my surprise, she proposed to me aboard ship and told me she wouldn't let Cody stand in the way of our happiness. She swore she loved me and I believed her. Of course I knew her feelings for me were different from what she'd felt for her husband. I told myself that in time, though, our love would take on a life of its own. I had gotten to the point where I wanted to settle down. I didn't want to look anywhere else."

He stopped pacing and put his hands on his hips. "We probably would have achieved a solid marriage if her husband hadn't returned. But the second she phoned me and told me the news that he was alive, I knew it was over. So did she."

"How were you able to do it?" Laura asked. "How were you able to let go?"

"It was hard. I won't lie about that. We'd been friends a long time."

"And lovers," she whispered.

"No, Laura, that's where you're wrong. We never slept together."

She couldn't comprehend what he was telling her. "You mean that over a two-year period you nev—"

"No," he cut in. "I didn't want to make love to her until I knew it would be *me* in her bed, not Nick. You see, I thought it didn't matter that she still clung to her first love. But when it came right down to it, I was greedy. I wanted it all. When I couldn't have it,

I decided to play a waiting game. I could afford to. I wasn't going anywhere.''

He sat down on the edge of the bed and ran a hand through his hair. Laura found *herself* wanting to do that, but she stayed still and listened. ''Because of that decision, we were both fortunate enough to walk away in the end without *that* complication to deal with. She was able to resume her marriage to Nick and not look back. They have an incredible relationship, like Richard and Bev's. Needless to say it made Cody deliriously happy.''

''Stop being so noble, Zach!'' she exclaimed. ''What about *your* happiness?''

''*My* happiness?'' He turned to her and his eyes narrowed. ''She's sitting right in front of me, exactly where I want her.'' His voice sounded husky.

Laura heard the words with a sense of unreality. ''Be serious.''

''I've never been more serious in my life. Haven't you listened to anything I've been saying?''

The next thing she knew, he stood up and reached for her, pulling her, still clutching the bedspread, into his arms.

''I've only known one great love, my darling. *You.*''

She couldn't deny the power of his declaration. All the emotion, all the love that was in him, had found the path straight to her heart. A small cry of joy escaped her. ''I love you, too, Zach.''

He molded her body to his, worshipping her with his hands and mouth. She couldn't get close enough.

"I never believed a person could fall in love at first sight, Laura, but it happened to me when I opened my hotel-room door and saw you standing there."

"That day was like a wonderful dream," she said. "I never wanted to wake up."

Zach sighed. "By the time I'd made up the excuse that I was out of razor blades so I could walk you to your hotel, I was in love. I knew you were Tony's wife, but it didn't seem to matter. You weren't anything like I'd imagined. I didn't want to leave your side, or you to leave mine."

"I know, darling, I know. Why do you think I invited you in *my* hotel room and fed you those granola bars? I was desperate to think up any idiotic excuse to detain you."

Burying his face in her neck, he whispered, "I loved those bars. With every delicious bite, I cursed the Fates that had made you Tony's wife, instead of mine. Talk about desperation…"

Laura clung to him, almost mindless with passion.

"The attraction I felt for you," he said, "drove me to inveigle Richard into taking you around the circuit with him. Not that he needed any coaxing once he'd met you. It was the only plan I could think of to legitimately see you every morning and every night."

"Then why did you stop joining the family?" she cried in remembered pain.

He held her away from him and shook her gently. "You *know* why. I'd already passed beyond the bounds of decency when I called you from the hospital.

"No, you—"

"Laura," he interrupted, "all my life I've tried to live by a certain code of ethics. Making love to another man's wife has always been verboten. I don't frighten easily, but that night when I knew you were alone, I came close to breaking that vow and I experienced real fear."

She closed her eyes tightly and buried her face in his chest. "You were right not to come. How could I have refused you? Not even Tony's death made a difference. After that scene with the press, I just wanted to curl up with you alone somewhere and shut out the world. I'll never know how I found the strength to turn away from you."

A tremor shook his powerful body. "I don't want to think about that. The only matter of any importance is marrying you. If it was up to me, I'd drive us to Nevada right now. But if you want a big wedding..."

She chuckled. "I'm afraid the wedding arrangements might already be out of our hands."

He looked down at her, confused. "What are you talking about?"

"Bev and Richard have been hoping for months that we'd get together. They'd be crushed if we just drove off without letting them plan a celebration."

"I love and need you so badly I don't know if I can wait. But since it's Richard and Bev—"

Laura silenced his mouth with her own. He returned

her kiss with an ardor that blocked out the rest of the world. When he finally let her catch her breath, she murmured, "Let's go upstairs and tell them the happy news. It's already morning. The sun's up. And you *know* they've been awake all night just waiting to find out if all their plots have hatched the way they hoped."

Zach smiled at her. "You love them as much as I do. That's just one of the many things I adore about you."

"They're the most wonderful people I've ever known."

"I agree."

So saying, he picked her up in his arms and headed for the door.

"First we'll have to go by the guest room so I can get dressed," she said.

"Really."

She blinked.

"Zach—"

"Hush, woman!"

Effortlessly he carried her up the stairs. Something told her she was in trouble.

"Zach, you can't let anyone see me like this!"

He cast her a positively wolfish leer. "Any spoils must be presented to the master of this house first. He and he alone will decide your fate."

"Uncle Zach!"

Richie appeared out of nowhere. "What're you doing with Laura and how come she's wrapped in my bedspread?'' He spoke loudly enough for all to hear. Within seconds the girls had run out of the master bedroom.

"Is she sick?'' Rachel wanted to know.

"How come she's not saying anything?'' Robin demanded.

Fire raged in Laura's cheeks. All she could do was hide her face in Zach's neck.

"She's in shock, Robin.''

"Does that mean the baby's coming?''

Laura could feel Zach shake with suppressed laughter. "It better not be. We've got to get married first.''

"Hooray!'' the girls shouted.

"It's about time, Uncle Zach,'' Richie declared.

"Is *that* right, Richie.''

"Yeah. Laura's the best. She's already part of the family.''

"Did you hear that, my love?'' Zach said in her ear as they swept through the doorway of Bev and Richard's room. "No greater praise.''

"Come all the way in, little brother. Let's see what you've got bundled up in there.''

"I've returned with precious plunder after a great voyage in my longboat.''

"What's a longboat?'' Robin wanted to know, but nobody answered.

"Come closer so I can inspect the goods,'' came the command.

"Richard Thorald Wilde!'' Bev cried indignantly on Laura's behalf.

"You started this, *wife,*" Richard teased.

Laura had the sinking feeling there was no stopping Zach or his brother. He carried her over to Richard's side of the king-size bed.

Richard reached out to smooth the fringe of Richie's bedspread away from her face. He winked. "What's this? A woman with strange black hair and dark eyes that can put the pox on a man so he doesn't know where he is or what he's doing. Don't you know this kind of creature makes a man useless and causes trouble in our world of blond-haired blue-eyed giants?"

"Richard, that's enough!" Bev tried again.

"She's with child, too, but I still want her." Zach swooped down and gave her a kiss in front of everyone.

"Hmm, yes, I can see that you do." Richard put a finger to his cheek thoughtfully. "If you claim her, you can't go on any more voyages."

"I don't want to go on any more voyages. I want my own castle, my own lands…my own woman."

"From here on out you'll have to do your share of the work and not cause any more havoc for me and mine."

"I swear by the oath of Thorald I shall."

"By the oath of Thorald, huh? In that case, she's yours! What do you call this creature?"

"Laura."

"That's a strange name."

"But I like it."

"The child's name will have to be Astrid in honor

of our great-great-grandmother, Queen Astrid, isn't that right, *wife?*"

"Astrid?" The shock in Zach's voice made Laura chuckle.

"It's Astrid, or there will be no ceremony."

Zach looked down at her in puzzlement. "Laura?"

"Do you mind?" Her eyes begged him. "She's going to be your daughter. I want her to be a true Wilde."

Zach's stunned gaze flicked back to Richard. "Astrid it is."

A huge grin transformed Richard's face. "I told you those brown eyes were going to be your downfall. Wife." He turned to Bev. "Name the date for the ceremony."

"Wednesday."

"But that's five days from now!" Zach protested. "I'm not waiting that—"

"Wednesday it is," Richard proclaimed with kingly authority. "Until then, this creature will have to stay with the womenfolk and be prepared."

Rachel squirmed her way through to sit on her father's lap.

"Daddy, you're funny."

"Yeah, Daddy—"

Robin was cut off by the ringing of the phone. It was a sound no one had heard since the quake.

"The phone's back on, thank goodness. Now we can call everybody and invite them!" Bev reached for the receiver and said hello. But the shining happiness in her face faded as she listened to whomever was on the other end.

Fearing it was bad news, everyone in the room fell quiet. Laura clung to Zach.

"He's fine. In fact, he's right here," Bev said quietly, her apprehensive blue eyes darting to her brother-in-law.

Covering the mouthpiece, she said, "It's for you, Zach. Salt Lake calling. You can take it downstairs. I'll wait and then hang up."

Laura felt as if someone had just slugged her in the stomach. *It's Rosie.*

She stiffened in Zach's arms. "Put me down in the hall, then go take your call," she urged him in a shaky voice.

Ignoring her request, Zach held her even closer in his arms and walked around to the phone on Bev's side of the bed.

"Hold the receiver up for me, will you, darling?"

In shock, Laura did as he asked, but her fingers were trembling.

"Rosie?" he began. "Is that you?"

"Yes. When I heard that the Newport area had been hit by the quake, I had to call to find out if you and your family were all right."

Warmed by her concern, Zach felt like he was talking to an old friend, nothing more. He could have no greater proof of his total and complete love for Laura. She was his whole world. Nothing else mattered.

He cleared his throat. "We were lucky," he murmured, looking at Laura, who stared up at him half-fearfully. "No one got hurt except my fiancée, and even she escaped with only minor injuries."

"Oh, Zach!" Rosie said happily. "You're engaged?"

"Yes. We're being married on Wednesday." He paused to kiss Laura on the mouth. He'd never get enough. "You were given your heart's desire when Nick returned from the war. Now that I've found mine I understand why you could never let him go. If I lost Laura…" He couldn't even think about it.

"Never," Laura mouthed before relaxing against him in total contentment.

"Your news has made me happier than you'll ever know," Rosie said.

"Laura's love has made me feel reborn."

"I can tell. God bless you, Zach."

"God bless you, too, Rosie. Give my best to Nick and Cody."

When he hung up the phone, the last door to his troubled past had closed. Zach lowered his head to kiss the woman who'd become his future, his *life*.

"Okay, everybody," Richard announced as he climbed out of bed. "It's time for breakfast. Last person downstairs has to do the dishes and clean up the kitchen!"

"That'll be Uncle Zach," Richie grumbled near the doorway. "If he ever *does* come down."

"I wouldn't count on it," his mother said, glancing at the oblivious couple locked in an embrace.

"But Laura promised to play baseball cards with me."

"I'm afraid you're going to have a long wait, son," Richard said. "Since I don't have to go to work today, how about me standing in for her?"

"You?" There was a brief silence. "Okay," he agreed, not sounding quite as grumpy, "but nobody's as smart as Laura."

"We don't have to go to school on Wednesday, do we, mommy."

"Of course not, Rachel honey. I'm going to need you girls' help to get everything ready. We want Zach and Laura's wedding day to be perfect!"

"Yeah!" they all chimed in at once.

CHAPTER FIFTEEN

"GOODBYE! HAVE A wonderful time!"

While family and friends stood on the front porch and waved to Zach and Laura as they drove off with *Just Married* spray painted on the trunk of the car, Richard reached for his wife. For some odd reason, he needed her more than usual tonight.

Loving her pregnant shape, he slid his hands around her from behind and instinctively searched for movement in her abdomen. He would never take the process of conception and birth for granted. Each time he felt the evidence of the baby they'd made inside her, he relived the wonder of it all—especially tonight because the brother he adored was finally going to experience real joy as a husband and father, too. In fact, he would probably end up having several children in quick succession to make up for lost time.

Suddenly Bev whirled around to face him. "I'm so happy I feel like I'm going to burst! Have you ever seen two people more in love? Honey, I can't believe I'm saying this, but I'm glad Zach had to go through what he did first. Otherwise he would never have met the perfect woman for him."

As Richard took in his wife's radiant beauty, his

heart overflowed with love. Swallowing with difficulty, he murmured, "If it hadn't been for you, if you
didn't love him as much as you do..." He gave up
and simply crushed her in his arms.

"Hey," she whispered, nestling even closer. "I
have a surprise for you."

When her words had fully computed, he pulled far
enough away to look down at her questioningly.

"I decided to save it until now to help you get over
your separation anxiety."

One brow quirked. "Separation anxiety?"

"Yes. You think I don't know you're feeling a little
abandoned now that your brother has cut the cord for
good, so to speak?"

Bev knows everything. How I love her.

"When Laura and I went in for our ultrasounds, I
found out we're going to have a new version of Zach
running around the house pretty soon."

"We're having another boy?" Richard almost
shouted. His parents and Laura's, who were standing
nearby talking, started to laugh.

Bev sent him a teasing smile.

"I thought that might cheer you up. In your old old
age you'll have this cute little towheaded guy who'll
follow you everywhere, who'll gaze up at you with
adoration in his eyes and think you're the greatest man
alive. Which, of course, you are."

As SOON AS Laura was dressed, she left the examining
room and more or less shuffled into her doctor's office.

"Full term" had taken on new meaning in the past couple of weeks, for both her *and* Zach.

Hard to believe February had finally arrived. With Valentine's Day just around the corner, this could be her last visit before the baby came.

Zach stood up as she entered the room. He gave her a hug and the doctor told them to be seated. Though her husband tried not to show it, he'd been on edge all week.

Yesterday he'd hung around their newly remodeled condo all morning with the excuse that he didn't need to go into work until later. Today he'd taken the whole day off just to accompany her to the doctor's office.

Of course, Laura wasn't complaining. She deemed any time she could spend with him precious. But she didn't like that brooding expression on his handsome face. It was too great a reminder of the Zach she'd confronted in the Galápagos.

Without preamble, Cindy Stewart, Laura's obstetrician, explained that everything looked good.

"The baby has dropped and you're two centimeters dilated. Don't plan another sailing trip down to Baja right now." She winked as she said it, but Laura noticed that Cindy's teasing had been wasted on Zach. He'd gone pale beneath his tan.

Now he got to his feet, rubbing his neck absently. "What you're saying is, our baby could come any time now."

"That's right. If you have some questions, I'd be glad to answer them."

Laura's heart went out to her husband, whose anxious gaze flicked from Cindy to her. "Do you have any, darling?"

"No."

She had several actually, but in Zach's nervous state, she thought it wiser not to voice them.

"If that's the case, I'll leave you two and go see my next patient." Cindy rose from her chair. "Call me when the pains start. You have the number of my beeper."

Laura nodded. "Thank you so much for everything."

"It's my pleasure, believe me." On her way out of the room the doctor patted Zach's arm. "Your wife is going to be fine."

Her reassurance didn't make a dent. The second she was out the door Zach cupped Laura's elbow. "Let's go home."

"All right."

On their way out to the parking lot her stomach grumbled, reminding her that it had been a long time since lunch. "Do you care if we stop for some souvlaki on the way?"

Grim-faced, he muttered, "We'll phone for take-out."

Laura frowned. As far as she knew, there were no Greek restaurants in the area that delivered. Her husband simply wasn't thinking clearly. He'd been cooped up all day and needed an outlet.

"I've got a better idea. Let's take a walk down on

the pier and find us a cozy little place that serves stuffed shrimp.''

It was a favorite dish of theirs, but judging by her husband's next question, it seemed he couldn't be tempted.

"Do you think that's wise this close to your time?''

She leaned into his side and kissed his cheek before they got in the car. "Darling, we both have to eat. As for walking, a little exercise is good for me.''

His jaw hardened. She recognized the signs.

"On second thought, home does sound inviting. Come to think of it, one of your Spanish omelettes sounds even better.''

"You'd like that?''

Obviously she'd said the right thing to temporarily appease him.

"I'd love it.''

Within minutes they'd arrived at the condo. The double decks overlooking the water had been destroyed by the quake and recently rebuilt. It was the kind of beachfront property Laura had always dreamed of.

Possessing a green thumb like her dad's, she had plants and tubs of potted flowers growing inside and out. Together she and Zach had chosen a Hapsburg-yellow color scheme, which they teamed with light oak and rattan furniture. The decor had transformed his former domicile into a comfortable sunny haven of beauty. Especially the nursery.

Of all the bedrooms in the house, the baby's room

had claimed her husband's undivided attention. Never had any expectant father taken his role so seriously. From the walnut-colored French-provincial-style crib to the colorful mobile of the seven dwarfs, everything was perfect.

For the past four months they'd been ecstatically happy. Why, she worried, had Zach's behavior undergone such a drastic change?

The second they entered the house he put his hands on her shoulders from behind and said, "Why don't you go on up and take a nice relaxing bath. By the time you're out, I'll have dinner ready and bring it to you in bed."

Laura didn't turn around.

You're frightened, my darling. What's wrong?

She kissed the hand nearest her warm cheek. She was always warm these days. "You must have been reading my mind. I'll be waiting for you."

All three bedrooms faced the water and so each had a spectacular view. Laura entered the master bedroom, her mind trying to fathom what was going on inside her husband.

By the time she'd had her bath and slipped into a fresh nightie, she'd made up her mind to get to the bottom of it.

No sooner had she climbed into their king-size bed than he appeared with a tray. She sat up against the headboard, already salivating over the omelette's delicious aroma.

"Mmm," she said as he placed the tray on her lap.

"Thank you, darling. Everything looks wonderful. Where's *your* dinner?"

His eyes were veiled. "I'll eat later."

Knowing better than to coax him, she started to eat and chatted about inconsequential matters. He sat in one of the chairs near the bed and watched her.

Ever vigilant, as soon as she'd eaten the last green pepper and drained her glass of lemonade, he took the tray and put it on the magazine table next to his chair.

As far as she was concerned, it was time for a serious talk.

After praising him for the superb cuisine, she patted his side of the bed. "Come and join me," she invited, her voice husky. "I miss you next to me."

It was true. Up until a week ago they'd been making love morning, noon and night, whenever they could. Every time was like the first time, filling her with rapture.

Then suddenly he'd stopped touching her. For the past few nights when he'd thought she was sleeping, he'd left their bed to stand out on the deck, sometimes until the morning fog rolled in.

Zach's hands tightened on the arms of the chair, but he made no move to get up. "I don't think that's a good idea."

She frowned. "I think it's a very good idea. All I want you to do is hold me."

"It's almost impossible for me to just hold you," he said gruffly.

"Then I'll hold *you*."

She heard his sharp intake of breath. "Don't, Laura."

"Don't what? Ask my husband to come to bed with me? It's a perfectly natural request—unless you've stopped loving me."

His savage imprecation made her jump. Like lightning he shot out of the chair, his hands balled into fists at his sides. "Don't ever say that!"

"Darling!" she cried, aghast. "What's wrong? For the past week you've been acting like a stranger. *Talk* to me! Please. Tell me why you're so upset."

His continued silence devastated her. He was in pain. On an impulse she asked, "Are you afraid something's going to happen to me?"

The second the question left her lips she saw the hardening of his features and knew she'd hit home.

"You heard the doctor. I'm going to be fine."

"Can she guarantee it?" he fired back.

Laura had been listening with all her senses. Suddenly her thoughts flashed back to his first fiancée, and then to Tony.

He thinks there's a chance I'm going to die.

She tossed the covers aside. Forgetting her protruding stomach, she pushed herself off the bed and threw her arms around his neck.

"Millions of women are having babies every day. You're going to be right there with me, holding my hand. How could anything go wrong? You'll be the first one to see our daughter born. I can picture you parading around with her right now."

His gray eyes had darkened with emotion. "If anything happened to you..."

She trembled. "Don't you think I feel the same way about you every time you leave this house to go to work? Every time you're out of my sight? All it proves is how much we love each other. But we can't let the past dominate our lives, not when we have everything to live for."

"I know," he whispered, but his eyes were glazed with moisture. For a moment she saw into his soul and read his anguished cry for help. Something else was still worrying him.

"Are you afraid for the baby? You don't have to be. The ultrasound indicates our baby is perfect."

He didn't say anything. The bleakness in his eyes alarmed her. Then she remembered a comment Richie had made to her in the car.

"Zach, you're going to be the first person our baby sees when she's born. You'll be her father, now and always. Someday when she's old enough, we'll tell her about Tony, but if you think for one second that will make any difference to her, you couldn't be more wrong."

"But every time you look at her, you'll—"

"No, darling. Haven't you been listening to me? Since the moment you guessed I was pregnant, I have always thought of you as her father. In fact, I can't remember a single second when I didn't. Her birth is going to make us even closer, because she'll be the best part of Tony. She's a gift we'll treasure forever."

They were the right words to say. Zach reached for her and they clung. Then, grasping him by the hand, she drew him onto the bed and into her arms. Thus began a communication of bodies and spirits that lasted well into the night. At some point they finally fell asleep with her back against his chest, his arm around her and the baby.

AROUND FIVE in the morning Laura was awakened by a dragging sensation that swept around from her lower back to the front. There was only one thing that feeling could be.

For a long time she lay there in awed silence, pondering the event that was about to happen.

By six she was convinced the pains coming at regular intervals weren't going to go away. When her first really hard contraction began, she let out a cry of surprise at its intensity.

With a smothered imprecation, Zach said, "I felt that, too!"

Masculine hands that could be at once provocative and tender moved over her taut belly.

"How incredible!" he said. "Where did you put Dr. Stewart's number? I have to call her. We've got to get to the hospital."

"It's written on the appointment card in my purse, but there's no big hurry. She says the first baby usually takes a while."

"Our baby is really coming!"

"Yes." Her face broke out in a grin because he

sounded so excited. The demons of last night seemed to have vanished. "We're about to become parents. Do you think you're ready?"

"As long as you never stop loving me, I'm ready for anything, Mrs. Wilde."

"FOR CRYING OUT LOUD, Uncle Zach, when's it going to be my turn to hold Astrid?"

Richie's frustrated voice carried from the nursery into the bedroom where Laura and Bev were having a heart-to-heart.

Leaving Richard and Zach with the awesome responsibility of deciding how long each child should be given time with the adorable new dark-haired arrival, Bev heaved a weary sigh and stretched out on the bed so she was facing Laura.

"Here I am, still great with child, and you're lying there looking gorgeous when you only gave birth five days ago. It's not fair!"

"A lot *you* know. As soon as I'm given permission, I'm going to have to whip out my mother's old exercise board, otherwise Zach will turn me in for a new model."

"That'll be the day. Honestly, Laura, you have my brother-in-law so womped, I don't recognize him anymore."

Laura's eyes shone. "You think?"

"Was there ever any question?" She raised herself on one elbow and said seriously, "There's a marked difference in him from a few days ago, too." She paused, then confided, "I know this might sound strange, but his behavior, I thought, was most peculiar lately. Then suddenly it's like this hidden part of him emerged. There's a new confidence I've never seen before."

Laura nodded sagely. "It's called *relief,* and it's because I didn't die in childbirth." The other reason didn't matter anymore. Besides, it was something private between her and her husband.

Bev's smile faded. The two of them stared hard at each other with an understanding born out of their love for Zach.

"I should have figured that one out long before now."

"Tell me about it," Laura groaned. "I was beginning to think he'd fallen out of love with me. Then it came like a revelation what was really going on. I'm afraid I've married a very complicated man."

Bev smiled. "Join the club. All the Wilde men are the same. Complex, but s-o-o-o wonderful. We just have to learn to stay one step ahead of them. Did you know Richard almost fell apart when Zach drove off with you after the reception?"

"You're kidding."

"Nope. For once in his life Richard had to face the fact that you now came first in his younger brother's life. After being the kingpin all these years, it was hard to relinquish it."

She patted her stomach. "That's why it's a good thing my baby is about to make an appearance. Little

Zach ought to expand my husband's role of guardian of the realm.''

Laura was shocked. "Bev, I had no idea. Honestly, Zach and I have been so happy I guess we've kind of ignored everyone else.''

"Don't you *dare* apologize!''

"Apologize for what?'' Zach said from the doorway. He was holding their hungry infant. Laura could see he was a natural-born father and so crazy about the baby his every fear had fled.

She smiled up at him. "For going into labor before *she* did.''

An answering smile transformed his features. "They don't call me King of the Mountain for nothing! Are you ready to feed my little girl?''

"I recognize that look,'' Bev whispered. "He wants to be alone with you. I'll gather up our brood and call you tomorrow. It might even be from the hospital.''

"I hope so.'' Laura squeezed Bev's hand. "I've got my fingers crossed. Thank you for the darling outfit and booties.''

"Anytime.''

With some difficulty Bev got off the bed and gave the baby's head a kiss on her way out of the room. The minute the door closed Laura held out her arms.

"I want both of you here with me.''

Zach eyed his wife for a moment. It seemed his life had always been a race toward something elusive, something that had no name. But as he stood there with their daughter in his arms, Laura's face aglow

with love, he knew that long race was over. He knew
what it was he'd been running toward all this time.

His share of heaven on earth.

COMING NEXT MONTH

#758 BEAUTY & THE BEASTS • Janice Kay Johnson
Veterinarian Dr. Eric Bergstrom is interested in a new
woman. A *beautiful* woman. He's volunteered his services at
the local cat shelter she's involved with. He's even adopted
one of the shelter's cats. But he still can't manage to get
Madeline to go out with him. That's bad enough. Then Eric's
twelve-year-old son comes to town, making it clear that he
resents "having" to spend the summer with his father. Well,
at least Eric's new cat loves him....

#759 IN THE ARMS OF THE LAW • Anne Marie Duquette
Home on the Ranch
Morgan Bodine is part-owner of the Silver Dollar Ranch;
he's also the acting sheriff in Tombstone, Arizona.
Jasentha Cliffwalker is a biologist studying bats on Bodine
property. Morgan and Jaz loved each other years ago, but it
was a love they weren't ready for. *Are they ready now?*
They'll find out when a stranger comes to Tombstone,
threatening everything they value most.... By the author of
She Caught the Sheriff.

#760 JUST ONE NIGHT • Kathryn Shay
9 Months Later
Annie and Zach Sloan had married for all the right reasons.
They'd fallen in love and neither could imagine life without
the other. But those reasons hadn't been enough to keep
them together. Then—six years after the divorce—a night
that began in fear ended in passion. And now there's a
new reason for Zach and Annie to marry. *They're about to
become parents.*

#761 THIS CHILD IS MINE • Janice Kaiser
Carolina Prescott is pregnant. Webb Harper is the father.
After his wife died, he forgot all about the donation he'd left
at a fertility clinic. Due to a mix-up, Lina is given the wrong
fertilized egg—but that doesn't make her less of a mother!
Both Lina and Webb have strong feelings about the baby
she's carrying and the ensuing lawsuit. Can their growing
feelings for each other overcome the trauma of the battle
for custody?

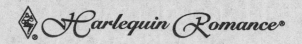

NO WIFE REQUIRED! (#3477)
by Rebecca Winters

She wants a husband....
Lacey West's biological clock isn't so much ticking as
sounding alarm bells! Then Max Jarvis moves into her
apartment block...six feet two inches of prime
bachelor! The perfect male, except for one thing...he
doesn't want a wife!

**Rebecca Winters's latest romance matches one
determined woman against one even more
determined bachelor!**

About Rebecca Winters:

"One of our favorite authors."   —*Romantic Times*

"Rebecca Winters writes from the heart. She has the
ability to make me laugh or cry. Mostly she makes me
care."   —*Debbie Macomber*

NO WIFE REQUIRED! will appear as part of
Harlequin Romance's *Simply the Best* promotion—a
showcase of the best of our new romance novels.

Authors you'll treasure,
books you'll want to keep!

Available in *Harlequin Romance* in October 1997.

Don't miss these Harlequin favorites by some of our most popular authors! And now you can receive a discount by ordering two or more titles!

HT#25700	HOLDING OUT FOR A HERO	
	by Vicki Lewis Thompson	$3.50 U.S. ☐/$3.99 CAN.☐
HT#25699	WICKED WAYS	
	by Kate Hoffmann	$3.50 U.S. ☐/$3.99 CAN.☐
HP#11845	RELATIVE SINS	
	by Anne Mather	$3.50 U.S. ☐/$3.99 CAN.☐
HP#11849	A KISS TO REMEMBER	
	by Miranda Lee	$3.50 U.S. ☐/$3.99 CAN.☐
HR#03359	FAITH, HOPE AND MARRIAGE	
	by Emma Goldrick	$2.99 U.S. ☐/$3.50 CAN.☐
HR#03433	TEMPORARY HUSBAND	
	by Day Leclaire	$3.25 U.S. ☐/$3.75 CAN.☐
HS#70679	QUEEN OF THE DIXIE DRIVE-IN	
	by Peg Sutherland	$3.99 U.S. ☐/$4.50 CAN.☐
HS#70712	SUGAR BABY	
	by Karen Young	$3.99 U.S. ☐/$4.50 CAN.☐
HI#22319	BREATHLESS	
	by Carly Bishop	$3.50 U.S. ☐/$3.99 CAN.☐
HI#22335	BEAUTY VS. THE BEAST	
	by M.J. Rodgers	$3.50 U.S. ☐/$3.99 CAN.☐
AR#16577	BRIDE OF THE BADLANDS	
	by Jule McBride	$3.50 U.S. ☐/$3.99 CAN.☐
AR#16656	RED-HOT RANCHMAN	
	by Victoria Pade	$3.75 U.S. ☐/$4.25 CAN.☐
HH#28868	THE SAXON	
	by Margaret Moore	$4.50 U.S. ☐/$4.99 CAN.☐
HH#28893	UNICORN VENGEANCE	
	by Claire Delacroix	$4.50 U.S. ☐/$4.99 CAN.☐

(limited quantities available on certain titles)

	TOTAL AMOUNT	$ _____
DEDUCT:	10% DISCOUNT FOR 2+ BOOKS	$ _____
	POSTAGE & HANDLING	$ _____
	($1.00 for one book, 50¢ for each additional)	
	APPLICABLE TAXES*	$ _____
	TOTAL PAYABLE	$ _____

(check or money order—please do not send cash)

To order, complete this form, along with a check or money order for the total above, payable to Harlequin Books, to: In the U.S.: 3010 Walden Avenue, P.O. Box 9047, Buffalo, NY 14269-9047; In Canada: P.O. Box 613, Fort Erie, Ontario, L2A 5X3.

Name: _____

Address: _____ City: _____

State/Prov.: _____ Zip/Postal Code: _____

*New York residents remit applicable sales taxes.
Canadian residents remit applicable GST and provincial taxes.

Look us up on-line at: http://www.romance.net

HBKJS97